FATAL TIDE

FATAL TIDE

IRIS JOHANSEN

RANDOM HOUSE
LARGE PRINT

The Library of Congress has established a Cataloging-in-Publication record for this title.

0-375-43226-4

www.randomlargeprint.com

FIRST LARGE PRINT EDITION

10   9   8   7   6   5   4   3   2   1

This Large Print edition published in accord with the standards of the N.A.V.H.

FATAL TIDE

Chapter One

Cool water, smooth as glass as Kelby swam through it. Jesus, he was thirsty. He knew all he had to do was open his lips and the water would flow down his throat, but he wanted to see beyond the arched doorway first. It was huge and ornately carved, beckoning him forward. . . .

Then he was through the arch and the city was spread before him.

Giant white columns built to stand forever. Streets laid out in perfect order. Glory and symmetry everywhere . . .

"Kelby."

He was being shaken. Nicholas. He came instantly alert. "Time?" he whispered.

Nicholas nodded. "They should be coming back for you again in five minutes. I just wanted to make sure we're on the same page. I've decided we scratch the plan and I take them out by myself."

"Screw you."

"You'll blow it for both of us. You haven't had anything to eat or drink in three days, and you looked like a truck ran over you when they brought you back to the cell."

"Shut up. It hurts my throat to argue." He leaned back against the stone wall and closed his eyes. "We go as we planned. I give the word. Just tell me when they start down the hall. I'll be ready."

Go back to the sea. There's strength there. No thirst that couldn't be satisfied. He could move without pain through the buoyant water.

White columns shimmering . . .

"They're coming," Nicholas murmured.

Kelby opened his eyes only a slit as the door was unlocked. The same two guards. Hassan had an Uzi cradled in his arm. Kelby was so hazy he couldn't remember the other guard's name. But he could remember the toe of his boot as he kicked in his rib. Yes, he could remember that.

Ali, that was the bastard's name.

"Get up, Kelby." Hassan was standing over him. "Is the American dog ready for his beating?"

Kelby groaned.

"Get him, Ali. He's too weak to stand up and face us again."

Ali was smiling as he came to stand beside Hassan. "He'll break this time. We'll be able to drag him into Baghdad and show the whole world what cowards the Americans are."

He reached down to grab Kelby's shirt.

"Now." Kelby's foot lashed upward and connected with Ali's nuts. Then he rolled sideways, knocking the Arab's legs from beneath him.

He heard Hassan mutter a curse as Kelby leapt to his feet. He got in back of Ali before he could get off his knees, and his arm snaked around Ali's neck.

He broke it with one twist.

He whirled to see Nicholas smashing the Uzi into Hassan's head. Blood spurted. Nicholas hit him again.

"Out." Kelby grabbed Ali's pistol and knife and ran to the door. "Don't waste time on him."

"He wasted a lot of time on you. I wanted to make sure he'd gone to Allah." But he was running after Kelby down the hall.

In the front office another guard jumped to his feet and reached for his gun. Kelby cut his throat before he could lift it.

Then they were outside the hut and running toward the hills.

Shots behind them.

Keep running.

Nicholas looked over his shoulder. "Are you okay?"

"Fine. Go on, dammit."

Sharp pain in his side.

Don't stop.

The adrenaline was draining away and weakness was dragging at every limb.

Go away from it. Concentrate. You're swimming toward the archway. No pain there.

He was running faster, stronger. The hills were just ahead. He could make it.

He was through the archway. White columns gleamed in the distance.

Marinth . . .

LONTANA'S ISLAND
LESSER ANTILLES
Present Day

Lacy golden fretwork.
Velvet drapery.
Drums.
Someone coming toward her.
It was going to happen again.
Helpless. Helpless. Helpless.
The scream that tore from Melis's throat jarred her awake.

She jerked upright in bed. She was shaking, her T-shirt soaked with sweat.

Kafas.

Or Marinth?

Sometimes she wasn't sure. . . . It didn't matter.

Only a dream.

She wasn't helpless. She'd never be helpless again. She was strong now.

Except when she had the dreams. They robbed her of power and she was forced to remember. But she had the dreams less often now. It had been over a month since the last one. Still, she might feel better if she had someone to talk to. Maybe she should call Carolyn and—

No, deal with it. She knew what to do after the dreams to rid herself of these trembling fits and get back to blessed normalcy. She tore off her nightshirt as she left the bedroom and headed toward the lanai.

A moment later she was diving off the lanai into the sea.

It was the middle of the night, but the water was only cool, not cold, and felt like liquid silk on her body. Clean and caressing and soothing . . .

No threat. No submission. Nothing but the night and the sea. God, it was good to be alone.

But she wasn't alone.

Something sleek and cool brushed against her leg.

"Susie?" It had to be Susie. The female dolphin was much more physically affectionate than Pete. The male touched her only rarely, and it was something special when he did.

But Pete was beside her in the water. She saw him out of the corner of her eye as she stroked toward the nets that barricaded the inlet. "Hi, Pete. How are you doing?"

He gave a subdued series of clicks and then dove beneath the surface. A moment later Susie and Pete came to the surface together and swam ahead of her toward the nets. It was strange how they always knew when she was upset. Ordinarily their behavior was playful, almost giddily exuberant. It was only when they sensed she was disturbed that they became this docile. She was supposed to be the one teaching the dolphins, but she was learning from them every day she spent in their company. They enriched her life and she was grateful that—

Something was wrong.

Susie and Pete were both squeaking and clicking frantically as they approached the net. A shark on the other side?

She tensed.

The net was down.

What the hell . . . No one could unfasten the net unless they knew where it was connected. "I'll take care of it. Go back home, guys."

The dolphins ignored her, swimming around her protectively while she examined the net. No cuts, no tears in the strong wire. It took her only a few minutes to fasten the net again. She set off back to the cottage, her strokes strong, purposeful—and wary.

It didn't have to be a problem. It could be

Phil back from his latest journey. Her foster father had been gone for nearly seven months this time, with only an occasional phone call or postcard to tell her if he was alive or dead.

But it could be trouble. Phil had been forced to go on the run almost two years ago and the threat was only partially eliminated. There could still be people out there who wanted to get their hands on him. Phil wasn't the most discreet person in the world, and his judgment wasn't as keen as his intellect. He was a dreamer who took more chances than—

"Melis!"

She became still, paddling in place, her gaze on the lanai a short distance away. She could see a man's silhouette outlined against the lights of the living room. It wasn't Phil's small, wiry frame. This man was big, muscular, and vaguely familiar.

"Melis, I didn't mean to scare you. It's me, Cal."

She relaxed. Cal Dugan, Phil's first mate. No threat here. She had known and liked Cal since she was sixteen. He must have moored his boat at the pier on the other side of the house, where she couldn't see it. She swam toward the lanai. "Why didn't you call me? And why the devil didn't you put the net back up? If a shark had gotten to Pete or Susie, I'd have strangled you."

"I was going to go back and do it," he said defensively. "Nah, I was going to persuade you to do it. I'd have to know Braille to be able to hook it up in the dark."

"That's not good enough. It only takes a minute to pose a threat to the dolphins. You're just lucky it didn't happen."

"How do you know a shark didn't get in?"

"Pete would have told me."

"Oh, yeah. Pete." He dropped a bath towel on the lanai and turned his back. "Tell me when I can turn around. I guess you haven't taken to wearing a swimsuit?"

"Why should I? There's no one to see me but Pete and Susie." She hoisted herself onto the tiles and wrapped the large towel around her. "And uninvited guests."

"Don't be rude. Phil invited me."

"Turn around. When's he coming? Tomorrow?"

He turned around. "Not likely."

"He's not in Tobago?"

"He was setting sail for Athens when he sent me here."

"What?"

"He told me to hop on a plane out of Genoa and come and give you this." He handed her a large manila envelope. "And to wait here for him."

"Wait for him? He'll need you there. He can't do without you, Cal."

"That's what I told him." He shrugged. "He told me to come to you."

She glanced down at the envelope. "I can't see out here. Let's go inside where there's light." She tightened the towel around her. "Make yourself some coffee while I take a look at this."

He flinched. "Will you tell those dolphins I'm not going to hurt you and to stop screeching?"

She'd barely been aware they were still beside the lanai. "Go away, guys. It's okay."

Pete and Susie disappeared beneath the water.

"I'll be damned," Cal said. "They do understand you."

"Yes." Her tone was abstracted as she went into the cottage. "Genoa? What's Phil been up to?"

"Search me. A few months ago he dropped me and the rest of the crew off in

Las Palmas and told us we were on vacation for three months. He hired some temporary help to sail the *Last Home* and took off."

"Where?"

He shrugged. "He wouldn't say. Big secret. It wasn't like Phil at all. It was like that time he went off with you. But this was different. He was on edge and he wouldn't say anything when he came back and picked us up." He grimaced. "It's not as if we haven't been with him for the last fifteen years. We have shared a hell of a lot together. I was there when he brought up the Spanish galleon, and Terry and Gary signed on a year later. It kind of . . . hurt."

"You know when he becomes focused on something he can't see anything else." But she had seldom known him to close out his crew. They were as close to family as Phil would permit near him. Closer than he would let her come.

But that was probably her fault. She found it difficult to be openly affectionate with Phil. She had always been the protector in a relationship that had sometimes been both volatile and stormy. She was often impatient and frustrated with his almost childlike single-mindedness. But they were a team, they fulfilled each other's needs, and she did like him.

"Melis."

She glanced at Cal to find him gazing awkwardly at her. "Would you mind putting on some clothes? You're one gorgeous woman, and even though I may be old enough to be your father, it doesn't mean I don't have the usual responses."

Of course he did. It didn't matter that he'd known her from the time she was a teenager. Men were men. Even the best of them were dominated by sex. It had taken her a long time to accept that truth without anger. "I'll be right back." She headed for the bedroom. "Make that coffee."

She didn't bother to shower before she put on her usual shorts and T-shirt. Then she sat down on the bed and reached for the envelope. It might be nothing, totally impersonal, but she didn't want to open it in front of Cal.

The envelope contained two documents. She took out the first one and opened it.

She stiffened. "What the hell . . ."

HYATT HOTEL
ATHENS, GREECE

"Stop arguing. I'm coming to get you." Melis's hand tightened on the phone. "Where are you, Phil?"

"At a tavern on the waterfront. The Delphi Hotel," Philip Lontana said. "But I'm not going to involve you in this, Melis. Go home."

"I will. We're both going to go home. And I'm already involved. Did you think I was just going to sit around doing nothing after I got that notification that you'd deeded the island and the *Last Home* over to me? That's the closest to a last will and testament I've ever seen. What the hell's happening?"

"I had to turn responsible sometime."

Not Phil. He was as close to Peter Pan as a man in his sixties could be. "What are you afraid of?"

"I'm not afraid. I just wanted to take care of you. I know we've had our ups and downs, but you've always stood by me when I needed you. You've pulled me out of scrapes and kept those bloodsuckers from—"

"I'll pull you out of this scrape, too, if you'll tell me what's happening."

"Nothing's happening. The ocean is unforgiving. You can never tell when I'll make a mistake and never—"

"Phil."

"I've written it all down. It's on the *Last Home*."

"Good. Then you can read it to me when we're on our way back to the island."

"That may not be possible." He paused. "I've been trying to get in touch with Jed Kelby. He's not been answering my calls."

"Bastard."

"Maybe. But a brilliant bastard. I've heard he's a genius."

"And where did you hear it? His publicity agent?"

"Don't be bitter. You've got to give the devil his due."

"No, I don't. I don't like rich men who think they can make toys of everything in the whole damn world."

"You don't like rich men. Period," Phil said. "But I need you to contact him. I don't know if I'll be able to reach him."

"Of course you will. Though I don't know why you think you have to do it. You've never called in help before."

"I need him. He's got the same passion I

have and the drive to make it happen." He paused. "Promise me you'll get him for me, Melis. It's the most important thing I've ever asked of you."

"You don't have to—"

"Promise me."

He wasn't going to give up. "I promise. Satisfied?"

"No, I hated to ask you. And I hate being in this spot. If I hadn't been so stubborn, I wouldn't have had to—" He drew a deep breath. "But that's water under the bridge. I can't look back now. There's too much to look forward to."

"Then why make out your last will and testament, dammit?"

"Because they didn't get a chance to do it."

"What?"

"We should learn from their mistakes." He paused. "Go home. Who's taking care of Pete and Susie?"

"Cal."

"I'm surprised you're letting him do it. You care more about those dolphins than anyone on two legs."

"Evidently I don't, if I'm here. Cal will take good care of Pete and Susie. I put the fear of God in him before I left."

He chuckled. "Or the fear of Melis. But you know how important they are. Go back to them. If you don't hear from me in two weeks, go get Kelby. Good-bye, Melis."

"Don't you dare hang up. What do you want Kelby to do? Is this about that damn sonic device?"

"You know it's never really been about that."

"Then what is it about?"

"I knew it would upset you. Ever since you were a child, you've always had a thing about the *Last Home*."

"Your ship?"

"No, the other *Last Home*. Marinth." He hung up.

She stood there, frozen, for a long moment before she slowly closed her phone.

Marinth.

My God.

THE *TRINA*
VENICE, ITALY

"What the hell is Marinth?"

Jed Kelby stiffened in his chair. "What?"

"Marinth." John Wilson looked up from

the pile of letters he'd been scanning for Kelby. "That's all that's written in this letter. Just the one word. Must be some kind of prank or advertising gimmick."

"Give it to me." Kelby slowly reached across the desk and took the letter and envelope.

"Something wrong, Jed?" Wilson stopped sorting the letters he'd just brought on board.

"Maybe." Kelby glanced at the name on the return address of the envelope. Philip Lontana, and the date stamp was over two weeks old. "Why the hell didn't I get this sooner?"

"You might have, if you'd stay in one place more than a day or two," Wilson said dryly. "I haven't even heard from you in two weeks. I can't be held responsible for keeping you current if you don't cooperate. I do my best, but you're not the easiest man to—"

"Okay, okay." He leaned back and stared down at the letter. "Philip Lontana. I haven't heard anything about him for a few years. I thought maybe he'd quit the business."

"I've never heard of him."

"Why should you? He's not a stockbroker

or banker, so he wouldn't be of interest to you."

"That's right. I'm only interested in keeping you filthy rich and out of the clutches of the IRS." Wilson set several documents in front of Kelby. "Sign these in triplicate." He watched disapprovingly as Kelby signed the contracts. "You should have read those. How do you know I didn't screw you?"

"You're morally incapable of it. If you were going to do it, you'd have taken me to the cleaners ten years ago when you were tottering on the verge of bankruptcy."

"True. But you pulled me out of that hole. So that's not really a test."

"I let you flounder for a while to see what you'd do before I stepped in."

Wilson tilted his head. "I never realized that I was on trial."

"Sorry." His gaze was still on the letter. "It's the nature of the beast. I've not been able to trust many people in my life, Wilson."

God knows that was the truth, Wilson thought. Heir to one of America's largest fortunes, Kelby and his trust fund had been fought over by his mother and grandmother from the time his father died. Court case had followed court case until he'd reached his twenty-first birthday. Then he'd taken control with a cool ruthlessness and intelligence, jettisoned all contact with his mother and grandmother, and set up experts to manage his finances. He'd finished his education and then taken off to become the wanderer he was today. He'd been a SEAL during the Gulf War, later purchased the yacht *Trina* and started a series of underwater explorations that had brought him a fame he didn't appreciate and money he didn't need. Still, he seemed to thrive on the life. For the past eight years he'd lived hard and fast and dealt with some pretty unsavory characters. No, Wilson couldn't blame him for being both wary and cynical. It didn't bother him. He was cynical himself, and over the years he'd learned to genuinely like the bastard.

"Has Lontana tried to contact me before?" Kelby asked.

Wilson sorted through the rest of the mail. "That's the only letter." He flipped open his daybook. "One call on the twenty-third of June. Wanted you to return his call. Another on June twenty-fifth. Same message. My secretary asked what his business pertained to but he wouldn't tell her. It didn't seem urgent enough to try to track you down. Is it?"

"Possibly." He stood up and walked across the cabin to the window. "He certainly knew how to get my attention."

"Who is he?"

"A Brazilian oceanographer. He got a lot of press when he discovered that Spanish galleon fifteen years or so ago. His mother was American and his father Brazilian, and he's something of a throwback to another age. I heard he thought he was some kind of grand adventurer and sailed around looking for lost cities and sunken galleons. He discovered only one galleon, but there's no doubt he's very sharp."

"You've never met him?"

"No, I wasn't really interested. We wouldn't have much in common. I'm definitely a product of this age. We're not on the same wavelength."

Wilson wasn't so sure. Kelby was no dreamer, but he possessed the aggressive, bold recklessness that typified the buccaneers of this or any other century. "So what does Lontana want with you?" His gaze narrowed on Kelby. "And what do you want with Lontana?"

"I'm not sure what he wants from me."
He stood looking out at the sea, thinking.
"But I know what I want from him. The
question is, can he give it to me?"

"That's cryptic."

"Is it?" He suddenly turned to face Wilson.
"Then, by God, we'd better get everything
clear and aboveboard, hadn't we?"

Shock rippled through Wilson as he saw
the recklessness and excitement in Kelby's
expression. The aggressive energy he was
emitting was almost tangible. "Then I take it
you want me to contact Lontana."

"Oh, yes. In fact, we're going to go see
him."

"*We're?* I have to get back to New York."

Kelby shook his head. "I may need you."

"You know I don't know anything about
all this oceanography stuff, Jed. And,
dammit, I don't want to know. I have de-
grees in law and accounting. I wouldn't be
of any use to you."

"You never can tell. I may need all the
help I can get. A little more sea air will do
you good." He glanced down at the envelope again, and Wilson was once more aware
of the undercurrent of excitement that was
electrifying Kelby. "But maybe we should

give Lontana a little advance warning that he shouldn't dangle a carrot unless he expects me to gobble it with one swallow. Give me his telephone number."

She was being followed.

It wasn't paranoia, dammit. She could *feel* it.

Melis glanced over her shoulder. It was an exercise in futility. She wouldn't have known whom she was looking for on the crowded dock behind her. It could be anyone. A thief, a sailor eager for a lay . . . or someone who was hoping she'd lead him to Phil. Anything was possible.

Now that Marinth was involved.

Lose him.

She darted down the next street, ran one short block, ducked into an alcove, and waited. Making sure you weren't being paranoid was always the first rule. The second was to know your enemy.

A gray-haired man in khakis and a short-sleeved plaid shirt came around the corner and stopped. He looked like any casual tourist who frequented Athens this time of year. Except that his annoyed attitude didn't match his appearance. He was definitely irritated as his gaze searched the people streaming down the street.

She was not paranoid. And now she would remember this man, whoever he was.

She darted out of the alcove and took off running. She turned left, cut into an alley, and then turned right at the next street.

She glanced behind her in time to see a glimpse of a plaid shirt. He was no longer trying to blend in with the crowd. He was moving fast and with purpose.

Five minutes later she stopped, breathing hard.

She had lost him. Maybe.

Christ, Phil, what have you gotten us into?

She waited another ten minutes to make sure and then reversed her path and cut back toward the dock. According to her street map, the Delphi Hotel should be on the next block.

There it was. A narrow, three-story building whose facade was old, paint-chipped, stained by smog, and yet breathing atmosphere as everything did in this town. It wasn't a hotel Phil would have ordinarily tolerated. He liked old and atmospheric, but decay wasn't his forte. He enjoyed his comforts too much. Another mystery that—

"Melis?"

She turned to see a small, graying man in jeans and T-shirt sitting at a café table. "Gary? Where's Phil?"

He nodded at the water. "On the *Last Home.*"

"Without you? I don't believe it." First Cal and now Gary St. George?

"Neither did I." He took a sip of his ouzo. "I figure I'll stick around for a few days and he'll come back and get me. What can he do without me? He'd have real trouble sailing the *Last Home* by himself."

"What about Terry?"

"Fired him in Rome right after he sent Cal away. Told him to go to you and you'd find him work. Told me the same thing." He grinned. "You ready to become a headhunter for us, Melis?"

"How long has he been gone?"

"An hour maybe. Took off right after he talked to you."

"Where was he going?"

"Southeast, toward the Greek Islands."

She moved toward the dock. "Come on, let's go."

He jumped to his feet. "Where?"

"I'm going to rent a speedboat and go after the idiot. I may need someone to run it while I look out for the *Last Home*."

"It's still daylight." He tried to catch up with her. "We've got a chance."

"No chance about it. We're going to find him."

They caught up with the *Last Home* just before darkness fell. The two-masted schooner looked like a ship from another age in the soft light. Melis had always told Phil that the ship reminded her of pictures of the *Flying Dutchman,* and in the hazy golden twilight it appeared even more mystical.

And, like the *Dutchman,* deserted.

She felt a ripple of fear. No, it couldn't be deserted. Phil had to be belowdeck.

"Spooky, huh?" Gary said as he gunned the motorboat toward the ship. "He's turned the engines off. What the hell is he doing?"

"Maybe he's having trouble. He deserves it. Getting rid of his crew and taking off like—" She broke off to steady her voice. "Get as close as you can. I'm going to board her."

"I don't think he's going to roll out the welcome mat." Gary squinted at the ship. "He didn't want you here, Melis. He didn't want any of us on this trip."

"Too bad. I can't help what he wants. You know Phil sometimes doesn't make the best choices. He sees what he wants to see and then goes full speed ahead. I can't let— There he is!"

Phil had appeared from below and was frowning as he gazed at them over the expanse of water.

"Phil, dammit, what are you doing?" she shouted. "I'm coming aboard."

Phil shook his head. "Something's wrong with the ship. The engine just stopped. I can't be sure—"

"What's wrong?"

"I should have known. I should have been more careful."

"You're talking crazy."

"And I don't have time to talk anymore. I have to go and see if I can find where he— Go home, Melis. Take care of the dolphins. It's important that you do your job."

"We need to talk. I'm not going to—" She was talking to air. Phil had turned and gone back down below.

"Get me closer."

"He won't let you board her, Melis."

"Yes, he will. Even if I have to hang on to the anchor all the way to—"

The Last Home *exploded into a thousand fiery pieces.*

Phil!

"No!" She didn't realize she'd screamed the word in an agony of rejection. The ship was burning, half of it gone. "Get closer! We have to—"

Another explosion.

Pain.

Her head was splintering, exploding like the ship.

Darkness.

Chapter Two

"Melis Nemid has a concussion," Wilson said. "One of Lontana's crew brought her here after the explosion. The doctors think she's going to be fine, but she's been unconscious for the last twenty-four hours."

"I want to see her." Kelby moved down the hall. "Get me permission."

"Maybe you didn't hear me. She's out, Jed."

"I want to be there when she wakes up. I have to be the first one to talk to her."

"This hospital is pretty strict. And you're not family. They may not want to let you in her room until after she becomes conscious."

"Get them to do it. I don't care if you

have to give a big enough bribe to buy the hospital. And check back with the coast guard and see if they've located Lontana's body yet. Then go find the man who brought Lontana's daughter here and pump him. I want to know everything there is to know about what happened to Lontana and the *Last Home*. What room is she in?"

"Twenty-one." He hesitated. "Jed, she's just lost her father. For God's sake, what's the hurry?"

The urgency was that for the first time in years Kelby had been given hope and it was being snatched away from him. He'd be damned if he'd let that happen. "I'm not going to give her the third degree. To use one of your favorite phrases, that would be nonproductive. I do have a certain amount of tact."

"When you want to use it." Wilson shrugged. "But you'll do what you want to do. Okay, I'll deal with the nurses first and then go see what else I can find out about the explosion."

Which probably wouldn't be much, Kelby thought. According to the news broadcast they had heard on the way here, the explosion had virtually ripped the ship apart. He'd gone first to the disaster site, and there had been practically nothing to salvage. At the moment they were calling it an accident. Not likely. There had been two explosions at opposite ends of the ship.

Twenty-one.

He opened the door and went into the room. A woman lay in the single bed dominating the pleasant, serene room. No nurses, thank God. Wilson was good, but he needed time to pave the way. He grabbed a chair from beside the door and carried it over to the bed. She didn't stir as he sat down and began studying her.

Melis Nemid's head was bandaged, but he could see strands of blond hair clinging to her cheeks. Jesus, she was . . . exceptional. Her body was small, fine-boned, and she appeared as fragile as a Christmas ornament. It was incredibly moving to see someone that delicate hurt. It reminded him of Trina and those times when—

My God, he hadn't run across anyone in years who had brought that period of his life rushing back to him like this.

So smother it. Turn it around. Transform it into something else.

He stared down at Melis Nemid with cool objectivity. Yes, she was fragile and helpless-looking. Yet, if you considered the other side of the coin, that very delicateness was oddly sensual and arousing. Like holding a gossamer-thin china cup and knowing you could break it if you only tightened your hand. His gaze shifted to her face. Beautiful bone structure. A large, perfectly formed mouth that somehow increased the appearance of sensuality. A damn beautiful woman.

And this was supposed to be Lontana's foster daughter? Lontana was in his sixties and this woman was maybe mid-twenties. Of course, it was possible. But it was just as likely that the designation was a way of avoiding questions about a May–December relationship.

It didn't make any difference what she had been to him. The only important thing was that the relationship was long-standing and intimate enough that the woman would be able to tell him what he needed to know. If she did know, then there was no question he would make very sure she told him.

He leaned back in his chair and waited for her to wake.

Jesus, her head hurt.

Drugs? No, they'd stopped giving her drugs when she'd stopped fighting. She cautiously opened her eyes. No lacy fretwork, she realized with relief. Cool blue walls, cool as the sea. Crisp white sheet covering her. A hospital?

"You must be thirsty. Would you like some water?"

A man's voice. It could be a doctor or nurse. . . . Her gaze flew to the man sitting in the chair next to the bed.

"Easy, I'm not offering you poison." He smiled. "Only a glass of water."

He wasn't a doctor. He was wearing jeans and a linen shirt with cuffs rolled to the elbow, and he was somehow . . . familiar. "Where am I?"

"St. Catherine's Hospital." He held the glass to her lips as she drank. She gazed warily at him over the rim. He was dark-haired, dark-eyed, somewhere in his thirties, and wore confidence with the same casualness as he did his clothes. If she had met him before, she would definitely have remembered him.

"What happened?"

"You don't remember?"

The ship splintering, hurling chunks of deck and metal into the air.

"Phil!" She jerked upright in bed. Phil had been in that inferno. Phil had been— She tried to swing her legs to the floor. "He was there. I have to— He went below and he was—"

"Lie down." He was pushing her back onto the pillows. "There's nothing you can do. The ship was destroyed over twenty-four hours ago. The coast guard hasn't given up looking yet. If he's alive, they'll find him."

Twenty-four hours. She gazed at him dazedly. "They didn't find him?"

He shook his head. "Not yet."

"They can't give up. Don't let them give up."

"I won't. Will you go back to sleep now? The nurses are going to kick me out if they think I've upset you. I just thought you should know. I have an idea you're like me. You want to know the truth even if it hurts."

"Phil . . ." She closed her eyes as pain washed over her. "Hurts. I wish I could cry."

"Then do it."

"I can't. I haven't—I can't ever— Go away. I don't want anyone to see me like this."

"But I've already seen you. So I think I'll just stick around and make sure you're going to be okay."

She opened her eyes and studied him. Hard . . . so hard. "You don't care if I'm okay. Who the hell are you?"

"Jed Kelby."

That's where she'd seen him. Newspapers, magazines, TV . . . "I should have known. The Golden Boy."

"I used to hate that nickname and everything that went with it. It's one of the reasons I became so damn belligerent with the media." He smiled. "But I got over it. I'm not a boy any longer. I'm a man. And I am what I am. You might find that what I am can be very useful to you."

"Go away."

He hesitated and then stood up. "I'll be back. In the meantime, I'll try to make sure the coast guard continues to look for Lontana."

"Thank you."

"You're welcome. Shall I ask the nurse to come in and give you a sedative?"

"No drugs! I don't take—"

"Fine. Whatever you say."

She watched the door close behind him. He had been very agreeable, some might have even said kind. She was too hazy and hurting to know what to think of him. She'd only been aware of that air of calm confidence and physical strength—and it disturbed her.

Don't think of him.

And try not to think of Phil. Twenty-four hours was a long time, but he could still be out there.

If he'd grabbed a life vest.

If he hadn't been blown up before he hit the water.

Jesus, she wished she could cry.

"Should you be up?" Gary frowned with concern as he saw Melis sitting in the chair by the window the next morning. "The nurse told me you regained consciousness only last evening."

"I'm fine. And I have to show them I don't need to stay here." Her hands tightened on the arms of the chair. "They want me to wait and talk to the police."

"Yeah, I've already given them my statement. They won't hassle you, Melis."

"They're already hassling me. The police can't get here till later this afternoon and I won't wait. But the hospital is tying me up with such a string of red tape I can't make a move. I think it's just an excuse. They say I shouldn't leave until tomorrow anyway."

"The doctors probably know best."

"The hell they do. I have to go back to where the ship sank. I have to find Phil."

"Melis . . ." Gary hesitated before he said gently, "I was out there with the coast guard. You're not going to find Phil. We've lost him."

"I don't want to hear that. I have to see for myself." Her glance shifted to the well-manicured lawns outside the window. "What was Kelby doing here?"

"Mainly turning the hospital upside down. They wouldn't even let me into your room, but Kelby had no problem. And before he came here, he was out helping the coast guard with the search. You don't know him, do you?"

"I never met him. But Phil told me he was trying to contact him. Do you know why?"

Gary shook his head. "Maybe Cal knows."

Melis doubted it. Whatever business Phil had with Kelby was evidently part of this deadly scenario that had taken his life. And it was a business he hadn't been willing to share with even his closest friends.

Dear God, she was thinking of him as dead. She was meekly accepting what they'd told her. She couldn't do that. "Go find Kelby for me, Gary. Tell him to get me out of here."

"What?"

"You said he could pull strings. Tell him to do it. I don't think you'll have any problem. He came here because he wants something from me. Well, he can't get anything from me while I'm in this hospital. He'll want me out."

"Even if it's not good for you?"

She remembered the impression Kelby had given her of rock hardness. "He won't care. Tell him to get me away from here."

"Okay." Gary grimaced. "But I still don't think you should do it. Phil wouldn't have liked it."

"You know Phil always let me do exactly what I wanted to do. It was much less bother for him." She had to steady her voice. "So please don't argue with me, Gary. I'm having a few emotional problems today."

"You're doing fine. You always do fine." He hurriedly left the room.

Poor Gary. He wasn't used to her not being in control, and it was upsetting him. It was upsetting her too. She didn't like feeling this helpless.

No, not helpless. She instantly rejected the word. There was always something she could do, another path to take. She was just sad and angry and filled with despair. Never helpless. It was just that right now she couldn't see clearly what path was open to her.

She'd better decide soon. Kelby was hovering on the threshold and she'd been forced to let him draw closer. He would use that slightly open door to gain purchase and solidify his position.

She leaned back in the chair and tried to relax. She ought to rest and garner all her strength while she had the chance. It would take all her resources to push Kelby out and slam that door again.

Kelby smiled with amusement as he watched Melis Nemid walk toward the front entrance. A nun was trailing behind her with the wheelchair Melis should have been occupying, and she wasn't at all pleased.

He had a fleeting memory of his first impression of how fragile Melis appeared. That provocative aura of delicacy was still present, but it was balanced by the force and vitality of her carriage, the way she moved. He'd known from the moment she'd opened her eyes she'd be a force to reckon with. How had a dreamer like Lontana managed to get hold of her? Or maybe she'd gotten hold of him. That was considerably more likely.

She stopped in front of him. "I suppose I should thank you for cutting through all that red tape and making them let me go."

"This isn't a prison, Ms. Nemid," the nurse said tartly. "We only needed to know you were going to be well taken care of. And you should have let me follow procedure and wheel you out."

"Thank you, Sister. I'll watch out for her from here." Kelby took Melis's arm and gently pushed her toward the door. "You have an appointment to give your statement to the police later tonight. I've taken care of all the medical paperwork and picked up your prescription."

"What prescription?"

"Just some sedatives in case you need them."

"I won't need them." She pulled her arm away from him. "And you can send me the bill."

"Fine. I always believe in keeping everything on an even playing field." He opened the door of the car parked in front of the hospital. "I'll have Wilson bill you on the first of the month."

"Who's Wilson? He sounds like a butler."

"My assistant. He keeps me solvent."

"Not much of a job."

"You'd be surprised. Some of my explorations are a big drain on the corporations. Get in."

She shook her head. "I'm going to the coast guard station."

"It won't do you any good. They've dropped the search."

It rocked her. "Already?"

"A few questions have come up regarding Lontana's state of mind." He paused. "It wasn't an accident. They've recovered traces of plastique and a timer among the salvage timbers. Do you think he may have set that charge himself?"

Her eyes widened. "What?"

"You have to admit it's a possibility."

"I won't admit any such thing. It's *not* a possibility. Phil was worried when his ship just went dead in the water. He was going below to try to find what had gone wrong."

"That's what Gary told the coast guard, but Lontana didn't say anything definite enough to rule out the possibility of suicide."

"I don't care. Phil loved every minute of his life. He was like a child. A new adventure was always just around the next corner."

"I'm afraid this was his final adventure. No one had much hope of his surviving from the beginning."

"There's always hope." She started to turn away. "Phil deserves his chance."

"No one's cheating him of his chance. I'm just telling you what— Where are you going?"

"I have to see for myself. I'll rent a motorboat at the dock and—"

"Your friend Gary St. George is already waiting for you on the *Trina*. He said you were determined to go and search. We can be at the position where the *Last Home* blew within an hour."

She hesitated.

"What can it hurt?"

"A foot in the door."

He chuckled. "True. But you knew what you were getting into when you told St. George to go and get me to spring you from the hospital. Play the game."

"This isn't a game to me."

His smile faded. "No, I can see it isn't. Sorry. You're an unknown quantity to me. Maybe I've mistaken toughness for callousness." He shrugged. "Come on, I'll let this trip be a freebie. No obligations, no payoffs."

She studied him for a moment and then turned and got into the car. "I'll believe it when I see it."

"So will I. This is a surprise to me too."

They searched the disaster area all afternoon and found only a few scraps of debris. With every passing hour her hope gradually faded.

He wasn't there. No matter how determined she was, how hard she looked, he would never be there again. The turquoise sea was so serene and beautiful here, it seemed obscene that it could hold such horror, she thought numbly.

But it wasn't the sea that had killed Phil.

It might be his burial place, but it was not his killer.

"Do you want to make another pass?" Kelby asked quietly. "We could widen our perimeter again."

"No." She didn't turn to look at him. "It would be a waste of time. He's not here. Are you going to say I told you so?"

"No, you had to see for yourself to make it real to you. I can understand that. Are you ready to go back to Athens now?"

She nodded jerkily.

"Do you want anything to eat? I had Billy make some sandwiches. He does a pretty miraculous job. Wilson and your friend Gary are in the main cabin practically inhaling them."

"Billy?"

"Billy Sanders, the cook. I stole him from a top restaurant in Prague."

Of course a luxury yacht like the *Trina* would have a cook. She'd read somewhere he'd purchased the yacht from a Saudi oil sheik. It was absolutely huge, and its two state-of-the-art tenders were also very impressive. The *Trina* herself was sleek, modern, with all the latest scientific equipment and bells and whistles. This ship was light-years different from the *Last Home*. Just as Kelby was different from Phil. Yet Phil had thought Kelby had something in common with him.

He's got the same passion I have and the drive to make it happen.

Phil had said that about Kelby during the last telephone conversation she'd had with him.

He was right. She could sense both Kelby's passion and drive as if they were a living force.

"Food?" he prompted.

She shook her head. "I'm not hungry. I think I'll just sit here for a while." She sat down on the deck and wrapped her arms tightly around her knees. "It's not been an easy afternoon for me."

"Do tell." His voice was suddenly harsh. "I've been expecting you to break down for the last two hours. For God's sake, no one is going to think less of you if you do."

"I don't care what anyone else thinks. And my weeping and wailing wouldn't do Phil any good. Nothing will help him now."

He didn't speak for a moment, and when she glanced at him she found his eyes narrowed on the horizon.

"What is it? Do you see something?"

"No." His gaze shifted back to her. "What are you going to do now? Do you have any plans?"

"I don't know what I'm going to do. I can't seem to think clearly right now. First I have to go home. I have responsibilities. Then I'll decide what comes next."

"Where's home?"

"An island in the Lesser Antilles, not far from Tobago. It belonged to Phil, but he deeded it over to me." Her lips twisted bitterly. "He left me the *Last Home* too. It would only take the next decade or so to retrieve the parts floating out there."

"He must have cared very much for you."

"I cared for him too," she whispered. "I think he knew. I wish I'd told him. Christ, I wish I'd told him."

"I'm sure he felt richly compensated."

There was an inflection in his tone. "What do you mean?"

"Nothing." He looked away from her. "Sometimes words don't mean much."

"And sometimes they do. Phil told me he couldn't get you to return his calls. What did he say to you to get you to come here?"

"He sent me a letter with just one word."

His glance shifted back to her face. "I imagine you know what that word was."

She didn't answer.

"Marinth."

She gazed at him, silent.

"I don't suppose you'd care to tell me what you know about Marinth?"

"I don't know anything." She stared him directly in the eye. "And I don't want to know anything."

"I'd be willing to give you a good deal of money for any information you might be willing to share."

She shook her head.

"If you're not willing to admit Lontana committed suicide, has it occurred to you there might be another explanation?"

Of course it had occurred to her, but she'd been pushing the thought away all afternoon. She couldn't cope with analyzing anything right now. And no matter how Phil had died, she wasn't aligning herself with Kelby.

"I don't know anything," she repeated.

He studied her. "I don't think you're telling me the truth. I believe you may know a good deal."

"Believe what you like. I don't intend to discuss it."

"Then I'll leave you alone." He turned away. "See how sensitive I'm being? If you change your mind about the sandwiches, come to the cabin."

He was joking, but he had been surprisingly sensitive since they'd boarded the *Trina*. He'd set to the job at hand with brisk efficiency. He'd let her run the show and taken orders without complaint. He'd made this agonizing search bearable.

"Kelby."

He turned to look at her.

"Thank you. You were kind to me today."

"Hey, everyone gets ambushed occasionally by an attack of sentimentality. It doesn't happen often with me. I got off easy."

"And I'm sorry you came to Athens on a wild-goose chase."

"I'm not." He smiled. "Because I have a hunch it wasn't a wild-goose chase. I want Marinth. I'm going to have it, Melis."

"Good luck."

"No, luck's not enough. I'm going to need help. I was going to get it from Lontana, but now I'm left with you."

"Then you have nothing."

"Until you get off the ship. I made you a

promise that I'd make no demands today. All bets are off once you step onto dry land."

She felt a surge of panic as she watched him walk away from her. It was difficult to ignore that absolute confidence in her emotional state.

Difficult, not impossible. All she needed to do was go home and heal her wounds and she'd be as strong as ever. She'd be able to think and make decisions. Once she reached the island she'd be safe from Kelby and everyone else.

"She's giving up." Archer's hands tightened on the rail of the cruiser. "Dammit, they're going back to Athens."

"Maybe she'll come back and search tomorrow," Pennig said. "It's getting dark."

"Kelby has enough strobe lights on that ship to light up the entire coast. No, she's giving up. She'll be running back to that damn island. Do you realize how difficult that's going to make it for us? I was hoping for just one more day here." Well, he wasn't going to get it. Nothing was going as it should. The woman should have been vulnerable. It was what he'd planned. But Kelby had stepped into the picture and formed a protective barricade around Melis Nemid by his very presence. "I need to *get* to the bitch."

"What if she doesn't go home? Kelby might have paid her enough to have brought her on board with him."

"Not if Lontana couldn't get her to go with him. He told me she wouldn't have anything to do with it. But she knows, dammit. The bitch *knows.*"

"Then Tobago?"

"Tobago's a small island and she's a familiar face there. That's why I wanted to get her here." He drew a deep breath and consciously smothered the rage surging through him. He'd been hoping to go the simple route and avoid complications. Patience. It would all come out right if he didn't make any foolish moves. "No, we'll just have to find a way to make her leave the island and come to us."

And make sure she broke down and gave him what he wanted before he put an end to her.

Kelby stood at the rail and watched as Gary helped Melis from the tender to the dock.

She didn't look back at either him or the ship as she moved quickly down the dock toward the taxi stand.

She had dismissed him. The realization brought Kelby a mixture of amusement and irritation.

No way, Melis. It's not going to happen.

"I didn't think she was going to hold up." Wilson had joined him at the rail. "Today had to be damn hard for her."

"Yes."

"Her friend Gary didn't have any doubts. He said he'd known her from the time she came to live with Lontana when she was a teenager, and she was always the toughest little scrapper he'd ever run across. You'd never guess it. She looks like she'd melt in the rain."

"No chance of that." He watched her get into a taxi. Still no look back. "And that air of fragility can be a powerful weapon for a woman."

"I don't think she'd use it. I think she'd hate to admit that she wasn't strong." He glanced at Kelby. "Not everyone's like Trina. So don't be so damn judgmental, you cynical bastard."

"I'm not judging. I couldn't care less. I

just have to take stock of any ammunition she might have."

"You didn't get what you wanted from her?"

"Not yet."

"So what do we do?"

"I take the next plane to Tobago. And you find out everything you can about Lontana and Melis Nemid."

"How far back?"

"All the way, but concentrate on the last year. He only tried to contact me in the last month, and according to what you found out from St. George he wasn't acting normally for the past six months."

"If the suicide theory is correct, his mental state may not have been—"

"Discard theories. Get me facts."

"How quick do you want the report?" Wilson asked.

"Fast. Have the preliminary findings waiting for me when I reach Tobago."

"Fine. Anything else?"

"Yes, there was a cruiser out there this afternoon while we were searching. I saw it several times. It never got close enough for me to get a number, but I think the first three letters of the name on the hull were *S-I-R*."

"Great. That's giving me zilch. And that's a popular cruise area. Maybe a fisherman? Or someone from the insurance company?"

"Find out if there were any cruiser rentals."

"Even if it was rented, it could have been leased anywhere along the coast. I suppose you want that by the time you get to Tobago too?"

The taxi was pulling away and Melis was still staring straight ahead.

"Don't be sarcastic, Wilson." Kelby turned and headed for his cabin. "You know you enjoy doing the impossible. It's great for your ego. That's the reason you've stayed with me all these years."

"Is it?" Wilson was already reaching for his phone. "That's news to me. And here I thought it was because I wanted to gouge enough loot out of you to retire on the Riviera."

Chapter Three

As usual, Susie and Pete met Melis at the net.

She had never figured out how the dolphins knew she was coming. Of course their hearing was phenomenal, but they often ignored the arrival of the mail boat or passing fishermen. Yet they were always there when she returned from any trip. She'd even run tests to try to fool them. Once she'd left the boat a mile from the net and swum the rest of the way. But their instinct was unerring. They were always there, waiting, squeaking, clicking, whistling, dipping, swimming joyously in giddy circles.

"Okay, okay, I've missed you too." She floated the motorboat over the net before fastening it again. "Have you been giving Cal a bad time while I've been gone?"

Susie gave her high, clicking squeak that was so like laughter.

Dear God, it was good to be home. After the ugliness and horror she'd gone through in Athens, being here with Pete and Susie was like having a loving hand stroking, soothing her.

"I thought so." She restarted the motor. "Come on, we'll get some supper and you can tell Cal you're sorry."

Again, that joyous laughter as the dolphins raced ahead of her toward the cottage.

Cal met her at the pier, his expression sober. "You okay?"

No, she wasn't okay. But she was better now that she was home. "Gary called you?"

He nodded as he tied up the boat. "I'm damn sorry, Melis. I'll miss him. We'll all miss him."

"Yes, we will." She got out of the boat. "Do you mind if we don't talk about Phil right now? I've got to come to terms with it in my own way."

"Sure." Cal fell into step with her. "Then can we talk about Kelby?"

She stiffened. "Why?"

"Because Kelby offered Gary a job on the *Trina.*"

She stopped and stared at him. "What?"

"Good wages. Interesting work. It wouldn't be like crewing on the *Last Home,* but we have to make a living."

"We?"

"Gary said that there was a job for Terry and me too. He gave me Kelby's cell-phone number. He said to call him if we wanted the job." He looked away from her. "And if you didn't mind."

She did mind. The thought of losing these men with whom she'd grown up made her feel a little lost. "You think you could be happy working for Kelby?"

"Gary likes him and he's talked to the crew on the *Trina.* They say Kelby's fair, and as long as you're square with him, he'll be square with you." He paused. "But we don't have to take the job. Not if you don't like the idea. I know you and Phil didn't agree about Kelby. But his rep is pretty good."

His reputation was better than good.

Kelby was the rising star in the profession Phil had loved so well. He'd already discovered two galleons in the Caribbean. It was one of the reasons she'd harbored resentment. In the relatively short time he'd been in the business, he'd effortlessly overshadowed Phil's accomplishments.

She was being selfish. She had felt so safe when she'd reached the island that it hurt to realize Kelby was able to reach out even here and take these old friends away. "It doesn't matter what I think. Do what's best for you."

"We'd feel bad if you—"

"Cal, it's okay. Call Kelby and take the job. It's not as if you're going to work for a group of terrorists. I would have had to find all of you new berths anyway. I can't keep you employed here, so you might as well go where you can get work." He was still frowning and she forced herself to smile. "Unless you want me to hire you to help take care of Pete and Susie?"

"God, no," he said, horrified. "Do you know what they did to me? They stole my trunks. I was taking a morning swim and that female came up from below and jerked them off me. I thought I was being attacked. A man's privates should be respected."

She smothered a smile. "Only a little prank. They don't understand clothing. It's just another toy to them."

"Yeah? Well, I don't understand being stripped down to my birthday suit."

He was so outraged she couldn't resist. "They must have found you appealing. Dolphins are very highly sexed, you know."

"Oh, my God."

She chuckled and shook her head. "They were just playing. Neither of them has reached sexual maturity yet. They're only about eight years old and it may still be a year or two."

"Remind me not to be around. And that's not all they did. I couldn't get in the boat without them tipping it over."

"I can see you've suffered. I'll talk to them about it." She opened the front door. "After supper I promise I'll have them apologize."

"I don't want an apology. They wouldn't mean it anyway." He scowled. "Just don't leave me alone with them again."

"Not unless I absolutely have to do it."

His gaze narrowed on her face. "What's that supposed to mean? You never leave the island these days unless you're forced."

"Things happen. I didn't want to leave

here when you brought me those documents from Phil, but I did." She headed for the kitchen. "Besides, you won't be here for me to call on if you're going to take that job with Kelby."

"I never leave a buddy in the lurch."

She was touched. "Thanks, Cal. I hope I won't have to subject you to any more of the dolphins' tricks."

"Don't worry. I can handle them." He hesitated. "Maybe."

"They really like you or they wouldn't play with you. You should be flattered. It's a wonderful comp—"

"I don't want to be flattered. I just want to keep my drawers on." He gave her a nudge toward the lanai. "You look tired. Go out and sit down. I'll make supper." He hesitated. "I was wondering . . . Is there anyone we should tell about Phil? He didn't have any family, did he?"

"No one he's kept in touch with over the years. You and the other guys were more his family than any relation." But there was one person she should call. Not for Phil's sake, but Carolyn would be concerned if she found out later that Melis hadn't told her. "Maybe I will make a phone call or two."

"Do you need me?" Carolyn asked quietly. "Say the word and I'll hire a seaplane here in Nassau and be outside those nets in a heartbeat."

"I'm okay." Melis gazed out at the sea where Pete and Susie were playing. "Well, not okay. But I'm pulling myself together."

"What are you feeling? Anger? Sadness? Guilt?"

"I don't know yet. I'm still numb. I know I was glad to get home. I feel as if everything is dammed up inside me and can't get out."

"I'm on my way."

"No, I know what your appointment book looks like. You have clients, for God's sake."

"And I have a friend who needs me."

"Look, I'm coping. If you want to come here this weekend, I'll be glad to have you. You haven't seen Pete and Susie for a while anyway."

There was a silence on the other end of the line, and Melis could almost see the thoughtful frown on Carolyn's café au lait face. "Are you alone?"

"No, Cal is here. And, even if he wasn't,

I'm never alone, Carolyn. I have the dolphins."

"Yeah, they're really great to confide in."

"Actually, they are. They don't talk back."

Carolyn chuckled. "Okay, I'll wait until the weekend. And next week I'll arrange a few days off and we'll take my boat over to Paradise Island. We'll lie on the beach and drink piña coladas and forget about the world."

"That sounds great."

"Yes, and totally unrealistic. But that's okay too." She paused. "You call me if you need me. This has been coming for a long time, you know. If that dam breaks, I want to be there for you."

"I'm fine. I'll expect you Friday afternoon." She was silent a moment. "Thanks, Carolyn. Have I ever told you how much it means to me to have a good friend like you?"

"In one of your more sentimental moments I'm sure it came up. I'll see you Friday." She hung up.

And today was Tuesday. Melis felt a wave of loneliness, and suddenly the weekend seemed a long time away. She had an impulse to call Carolyn back and—

Stop it. What would she do if she did call her back? Whine and tell her she'd changed her mind? She couldn't lean on anyone, not even Carolyn.

Just keep busy with the dolphins. Let the island soothe and heal her.

If that dam breaks, I want to be there for you.

There wasn't going to be a dam break. She was in control just as she'd always been.

And Friday wasn't that far away.

Fifteen minutes after Kelby got off the plane in Tobago, his phone rang.

"Is this soon enough for the first report?" Wilson asked. "I didn't want to keep you waiting."

"Did anyone ever tell you that you're an overachiever?" He paid the porter as he got into the cab. "The docks," he told the driver as he sat back in the cab. "What have you got for me?"

"Not as much as I'd like. You know about Lontana's professional background."

"Not in the last year or so."

"That's because he disappeared from sight about two years ago. No one knew where he was or what he was doing."

"Some sort of exploration?"

"His ship never left Nassau harbor until about a year ago. Then he flew in and sailed out in the *Last Home* in a big hurry. He didn't tell anyone where he was going or when he'd be back."

"Interesting."

"And right after he left, some pretty rough types were searching for him in Nassau, asking questions in a very ugly way."

"Where was Melis Nemid all this time?"

"On her island taking care of her dolphins."

"Did she know where he was?"

"If she did, she wasn't talking."

"Tell me about Melis Nemid."

"Some more blanks. She seems to have hooked up with Lontana when she was a kid of sixteen. He was studying oceanic thermal vents off the coast of Santiago, Chile, and she was in the custody of a Luis Delgado. She was going to school and working for his Save the Dolphin foundation. According to Gary St. George, she was a quiet, withdrawn child, and her whole life seems to have been geared toward study and working with the dolphins. She's evidently one very smart cookie. Most of her education was home schooling on the Internet and on-the-job training. But she was accepted for college courses at sixteen and has earned an advanced degree in marine biology over the years."

"Very smart."

"And she seems to like her dolphins better than people. She's alone on that island most of the time. Of course, she did leave the island about six months ago to go to Florida. But that was to protest the bureaucracy that was interfering with the saving of stranded dolphins."

"What happened to this Luis Delgado?"

"He moved to San Diego when she was sixteen."

"And just left her?"

"That's one of the blanks. I only know that same week she sailed out of Santiago with Lontana and has been with him ever since. She's been on several of his explorations on the *Last Home,* but they seem to pretty much live their own lives."

"And what about this island where she lives?"

"Lontana bought it with the money he received from salvaging that Spanish galleon. If you're thinking about paying her a visit,

I wouldn't do it without an invitation. The only access is an inlet on the south side of the island, and that's barricaded by an electrified net to protect the dolphins. The vegetation is so lush that you can't even land a helicopter."

"I wasn't going to pay her a visit yet. I'm renting a cruiser and staying here until you give me something to use. I think she needs a little time to come to terms with Lontana's death."

"Then why are you there?"

Kelby ignored the question. "What did you find out about that cruiser I saw while we were searching for Lontana?"

"I'm still working on it. There's a possibility we may track it down soon if it's a lease. The *Siren* is owned by a British leasing company in Athens. There are lots of other *Sirens* registered, but they all have an adjective preceding the noun. Of course, I may be on the wrong track entirely." He paused. "You think someone may have followed her?"

"Maybe. Get me names and descriptions as soon as you can."

"Tomorrow."

"Today."

"You're a hard man, Kelby. Anything else?"

"Yes, try to locate Nicholas Lyons and get him down here."

"Oh, shit."

He chuckled. "It's okay, Wilson. The last I heard from him he was being very circumspect and legal—for him."

"Which isn't saying much. I suppose I'm going to have to look forward to bribing you both out of jail again?"

"You only had to do it once. And that jail in Algiers was very secure or we'd have managed to get out ourselves."

"I think you chose the worst elements possible to befriend while you were in the SEALs."

"No, I was the worst element possible, Wilson."

"Well, thank God you decided to grow up and stop playing commando. It would have been just like you to get killed and leave me with all that paperwork to straighten out."

"I wouldn't do that to you."

"Yes, you would." Wilson sighed. "Do you have any idea where Lyons is?"

"St. Petersburg."

"Can you call him?"

"No, he changes phones frequently."

"Which all circumspect and legal citizens do."

"Wilson. Find him. Get him to call me."

"It's against my better judgment." He paused. "I found out one more thing from Gary St. George about Melis Nemid. For the first two years she was with Lontana, she paid regular visits to some shrink in Nassau. Dr. Carolyn Mulan."

"What?"

"She didn't make any secret of it. She was very matter-of-fact about the visits to this Dr. Mulan. She even joked about it. He thought she'd been under a psychiatrist's care in Santiago too."

"That's a surprise. I'd judge her to be one of the most well-balanced people I've ever run across."

"Do you want me to try to contact her doctor and try to pump her?"

"There's such a thing as patient confidentiality."

"A little well-placed bribery could jump over that barrier."

Kelby knew that better than Wilson.

Money talked; money could turn black into white. He'd lived with that truth since he was a child. Why was he so reluctant to turn Wilson loose on Melis Nemid's records? It was very nasty. She'd probably bared her soul to that shrink, and it would be like stripping her naked to delve into her secrets.

But she might also have told this doctor about Marinth.

"See what you can find out."

NASSAU

Jesus, it was hot today.

Carolyn Mulan wiped the back of her neck with her handkerchief before wandering over to the window to look down at Parliament Street. The air conditioner in the building was on the fritz again, and she couldn't wait to get out of the office and drive down to the beach for a swim. Maybe she'd go out on the boat and sail over to Paradise Island. No, she'd wait until she could do that with Melis. With any luck she'd be able to coax her away from the dolphins next week.

Just one more patient and she'd be free to leave.

A knock and then the door opened. "Dr. Mulan? I'm sorry to barge in like this, but it seems your secretary has stepped away from her desk." His voice was hesitant and so was his demeanor. He was fortyish, small and pale and dressed in a neat blue suit. He reminded her vaguely of a milquetoast stereotype from some classic TV show. Only she'd learned there were no stereotypes. Each patient was an individual and deserved to be treated as such.

"Has she? That's not like Maria. I'm sure she'll be back soon." She smiled. "Please come in. I'm sorry. I don't recall your name."

"Archer. Hugh Archer." He came in and closed the door. "And don't apologize. I'm used to it. I know I'm one of those men who tend to fade into the background."

"Nonsense. It's just that I usually have Maria's notes in front of me." She headed for the door. "I'll get the new-patient forms from Maria's desk and then we can talk."

"Splendid." He didn't move from in front of the door. "I can't tell you how I'm looking forward to talking to you."

It was after three A.M. when Kelby's phone rang.

"I've reached Lyons," Wilson said. "He's on his way to Tobago. I think he was glad to leave Russia."

"Why not? The Antilles are much more pleasant."

"Yeah, and the police aren't nearly as grim about smuggling."

"That's true."

"And I may have to get on a plane and head for Nassau."

"Why?"

"I can't reach Carolyn Mulan. I'll keep trying to phone her, but I may have to search her out myself."

"You tried her office?"

"I got a recording. She has a secretary, Maria Perez, but I can't reach her either."

"That's not good."

"It's not unusual for her not to come home. According to her roommate, Maria has several very healthy and torrid relationships with men in town."

"And Carolyn Mulan?"

"She's divorced and in her fifties. She has

no significant other at the moment. She practically lives on her boat when she's not in her office."

"Let me know as soon as you contact her." He hung up and moved out onto the deck. It was hot and humid and the sea stretched like a dark, placid carpet before him. Dammit, he didn't like the way the situation was shaping up with Carolyn Mulan. If he'd decided Melis's doctor might be of use, someone else might have come to the same conclusion.

He was tempted to start the engines and head out for Melis's island. He was tired of twiddling his thumbs and waiting. He'd never been a patient man, and now that he was coming so close to Marinth he was filled with restlessness.

He was acting like a kid. Wilson would find Carolyn Mulan. And he could blow everything if he didn't play Melis Nemid right. No, he would do the smart thing and wait.

At two thirty-five in the morning, Melis was woken from a deep sleep by the ringing of the telephone.

"Melis?"

The voice was so hoarse, Melis didn't recognize it for a moment.

"Melis, I—need you to come here."

Carolyn.

She sat upright in bed. "Carolyn, is that you? What's wrong? You sound—"

"I'm okay. I need you to—" Her voice broke. "I'm sorry. God, I'm sorry. Cox. I never meant— Don't come. Lies. For God's sake, don't come."

The connection was broken.

Melis reached for her telephone book, and a moment later she was dialing Carolyn's cell number.

No answer.

She called her office and home. She got the recording at both places. She sat there, frozen, trying to clear her mind.

What the hell was happening? She'd known Carolyn since she was a teenager, and she'd been Melis's friend as well as her doctor. Melis had always counted on her as a rock of strength, but she hadn't been a rock tonight. She'd sounded . . . shattered.

Panic surged through her.

"Christ." She swung her feet to the floor

and ran down the hall to the guest room. "Cal. Wake up. I've got to call the police and then leave for Nassau."

Hurry. She had to hurry.

Melis jumped out of the cab at the small terminal and hurriedly paid the driver. She whirled and headed for the front entrance.

"Melis."

Kelby was waiting inside the terminal door.

She stopped. "Jesus, that's all I need." She went past him and started for the ticket counter. "Don't bother me, Kelby. I have a plane to catch."

"I know. But you'll have to change planes in San Juan to get to Nassau by commercial jet. I've rented a private jet and a man to pilot it." He took her elbow. "We'll be there two hours earlier."

She shook him off. "How did you know I was flying out tonight?"

"Cal. He was concerned about you and you wouldn't let him go with you."

"So he called you?"

"The night he called to accept my job offer, I asked him to keep an eye out for any problems you might be having."

"Christ, I can't believe he phoned you."

"He wasn't betraying you. He was trying to help."

Her lips twisted. "And doing a favor for the new boss."

He shook his head. "He's loyal to you, Melis. He's just worried. He didn't like that phone call from Carolyn Mulan. Neither did I."

Neither did Melis. She had been frightened when she received it and her fear had been steadily growing. "It's none of your business. *I'm* none of your business."

"But Marinth is my business because I've chosen it to be. And you're part of the big picture." He stared her in the eye. "And so is Carolyn Mulan. Wilson has been trying to contact her for the last two days. Someone might have become aware that we were trying to reach her and gone after her themselves. Or maybe they got to her first and that's why we couldn't make contact."

"And who is this 'someone'?"

"I don't know. If I did, I'd tell you. There was a cruiser roaming the area when we were searching for Lontana. It could have been perfectly innocent, but I'm trying to trace it. Or I may be completely off base. Maybe Carolyn Mulan's disappearance has nothing to do with Lontana's death." He added grimly, "But I don't like the fact that she was obviously being forced to lure you to Nassau. It doesn't look good."

"Good? It's damn well terrible. You don't know what it would take to make Carolyn—"

"But you're going to Nassau, and that's what she told you not to do."

"I can't do anything else. I called the Nassau police before I left the island and they're searching for her now."

He nodded. "I called them too. I thought it might help. Anyway, I'll be on my way to Nassau to find her tonight whether or not you're coming. I'm just offering you a lift."

Her hands clenched into fists at her sides. Carolyn caught in the middle. Carolyn clawing at a cage, helpless. Nightmare. Nightmare. Damn him. Damn them all. "Is your plane ready to go?"

"Yes."

She turned away jerkily. "Then let's get out of here."

She didn't speak again until they were almost to Nassau. "Why? Why were you trying to reach Carolyn?"

"You wouldn't talk to me. I was hoping she would."

"About Marinth? She doesn't know anything. I never told her anything about Marinth."

"I didn't know that."

"And she wouldn't have told you anyway. She'd never reveal anything I told her in our sessions. She believes in doctor-patient confidentiality. Besides, she's my friend."

"I was working in the dark. I thought a bribe might tip the scales."

"Never," she said fiercely. "She's one of the most honorable people I've ever met. She's smart and kind and never gives up. God knows she never gave up on me. If I had a sister, I'd want her to be like Carolyn."

"That's saying a lot. Did Lontana like her?"

"He didn't know her very well. He found her for me, but he didn't have much to do with her. He was always a little embarrassed around Carolyn. Psychiatrists were out of

his realm. But he'd promised, so he made
sure I kept going."

"Promised you?"

"No, Kem—" She was talking too much.
None of this was his business. It was evi-
dence of her panicky desperation that she
was babbling like this to him. "The police
were very concerned. She's a very respected
citizen. Maybe they'll have found her by the
time we arrive."

"Possibly."

"She sounded— She wasn't herself." Her
voice was shaking and she stopped to steady
it. "I can't tell you how strong she is. When
I first came to her, it was like being— I'd
never permitted myself to lean on anyone
before. She could have let me become de-
pendent, but she didn't. She wouldn't let me
lean. She just gave me her hand and told me
she'd always be my friend. She never broke
her word."

"I understand the psychiatrist-patient relation can become very close."

"It wasn't like that. After those first years,
she was my best friend." She leaned back in
the seat and closed her eyes. "When she
called . . . her voice . . . I think she was
hurting."

"We don't know. We'll find out." His hand closed on hers on the arm of the seat. "Don't borrow trouble."

He wasn't denying or confirming any possibility. She wouldn't have believed him if he had. But his touch was warm and comforting and she didn't try to withdraw her hand from his grasp. She needed comfort right now, and she'd take it where she could get it.

God, she hoped the police had found Carolyn.

Chapter Four

"Ms. Nemid? Mr. Kelby?" A heavyset black man in a tan suit was waiting at the hangar when they got off the jet. "I'm Detective Michael Halley. I talked to you on the phone?"

She nodded. "Have you found Carolyn?"

He shook his head. "Not yet. But we're looking very hard for her."

Her hopes plummeted. "It's a small island. Practically everyone knows Carolyn. Someone must have seen her or heard from her. What about Maria Perez?"

He hesitated. "Unfortunately, we have found Ms. Perez."

Melis stiffened. "Unfortunately?"

"She was discovered on the beach by a group of teenagers. Her throat had been slit."

Melis felt as if she'd been punched in the stomach. She was vaguely aware of Kelby's hand closing on her arm in silent support. "How . . ."

"We don't believe the homicide took place on the beach. There were traces of blood in the outer office, Dr. Mulan's office, and also in the alley in back of the office building. The other tenants vacate the building at six, so the body was probably removed after dark and dumped on the beach."

Dumped. He made her sound like a piece of garbage, not the funny, bawdy Maria that Melis had known for years. "You're sure it was Maria? There's no mistake?"

Halley shook his head. "We've had her roommate down to the morgue and it was a positive ID. We'd like you to come down to the station and give us a statement."

She nodded numbly. "I'll do anything I can to help find Carolyn. But I don't know why anyone would want to kill Maria."

"Blackmail?" Halley shrugged. "It's a possibility. One of the file cabinets was half empty and records were stolen."

"What records?" Kelby asked.

"*M* through *Z*." He paused. "She kept your file in the office, Ms. Nemid?"

"Of course. It was safe. The cabinet was always locked."

"Evidently not that safe." He frowned. "And I don't like the fact that other files were stolen. From the worried phone calls we've been receiving, it appears Dr. Mulan has had patients in all levels of the government. It could be extremely awkward if their records are made public."

"Awkward?" Her numbness disappeared in a surge of anger. "It's too bad that your politicians may be embarrassed. I don't care if the files were stolen. Carolyn is gone, damn you. Find her."

"Easy, Melis." Kelby took a step forward and nodded at a Mercedes parked by the hangar. "I have a car waiting, Detective. We'll follow you down to the station."

Halley nodded. "I'm sorry. I didn't mean to be insensitive. It's just that this crime is posing a problem for us on a number of levels." He turned and headed for a brown sedan. "I'll be waiting for you."

"Come on." Kelby nudged Melis toward the Mercedes. "Let's get this over with." He retrieved the key from a magnet box under the rear bumper and unlocked the car. "Or I can get Halley to wait until you're less upset."

"I'm not going to be less upset. Not until we find Carolyn." She got into the passenger seat. "I was hoping— It's much worse than I thought. Maria . . . they killed Maria."

"You knew her well?"

She nodded. "She's worked for Carolyn as long as I've been her patient. She went along on a few of our trips. Carolyn thought she was good for me."

"Why?"

"She was . . . different. My exact opposite. But . . . I liked her. She was always . . ." She stared blindly out the window as he started the car. "They slit her throat. My God, they slit her throat. Why?"

"The knife is quiet and quick."

Yes, he'd know about that, she thought. She remembered reading somewhere that he'd been in the SEALs and they were accustomed to inflicting quick, quiet death. "She never hurt anyone. She just wanted to have a good time and squeeze joy out of every minute."

"Then she must have gotten in the way."

He started the car. "It's usually how the innocent are made victims."

"In the way of someone who wanted to
get to Carolyn?"

"Or the files. Halley seems to think you
may not be the only target."

"What do you think?"

"Unless your friend made more than one
phone call last night to people on her client
list, then I think you're the target and the
other records were taken as red herrings."

"And Halley would have told us if someone had come forward and said anything
about hearing from Carolyn."

He nodded. "But if those records were
compromising, they might not have come
forward. I'm only telling you what my gut
feeling is."

And that was what she was feeling too.
"Carolyn wanted to come to the island to
see me right away. I knew she was busy and
told her to wait until the weekend. Jesus, I
wish I'd let her come."

"So do I. But how could you know this
was going to happen?" He reached and
touched her hand that lay on her knee.
"Hindsight is easy. You can't blame yourself
for not being psychic. You were focusing on

me as the only threat in the entire scenario. And I don't believe you'd consider me a murder suspect."

"I was followed from my hotel to the docks in Athens. I just didn't want to think about anything concerning Phil until I could come to terms with it. I thought I was the only one who might be at risk."

"Do you have any idea—" He shook his head. "Sorry. You don't need any more questions thrown at you right now. Halley is going to be doing enough of that when we get to the station."

"I never saw him before." She hadn't moved her hand from beneath his, she realized dully. Strange. She didn't like to be touched, yet she had accepted physical contact from Kelby without question. "And I couldn't be sure that he had anything to do with Phil. I was a woman alone, and there are a lot of sexual predators out there."

"And I can see you'd be a prime target."

She stiffened and tried to move her hand.

His grasp tightened. "Not for me, dammit. Not now. It would be like kicking a puppy."

"A puppy is helpless. I'll never be helpless."

"Perish the thought. But since we're in this together and I'm no threat at present, there's nothing wrong with letting me stand by you in a bad situation." His lips tightened. "And I'd say this is one hell of a bad situation."

"I don't need you." *Bad* didn't describe the horror swirling around her. She felt as if she were enveloped in an icy, smothering fog. But Kelby was strong and full of life, and he had promised her he was no threat.

She didn't move her hand.

"Coffee?"

She looked up to see Kelby standing in front of her with a styrofoam cup in his hand. "Thanks." She accepted the cup and took a sip of the hot liquid. "You're done already?"

"It seemed pretty long to me. Halley is thorough. I had nothing to do with your friend apart from asking Wilson to try to see her. There wasn't much I could tell him."

"Or maybe he didn't want to offend you. You have big investments over in the Atlantis complex, don't you?"

"Yes, but that wouldn't stop Halley from

treating me with the same thoroughness as he did you. Dr. Mulan is evidently very important." He sat down beside her. "You've been here at the station almost six hours and this waiting room isn't very comfortable. How about letting me take you to a hotel? I'll stay here and get word to you if there's any—" She was shaking her head. "I didn't think so." He sipped his coffee. "Well, at least the coffee in the machine is decent. I've been in a few jails where it's tasted like mud."

"You have?"

"You act surprised. That's right, Wilson kept my checkered past out of the media. It's one of the only things he was able to keep from them."

"Why were you in jail?"

"Nothing too terrible. I was sowing a few wild oats after I got out of the SEALs. I was at loose ends and I wasn't sure what direction I needed to follow. I batted around from country to country trying to decide."

"And you chose oceanography."

"It kind of chose me. I loved sailing from the time I was a boy, and it was a natural progression." He took another swallow of his coffee. "Have you always known what you wanted to do?"

"Yes, since I was twelve years old. I saw the ocean, I saw the dolphins, and I knew I never wanted to leave them. They brought me peace."

"And that was important to a twelve-year-old?"

"To this twelve-year-old." She glanced at Halley through the glass partition that separated his office from the waiting room. He was picking up the phone and speaking into it. "Why is it taking so long? Do you think he knows what he's doing?"

"He seems pretty savvy. And he wants to find her, Melis."

Then why wasn't it happening? They hadn't heard anything in the hours they'd spent here. "It seems impossible that there weren't any witnesses who saw Maria and Carolyn being taken from their office."

"I'm sure they haven't interviewed everyone yet. It's still possible that— Shit." His gaze was on Halley, who had just hung up the phone. "I don't like his body language."

Melis stiffened. Halley was standing, moving toward the door leading to the waiting room. His shoulders were squared and his expression . . .

"Ms. Nemid. I'm sorry." His voice was

very gentle. "A body has washed ashore near the Castle Hotel. A woman in her fifties, tall, gray hair. We think it may be Carolyn Mulan."

"Think? Why don't you know?"

"There was some . . . damage. They're bringing the body to the morgue for identification."

"I want to see her. I can tell you if it's Carolyn."

"You may not be able to do that. Her face is pretty . . . lacerated."

Melis's nails dug into her palms as her hands clenched. "I've known her for years. She was closer than a sister to me. I can tell you if it's her."

"You don't want to see this body, Ms. Nemid."

"The hell I don't." Her voice was shaking. "It may not be her. I don't want you to stop looking while you get DNA or dental records on this woman. I want to see for myself."

Halley looked at Kelby. "If she believes she can give us a positive ID, I can't refuse. In a murder case, time is always important. But I sure as hell don't like it. Can you talk her out of it?"

Kelby shook his head. "I wish I could. No way."

"It's probably not her." Melis moistened her lips. "You don't know her. She's so strong, the strongest woman I've ever met. She wouldn't let anything happen to her. I'm sure it's someone else."

"Then why go through this?" Kelby asked roughly. "A few hours, a day, can't make—"

"Shut up, Kelby. I've got—" She turned to Halley. "Will you take me to this . . . morgue?"

"I'll take you." Kelby took her hand. "Let's get this over with, Halley."

The room was cold.

The glare of the stainlesss-steel table where the body lay covered by a white sheet was colder.

The whole world was cold. That must be why she couldn't stop shaking.

"You can change your mind," Kelby murmured. "You don't have to do this, Melis."

"Yes, I do." She stepped closer to the table. "I have to know—" She drew a deep breath and then told Halley, "Uncover her face."

Halley hesitated and then slowly drew back the sheet.

"Oh, God." She shrank back against Kelby. "Oh, Jesus, *no.*"

"Out." Kelby's arm went around her. "Let's get her away from here, Halley."

"No." She swallowed and took a step nearer. "There's still . . . It might not . . . She has a birthmark beneath the hair on her left temple. She was always going to have it removed, but she never got around to it." She gently brushed the hair back from the ruin of the woman's face.

Please. Jesus, let it not be there. Let this poor, savaged woman not be Carolyn.

"Melis?" Kelby said.

"I'm . . . sick." She barely made it across the room to the stainless-steel sink before she threw up. She hung desperately to the curled metal edge to keep from falling.

Then Kelby was there beside her, holding her. She could hear the pounding of his heart beneath her ear. Life. Carolyn's heart would never beat like that again.

"It's your friend?" Kelby said gently.

"It's Carolyn."

"You're sure?" Halley asked.

She had been sure the moment he drew

down that sheet. But she had not wanted to admit it to herself. "Yes."

"Then get the hell out of here." Halley turned away and began to draw the sheet over Carolyn's face.

"No." Melis broke free of Kelby's hold and moved back across the room. "Not yet. I have to—" She stood looking down at Carolyn's face. "I have to remember. . . ."

The pain was twisting hot and sharp through her, dissolving the ice and leaving only despair.

Carolyn . . .

Friend. Teacher. Sister. Mother.

Dear God in heaven, what did they do to you?

"This is your room." Kelby unlocked the door and turned on the light of the hotel room. "I'm next door in the adjoining room. Keep that door ajar. I want to hear you if you call out. Don't open the hall door at all."

Carolyn lying still and cold.

"Okay."

Kelby cursed beneath his breath. "You're not listening. Did you hear what I said?"

"Don't open the door. I won't. I don't want to let anyone in." She just wanted to be alone. Close the world out. Close the pain out.

"I guess that's as good as it's going to get. Remember, I'm here if you need me."

"I'll remember."

He looked at her with frustration. "I don't know what to do, dammit. This isn't my— Tell me what I can do for you."

"Go away," she said simply. "Just go away."

He didn't move, a multitude of expressions chasing across his face. "Oh, what the hell." The door closed behind him and an instant later she heard him check to make sure it was locked.

He hadn't trusted her to lock the door, she realized vaguely. Perhaps he was right. She couldn't seem to keep two thoughts together.

But she had no problem with memories. The memory of Carolyn when she'd first met her. The memory of her at the wheel of her boat, laughing at Melis over her shoulder.

The memory of the broken, torn Carolyn lying on that slab in the morgue.

She switched off the light and sank down
in the easy chair by the window. She didn't
want light. She wanted to crawl into a cave
and be alone in the darkness.

Maybe the bad memories wouldn't follow
her there.

"Jesus, you're a hard man to find, Jed."

Kelby whirled around to see a giant of a
man coming toward him down the hall.

He relaxed as he recognized Nicholas
Lyons. "Tell that to Wilson, Nicholas. He
had to scour St. Petersburg for you."

"I was having a few difficulties." He
added dryly, "But I didn't leave a trail of
bodies behind me. Wilson tells me you've
got yourself into a bit of first-class nastiness
here." He glanced at the door. "Is that her
room?"

Kelby nodded. "Melis Nemid." He
moved a few feet down the hall and unlocked his door. "Come in and I'll order you
a drink and fill you in."

"I can hardly wait." Nicholas grimaced as
he followed him. "It might be safer for me
to go back to Russia."

"But less profitable." He turned on the

light. "If you're going to risk getting yourself killed, it might as well be for something
worthwhile."

"Marinth?"

"Wilson told you?"

Lyons nodded. "It's the bait that drew me
here. I decided that you need the services of
a first-rate shaman like me if you're going to
try to mess around with Marinth."

"Shaman? You're a half-breed Apache
who grew up in the Detroit slums."

"Don't bother me with truth when I'm
concocting such a great lie. Besides, I spent
summers on the reservation. You'd be surprised what I learned about magic when I
applied myself."

No, Kelby wouldn't be surprised. He'd
realized Lyons was multifaceted from the
moment he'd met him at SEAL training in
San Diego. On the surface he was all
friendly, casual charisma, but Kelby had
never run into anyone more coolly efficient
and savage when called into action. "What
kind of magic?"

"White magic, naturally. We Indians have
to be politically correct these days." He
smiled. "Want me to read your mind?"

"Hell, no."

"What a spoilsport. You've never really let me show you my talents. I'll tell you anyway." He closed his eyes and put his hand to his forehead. "You're thinking about Marinth."

Kelby snorted. "That's an easy enough guess."

"Nothing about Marinth is easy." He opened his eyes and his smile faded. "Because it's your dream, Jed. Dreams are never simple. There are too many interpretations."

"It's your dream, too, or you wouldn't be here."

"I dream about the money it could bring. Hell, I don't know enough about Marinth for anything else. I didn't want to know. But now it appears you're going to have to fill me in."

"Okay, you've got to know that word first broke on Marinth in the late 1940s."

"Yeah, I saw that old copy of *National Geographic* you've had on the *Trina*. They did a spread on the discovery of the tomb of some scribe buried in the Valley of the Kings."

"Hepsut, scribe of the royal court. It was a great find since he'd covered the walls of his future burial place with the history of his time. Yet an entire wall was dedicated to the tale of Marinth, an island city destroyed in a great flood. It was an ancient tale even in the scribe's lifetime. Marinth was wealthy beyond belief. It had everything. Rich farmlands, a navy, a prosperous fishing industry. And it was reputed to be a technological and cultural mecca for the whole world. Then one night, the gods took back what they had created. They sent a great wave and drew the city back into the sea where it was born."

"Sounds suspiciously like Atlantis."

"That was the general consensus. Marinth was just another name for a tale about Atlantis." He paused. "Maybe it was. It doesn't matter. What does matter is that this scribe devoted an entire wall of his final resting place to Marinth. Everything else in the tomb pertained to the history of Old Egypt. Why would he change horses in midstream and tell a fairy tale?"

"So you think it's not a legend?"

"Perhaps part of it is legend. But if even a tenth of it is true, the possibilities are damn exciting."

"Like I said, your dream." His gaze went to the adjoining door. "But it's not her dream, is it? After all that's happened, it has to be more like a nightmare."

"I'll see that she reaps a profit."

"*Profit* can have a number of interpretations too."

"God, I can't stand you when you're philosophical."

"I was more enigmatic than philosophical."

Kelby crossed to the phone. "I'll order you a bourbon. Maybe it will blur your—"

"Don't bother. You know we Indians can't take firewater."

"I don't know any such thing. You've drunk me under the table any number of times."

"Well, I have to keep a clear head when you're trying to get it blown off. Besides, I don't think you're in any mood to amuse me tonight. My shaman powers sense a definite emotional downswing." He turned and headed for the door. "I still have to check into this hotel. I'll call you when I have a room number."

"You haven't asked what I want you to do."

"You want to make me rich. You want me to make your dream come true." He

paused to glance again at Melis's adjoining
door. "And you want me to help keep her
alive while we're doing it. Does that
cover it?"

"That covers it."

"And you said I wasn't a true shaman."
The door closed behind him.

Nicholas was right, Kelby thought
wearily. He was tired and frustrated and his
mood was definitely somber. It was good to
have Nicholas here, but he didn't want to
deal with him right now. He couldn't shake
the memory of Melis Nemid's face as she
had looked down at the horror that had once
been her friend. He had wanted to curse and
rage and then scoop her up and carry her out
of there.

An unusual reaction from him. But then,
his every response had been unusual since
he'd met Melis. He could generally transform any softening in his feelings toward her
by concentrating on some other element,
such as her sexuality, as he had in the hospital in Athens. But he hadn't been able to do
that since he'd met her at the airport in
Tobago. Yes, he'd been sexually aware of
her, but there had been so damn much

more. She seemed to trigger emotions that he wasn't even aware he had anymore.

And she hadn't opened the adjoining door as he'd told her to do.

Kelby crossed the room and opened it a narrow crack. There was no light in her room, but he could sense she was awake—and in pain. It was as if he were connected to her in some way. Crazy.

He'd be glad when she was less vulnerable and he could get more perspective on the situation.

Don't think about her. He'd call Wilson and see if he'd managed to trace that cruiser. Then he'd contact Halley and give him his room number in case he had any new info.

Don't think about Melis Nemid sitting in that room. Don't think of her pain. Don't think of her courage. Just keep busy and work toward the goal. The dream. Marinth.

Kelby knocked on the adjoining-room door and then opened it all the way when she didn't answer. "Are you okay?"

"No."

"Well, I'm coming in anyway. I decided

to let you alone to grieve for a while, but you've been sitting here in the dark for the past twenty-four hours. You need to eat."

"I'm not hungry."

"Not much." He flipped on the light as he entered the room. "Just enough to combat the shock. I've ordered some tomato soup and a sandwich." He grimaced. "I know you don't want me here, but you'll have to tell me if there's someone else you need me to call."

She shook her head. "Have they finished with the autopsy?"

"You don't want to talk about this."

"Yes, I do. Tell me."

He nodded. "They rushed it and the DNA test. They wanted a final confirmation for a number of reasons."

"The people whose records were stolen."

"I admit Halley's taking some heat. It's—" He broke off at a knock on the door. "There's your meal." He crossed the room and she heard him talking to the waiter. Then he was shutting the door and wheeling in a cart. "Sit down and eat something. I'll answer any questions you want after you finish."

"I'm not—" She met his gaze. He wasn't

going to budge and she needed information. It was a small price to pay. She sat down and began to eat. She finished the sandwich, left the soup, and pushed the cart aside. "When will they release Carolyn's body?"

He poured her a cup of coffee from the carafe. "Do you want me to ask Halley?"

She nodded. "She wanted to be cremated and her ashes thrown into the sea. I want to be here when that's done. I need to say good-bye."

"Her ex-husband, Ben Drake, is already taking care of the arrangements. All that's left is the release."

"Ben must be heartbroken. He still loved her, you know. They couldn't live together, but that didn't mean anything. Everyone loved Carolyn."

"You most of all." He studied her. "You're more composed than I thought you'd be. You're pale as a ghost, but I was expecting a complete breakdown when I brought you here. You were on the brink."

She was still on the brink. She felt as if she were walking on the edge of a cliff, putting one foot in front of the other, and never sure if the ledge would collapse beneath her. "I wouldn't do that to Carolyn." She kept her voice steady with an effort. "She would have been disappointed in me if I let myself go to pieces. She would have felt as if she'd failed me."

"If she was as kind as you say, I don't think she'd mind if you let go and—"

"I'd mind." She stood up and moved toward the window that overlooked the sea. "Have they found anything more about Carolyn's death?"

"The official verdict is loss of blood."

She braced herself. "She was tortured, wasn't she? Her poor face . . ."

"Yes."

"What . . . did they do to her?"

He was silent.

"Tell me. I have to know."

"So that you can hurt more?" he asked roughly.

"If they tortured her, it was because they wanted her to get me here. They almost succeeded, so they must have hurt her terribly." She folded her arms across her chest. Hold tight. Draw into a shell and the words won't hurt so much. "If you don't tell me, I'll ask Halley."

"They used a knife on her face and breasts. They pulled two molars out by the roots from the back of her mouth. Are you satisfied now?"

Pain. Hold tight. Hold tight. Hold tight.

"No, I'm not satisfied, but I know the tally now." She swallowed. "Halley has no clues? No witnesses?"

"No."

"What about the name she said? Cox."

"Immigration has one Cox who's recently arrived here. But he's a solid citizen in his seventies, a philanthropist. Besides, I don't think the scumball listening to Dr. Mulan's conversation would have permitted her to tell you his name. Maybe she was confused."

"No names in her appointment book?"

"No appointment book. Gone with the file records."

"When are they having Maria's funeral?"

"Tomorrow at ten. Her mother's coming in from Puerto Rico tonight. You're going?"

"Of course."

"There's no 'of course' about it. There have been two murders in the last forty-eight hours, both of them linked to you. Someone wants to get hold of you very badly. Yet you're going to go to that funeral as if nothing has happened."

"Why not?" She smiled crookedly. "You'll keep me safe. You don't want anyone else to know anything about Marinth. Isn't that why you've been parked on my doorstep?"

He stiffened. "Sure. Otherwise I'd just let the people who carved up your friend have their go at you. What the hell do I care?"

He was angry. Maybe even hurt? She didn't know and she was in no shape to analyze what Kelby was feeling. She hardly knew the man.

No, that wasn't true. After what they had gone through together, she realized Kelby was not the spoiled, ambitious man she'd imagined him to be. He was hard, but he wasn't totally ruthless. "I spoke without thinking. I guess I have a suspicious nature."

"Yes, you do. But you're right. You just caught me off guard." He moved toward the door. "I'll be here tomorrow morning to pick you up and take you to the funeral. I'm going to go down to the station and try to harass Halley into giving me more information. I have a friend in the hall keeping an eye on you. His name is Nicholas Lyons. He's big, ugly, has long black hair, and looks

like Geronimo. Keep your door locked."
The door slammed behind him.

She was glad he was gone. He was too
strong, too vibrant. She didn't need her con-
centration divided, as it always was when
Kelby was near. She had to devote all her attention and effort to just getting through the
next hours, the next days.

And decide how to even out the tally.

Chapter Five

Melis's phone rang at nine-thirty the next morning. "I'm Nicholas Lyons, Ms. Nemid. Jed's down at the police station and running a little late. He asked me to take you to the funeral. He'll join us there."

"I'll meet you in the lobby."

"No, I'll come and get you. There are too many exits, and elevators are never safe. Jed wouldn't like it if I let you get snatched out from under us. Look through the peephole when I knock. I'm sure Jed described me. Tall, handsome, and chock-full of dignity and charm. Right?"

"Not exactly."

"Then you'll have a pleasant surprise." He hung up.

She glanced at the mirror in the foyer. Thank God she didn't look as bad as she felt. She was pale but not haggard. Not that Maria's mother would notice. She would be too devastated to be aware—

A knock.

She glanced through the peephole.

"Nicholas Lyons. See? Jed lied to you." He smiled. "He's always been jealous of me."

Kelby hadn't lied. Lyons was at least six foot five, powerfully built, and his shiny black hair was tied back in a queue. His features were so rough-hewn, they could have been called ugly if they hadn't been interesting. "Well, he wasn't right when he said you looked like Geronimo." She unlocked the door. "The only pictures I've ever seen of Geronimo were taken when he was an old man."

"He was talking about the movie version. Young, dynamic, intelligent, fascinating." His smile faded. "I'm sorry about your loss. Jed says you've been having a bad time. I just want you to know that nothing's going to happen to you when you're with me."

Strange. She believed him. He exuded a solid strength and determination that was reassuring. "Thank you. It's good to know I have Geronimo on my side."

"And at your side." He stepped back and gestured. "Let's get moving. Jed will be worried, and that always makes him difficult."

She closed the door and started toward the elevator. "You must know him very well."

He nodded. "But it took a hell of a long time. His upbringing didn't encourage him to give either trust or affection freely."

"Did yours?"

"My grandfather was awesome. Sometimes it only takes one person to make the difference."

"You didn't answer me."

"Oh, you noticed that?" He smiled. "What a perceptive woman you—" He suddenly whirled and moved in front of her as the exit door opened beside them. In the space of seconds his entire demeanor had changed from easygoing casualness to threatening intimidation. The waiter carrying a tray who stepped out of the stairwell stopped in his tracks and then took a step back. Melis didn't blame him. She would have been taken aback too.

Then Nicholas smiled, nodded at the waiter, and motioned for him to go ahead of them.

The man scurried quickly down the hall.

"What was I saying?" Nicholas asked. "Oh, yes, I was saying what a perceptive woman you are."

And what an intriguing man he was, she thought. But that was okay. It didn't surprise her that Kelby's friend had sharp edges. Like to like. And she didn't have to solve any puzzles right now. All she had to do was make it through Maria's funeral and try to give some small comfort to her mother.

Hold tight. Don't free the grief and fury. Take one step at a time.

"The Nemid woman attended the secretary's funeral today," Pennig said as soon as Archer picked up the phone. "There was no chance to get to her. Kelby was with her every minute, and she was surrounded by police and mourners."

"You kept your distance?"

"Of course I did. She saw me in Athens. The bitch stared right at me. She could recognize me."

"That's because you were clumsy. You should have been more careful."

"I was careful. I don't know how she knew I was behind her."

"Instinct. It's a quality you're short on, Pennig. But you have other talents I admire. It's those talents that I've tried to nurture. Though I was a little disappointed that you failed with Mulan after all I've taught you."

"I almost had her," Pennig said quickly. "And she wasn't easy. Sometimes the women are tougher."

"But you assured me she was broken or I'd never have let her phone Melis Nemid. That was a serious lack of judgment on your part."

"It won't happen again."

"I know it won't. Because I won't permit it."

Pennig felt a ripple of anxiety that he quickly suppressed. "Do you want me to stay here? I don't know how close I can get to her."

"Stay there for a little while. You never know when opportunity will knock. In the meantime I want you to find out everything you can about Kelby and any associates. Including his telephone number and where his boat is docked. Join me in Miami in two days if it's a no-go there in Nassau. And don't let anyone see you, dammit. Did your contacts in Miami find the two men I told you to line up?"

"Yes, two Miami locals, Cobb and Dansk. Small-time, but they'll do for surveillance of the island."

"I hope they won't be necessary. I'd be exceedingly pleased if you were able to get to Melis Nemid there in Nassau."

Pennig was silent a moment. "And what do we do if I can't?"

"Why, I find a way to stab Melis Nemid where it hurts the most," Archer said gently. "And I promise you that I won't be as inefficient as you were with Carolyn Mulan."

So quick, Melis thought as she watched Carolyn's ashes drift into the sea. Her final remains disappeared beneath the waves in seconds.

Just in that short span, the last vestige of a life was gone. But she had left so much behind. Melis took the silver whistle Carolyn had given her, kissed it, and threw it into the sea.

"What was that?" Kelby asked.

"Carolyn gave it to me for luck when I brought the dolphins home." She swallowed. "It was too pretty to use, but I always carried it with me."

"Don't you want to keep it?"

She shook her head. "I want her to have it. She'd know what it meant to me."

"Bastards."

She turned to see Ben Drake, Carolyn's ex-husband, standing beside her, staring over the rail of the cruiser into the water. His eyes were bloodshot and moist with unshed tears.

"Sons of bitches. Why the hell would anyone—" He turned away and pushed his way through the crowd to the other side of the cruiser.

"You were right, he's taking it bad." Kelby gazed around the deck at the mourners. "She had a lot of friends."

"If they'd let everyone on board who wanted to come, they'd have sunk the ship." Melis looked back at the water. "She was very special."

"It's pretty clear everyone thought so." Several minutes passed and the cruiser had turned around and was going back to dock before he spoke again. "What now?" Kelby asked quietly. "You said everything was on hold until the service for your friend was over. You can't stay here. It's too dangerous for you. Are you going back to your island?"

"Yes."

"Will you let me go with you?"

She could tell he was expecting her to refuse. She glanced back over her shoulder at the sea where Carolyn's ashes had been scattered.

Good-bye, my friend. Thank you for all you gave me. I won't forget you.

Her lips tightened as she turned back to face him. "Yes, by all means, come with me, Kelby."

"Quite a setup." Kelby watched her lower the net. "And your dolphin friends never try to get out?"

"No, Pete and Susie are happy here. Once I attached a radio tag and tried to release them, but they kept coming back to the net and calling me to let them in."

"They didn't like the big world?"

"They know it can be dangerous. And they've had all the adventures they wanted." She fastened the net after they floated over it. "Not everyone loves dolphins."

"It's hard to believe. Pete and Susie are certainly appealing." He grinned as he watched the dolphins swim giddily around the boat. "And they appear to love you."

"Yes." She smiled. "They love me. I'm family." She started the motor. "And family is important to dolphins."

"Did they adopt your friend Carolyn?"

She shook her head. "They liked her. Maybe they would have gotten closer if she'd been able to spend more time with them. She was always busy with her practice." She waved. "There's Cal on the pier. He'll be relieved I'm back. Pete and Susie make him uneasy. They sense he gets nervous and play tricks on him." She guided the boat to the pier and cut the engine. "Hello, Cal. Everything okay?"

"Fine." He helped her from the boat. "The dolphins have actually been good while you've been gone."

"I told you they liked you." She gestured to Kelby. "Jed Kelby, this is Cal Dugan, your new employee. You've talked to each other on the phone. Cal can show you your room. I'll go and shower and leave you to get to know each other. I'll see you at supper." She moved down the pier toward the house.

"I seem to have been dumped," Kelby murmured, his gaze on Melis. "I guess you have to be a dolphin to get her attention here."

"Pretty near," Cal said. "But at least she let you come. She doesn't issue many invitations."

"Unless she has a hidden agenda."

"There's nothing much hidden about Melis. She's up-front and out in the open." He grimaced. "She always tells you exactly what she thinks."

"Then she's not ready to tell me why I'm her guest." He stared after her speculatively. "At least not yet."

The sun was setting when Kelby came out on the lanai. Melis was sitting with her feet dangling in the water, talking softly to Pete and Susie.

He stopped for a moment, watching her. Her expression was soft, radiant. She looked completely different from the woman he had known since Athens.

That didn't mean she wasn't one tough cookie. He had to remember that and ignore this woman who looked like a child talking to her dolphins. Women were always the most dangerous when they seemed no threat at all. He was here for one reason, and nothing must get in the way.

Yeah, sure, a hell of a lot had already gotten in the way. But they had made it through that mess in Nassau. Now he could zero in and move toward the objective.

He strolled across the lanai toward her.

"They act as if they understand you."

Melis stiffened and looked up at Kelby. "I didn't know you were there."

"You were totally absorbed. Do they always come up and visit you after supper?" Kelby sat down on the edge of the lanai and watched Pete and Susie speed away and start playing in the sea.

"Most of the time. They usually come right at sunset. They like to say good night."

"How do you identify them in the water? Or should I say how would I identify them? You seem to have a second sense."

"Pete is larger and has darker gray markings on his snout. Susie's dorsal fin has a *V* in the center. Where's Cal?"

"I sent him to Tobago to get supplies and meet Nicholas's plane. They'll be back tomorrow."

"Nicholas Lyons is coming here?"

"Not unless you give the word. It's your island. He can stay in Tobago. I just wanted him nearby."

"He can come. I don't care."

"That's not what Cal said. According to him this is a very private island."

"That's the way I like it. But sometimes we have to ignore what we like or don't like. You may need him."

"Really?"

"Good night, guys," she called to the dolphins. "See you in the morning."

They gave a final chattering series of clicks and then disappeared beneath the water.

"They won't come back unless I call them."

"Why do you call them guys when Susie is a female?"

"When I first got to know them, they wouldn't let me get close enough to find out their sex. They're built for speed, and their genitals are tucked neatly out of sight until they have use for them. I just got in the habit of calling them that." She got to her feet. "I've made some coffee. I'll go get the cups and carafe."

"I'll come with you."

"No, stay here." She didn't want him with her. She needed a few minutes alone. Jesus, she didn't want to do this. Well, it didn't matter what she wanted. She'd made a decision and she had to stick to it.

He was standing looking out at the sunset when she came back with the tray. "God, it's beautiful. No wonder you never want to leave this place."

"There are lots of beautiful places in the world." She set the tray on the table. "And you've probably seen most of them."

"I've tried." He poured coffee and took his cup to the edge of the lanai. "But sometimes beautiful turns ugly. It depends on what happens there. I hope this place never does."

"That's why I had Phil install safeguards to protect the island."

"Cal told me that you could rev that electricity up on the net from low voltage to lethal." He paused. "And you did it before any of this particular ugliness was in the works. You evidently don't place much faith in law enforcement."

"The coast guard usually shows up after a crime. If you're going to maintain your independence, I've learned you can't really count on anyone but yourself." She looked him in the eye. "Haven't you?"

"Yes." He lifted his cup to his lips. "I wasn't criticizing your methods of taking care of yourself. I was only commenting." He turned to face her. "Okay, we've discussed scenic beauty, security, and independence. Now are you going to tell me why I'm here?"

"Why, I'm going to give you what you want. What you all want." She paused. "Marinth."

He stiffened. "What?"

"You heard me. The ancient city, the fortress, the treasure trove. The grand prize." Her lips twisted bitterly. "The trophy that was worth Carolyn and Phil giving their lives."

"You know where Marinth is?"

"I know the approximate area. It's in the Canary Islands. There are obstacles. It's not going to be easy. But I can find it."

"How?"

"I'm not going to tell you. It's important that you continue to need me."

"Because you don't trust me."

"I don't trust anyone where Marinth is concerned. I lived with Phil for years, and every one of those years he dreamed about finding Marinth. He'd read me the legends and tell me about the expeditions that went in search of the lost city. He even named his ship *Last Home* because that's how Hepsut referred to Marinth on the wall of his tomb. Phil wasn't nearly as excited about Atlantis. He was sure Marinth was the technological and cultural end of the rainbow. He spent half his life on wild-goose chases to find the city." She paused. "And then six years ago he thought he'd discovered the location. He wanted to keep it a big secret so other oceanographers wouldn't show up. He left the crew in Athens and took only me along to the site."

"And he found it?"

"He found a way to find it. And proof that it existed. He was over the moon with joy."

"Then why didn't he go after it?"

"There was a problem. He needed my help and I refused to give it."

"Why?"

"If he wanted to find it, then he could do it himself. Maybe some places need to stay buried in the ocean."

"But you're willing to help now."

"Because it's a price I have to pay. You want Marinth, just like Phil did."

"And what do you want?"

"I want the men who killed Carolyn and Phil. I want them punished."

"Dead?"

Carolyn lying on that cold metal slab.

"Oh, yes."

"And you don't believe the law will catch them?"

"I can't take the chance. And there's a chance I'd spin my wheels for a long time if I tried to find them myself. I don't have influence or money. This island is the only asset I have in the world. No, you're my best bet. You have as much money as Midas. Your background in the SEALs has taught you how to kill. Now you have motivation. I just gave it to you."

"But I have to give you what you want before I get my reward."

"I'm not a fool, Kelby."

"Neither am I. You didn't help Lontana

find Marinth, and you cared about him. Why should I believe you'll meekly lead me to it?"

"You won't believe me. But you're obsessed like Phil, so you'll take a chance that I'll keep my part of the bargain."

"You're sure of that?"

"Sure enough."

"Give me proof you know where Marinth is located."

"I don't have proof here I can show you. You'll have to trust me."

"If it's not here, where is it?"

"It's near Las Palmas."

"That's vague enough. Why don't we fly out there and you can show me?"

"If I showed you the proof, you might decide you didn't need me."

"Then you'd have to trust me, wouldn't you?" He shook his head. "We're at a stalemate. Outfitting a ship for this kind of expedition can be very expensive. I'm supposed to spend all that cash on the chance you're telling me the truth? Wilson wouldn't approve of me going on a wild-goose chase."

"Why are you arguing?" She frowned. "This is what you've wanted from me since you met me. Now I'm giving it to you."

"You're telling me you're giving it to me. Do you know how many times in my life I've trusted people and had them bite me in the ass? A long time ago I swore it would never happen to me again. You show me why I should think you're any different. I don't see any sign of either proof or bond." He was silent a moment. "I'll think about it."

She felt a ripple of panic. She hadn't expected his hesitation. Phil wouldn't have hesitated. Anything and everything for the dream. "What else do you want?"

"I said I'd think about it."

"No, I need you to do this. Carolyn was . . . I can't let them go free after what—" She drew a deep breath. "What do you want from me? I'll do anything. Do you want me to go to bed with you? I'll do it. That's a sort of promissory note, isn't it? Whatever it takes to make sure—"

"For God's sake, shut up. I don't want to screw you."

"You've never thought of it?" Her lips twisted. "Of course you have. Men . . . like me. They always have. It's something about the way I look. Carolyn used to say it aroused the conqueror instinct, that I had to accept it and deal with it. Well, I'm dealing with it, Kelby. You want a little something extra added to Marinth? You can have it. Just give me your promise."

"Son of a bitch."

"Just your promise."

"I'm not giving you anything." He took a step toward her, his eyes glittering in his taut face. "Hell, yes, I want to fuck you. I've wanted to do it from the first time I saw you in Athens. But you don't try to jump a woman who's already walking wounded. Dammit, I'm not an animal. I won't treat you like a whore even though you're offering to be one. If I decide to go after Marinth, it won't be because I want to get in you."

"Am I supposed to thank you for that? You don't understand. I don't care what you do. It won't mean anything to me."

He muttered an oath. "Jesus, no wonder you're a target. I don't know a man who wouldn't want to fuck you just to prove you wrong." He turned on his heel and headed for the lanai doors. "I've got to get the hell away from you. I'll talk to you in the morning."

She had blundered, she thought in despair when he'd disappeared inside the cottage. She had meant to be cool and businesslike, but at the first hint of opposition she'd panicked. She'd offered him the one commodity she knew was acceptable.

But it hadn't been acceptable to him. For some reason she'd made him both angry and indignant.

Not that he hadn't wanted it. She knew all the signs. His body had been tensed, primed, and she had sensed a raw sexuality.

And she hadn't drawn back from it.

The realization stunned her. There had not been the usual instinctive rejection. Perhaps it was because she was still in an emotional vacuum. Though she had been emotional enough to feel panic when she thought he was refusing to help her.

Forget it. She'd try to persuade him again in the morning. He would have all night to think about Marinth and all it would mean to him. Sex was only a temporary lure for a man anyway. Ambition and the hunger for riches were solid and permanent and swept everything else away in their wake. Who should know that better than she?

The moon was coming up, and the light was clear and beautiful on the water. She would stay here a little while and maybe she'd become more calm before she went to bed. Right now she felt as if she'd never sleep again. Her gaze went to the net across the inlet. So much evil beyond that net. Sharks, barracuda, and the vermin who had killed Carolyn. She had always felt safe here on the island, but not now.

Not now . . .

Christ, he was hard.

And stupid, Kelby thought in disgust. Bonehead stupid. Why walk out on her? He wasn't usually into self-denial. Sex was there. Take it.

It had to be the unexpectedness of the offer that had thrown him for a loop. She'd never indicated she'd been aware of the underlying sexual tension he felt. Hell, she'd been in an emotional tailspin since the moment he'd met her.

And that was the damn problem.

Okay, forget sex and concentrate on what was important. Could he believe her when she said she could give him Marinth? She was obsessed with finding the men who had killed her friend. She could be lying about knowing where it was located. She could also be lying about fulfilling her part of the bargain. It was a loaded situation.

And one he couldn't view objectively without a cold shower.

Kelby's phone rang as he was heading for the bedroom.

"I've found out who leased the *Siren*," Wilson said as soon as he picked up. "Hugh Archer. He was accompanied by a Joseph Pennig. It wasn't easy. I spent a hell of a lot of your money. Spiro, the owner of the rental company, was scared shitless to talk."

"Why?"

"I gather there were some ugly threats involved. Spiro's a tough old bird and not above renting his boats to the drug runners out of Algiers. So the threats had to be very nasty. He said that Pennig threatened to cut off his dick if he didn't forget he had ever seen them."

"Yes, I'd say that would give any man pause. Did you get any background information on Archer from Spiro?"

"Well, he didn't make him fill out a credit application," Wilson said dryly. "But he asked a few discreet questions after Archer paid up front in cash for the lease."

"Drug runner?"

"Not currently. He's into buying and selling

arms. Very big player. He's rumored to have smuggled nuclear components into Iraq."

"Then he'd have had no problem getting the plastique that blew up the *Last Home*."

"But why? Unless Lontana was involved in transporting some of his merchandise."

"I don't know why. Marinth could be enough of a draw. Maybe Lontana was helping Archer, then got in the way. Though dredging up a lost city is never get-rich-quick. You have to invest time and a hell of a lot of money before you see the bonanza. But I'm still leaning toward Marinth. Carolyn Mulan was kidnapped because they wanted to get their hands on Melis. And Melis knows about Marinth."

"And Lontana tried to contact you to talk about Marinth. You want me to try to get a background on Archer and find out where he's coming from?"

"You know it. Try to find out if he was in the Bahamas in the last week. How long do you think it will take you?"

"How the hell do I know? I don't have any contacts with Interpol."

"Then make them. I don't know how much time we have."

"Talk to Lyons," Wilson said sourly. "I'm sure he's been on an intimate footing with the police on several continents."

"Intimate maybe. But not exactly friendly."

"Melis is giving you a lead on Marinth?"

"Yeah, you could say that. Get back to me." He hung up.

Archer. The man in the cruiser now had a name and a past. A very dirty past. Well, if he'd been responsible for the deaths of Lontana, Maria Perez, and Carolyn Mulan, he had an even more ugly present. He'd be no loss if Kelby decided to go after him.

If? The decision was already made. Why should he hesitate? Since he'd first met Melis he'd been weak as water and he was sick of it. He had a line on Archer. He could find ways to pressure Melis into keeping her bargain. Marinth was on the horizon waiting for him.

So do what he wanted. Go after Marinth. Take the bargain.

And definitely take the sex.

Chapter Six

Melis's phone rang at twelve-thirty in the morning.

Carolyn.

She hadn't been sleeping, but the sound still caused her to jerk upright in bed. It was too reminiscent of that night when Carolyn had called her. Hurt. Dying . . .

The phone rang again.

Cal calling from Tobago?

She pressed the button.

The male voice was smooth, soft. "Melis Nemid?"

It wasn't Cal. "Yes. Who is this?"

"Special delivery."

"What?"

"I have a package for you."

"Is this some kind of joke?"

"Oh, no, I'm very serious. I've left your present tied to the net. I got a nasty shock. It left me with a very bad feeling toward you."

"What the hell is this all about?"

"You know, you really shouldn't have been so stubborn about Marinth. It's good for me, but you're not going to like the consequences."

"Who is this?"

"We'll talk later. Go get your present."

"I'm not going anywhere."

"I think you will. Curiosity is such a lure. You know, those dolphins squealing at me were very annoying."

She stiffened. "If you hurt them, I'll cut your throat."

"Such violence. You have a lot in common with one of my employees. You must meet him." He paused. "It was delightful talking directly to you. It's much better than just listening in on your conversation." He hung up.

She sat there, frozen.

That last sentence could mean only one thing.

Carolyn. He'd been the one listening, forcing Carolyn to lie to her.

"Christ." She jumped out of bed, pulled on her shorts and T-shirt, and ran out of the bedroom. She opened the electric box and pulled the lever to up the power. The front door slammed behind her as she darted out of the house.

"Where the hell are you going?" Kelby was standing in the doorway as she ran down the pier.

"Susie and Pete. That son of a bitch is going to hurt my guys." She untied the motorboat. "I won't let—"

"What son of a bitch?" Kelby was beside her, jumping into the boat. "And why should he want to hurt the dolphins?"

"Because he's a bastard." She started the engine. "Because that's what he does. He hurts things. He cuts and slashes and makes—"

"Will you tell me what the hell is happening?"

"I got a call from the son of a bitch who killed Carolyn. He told me he had a present for me. And then he started talking about Pete and Susie and how—" She drew a deep, shaky breath. "I'll kill him if he's hurt them."

"That's what you had in mind for him anyway. Did he tell you his name?"

"No, but he as good as told me he was the one listening when Carolyn called me." She reached down and grabbed two powerful lanterns and tossed them to him. "Make yourself useful. Shine those beams beyond the net. He could be out there with a rifle waiting for me."

"It's not logical." He lit the lanterns and shone the beam on the black waters beyond the net. "Nothing. I don't think he wants you dead."

"Screw logic." She slowed the boat as she approached the net. "Oh, God, I don't hear Pete and Susie."

"Maybe they're underwater."

"Not if someone was fooling around with the net. They're like guard dogs." She took the whistle she wore around her neck and blew into it. She still didn't hear them. Panic surged through her. "They could be hurt. Why aren't they—"

"Easy. I hear them."

She heard them, too, she realized with relief. A high clicking near the south bank of the inlet. She turned the boat. "Shine the light on them. I have to make sure they're okay."

Two sleek gray heads lifted as she approached. They didn't appear to be injured, only agitated. "It's okay, guys," she called soothingly. "I'm here. Nothing is going to happen to you."

They chattered excitedly and Susie started to swim toward her.

But Pete was staying at the net, swimming back and forth as if on guard.

"Get closer. There's something on the other side of the net." Kelby was focusing the lantern on the area beyond Pete. "I see it glittering in the water."

"Glittering?" Now she could see it too. It looked like a section of a fence, perhaps two by three feet. "What the hell is it?"

"Whatever it is, it's been fastened to the net," Kelby said. "And we won't be able to retrieve it until you lower the net and turn off the power."

She moistened her lips. "My present."

"It doesn't look very lethal. But it's your call."

"I want to know what it is. Keep that lantern on." She started toward the disconnect point. In three minutes she'd lowered the net, disconnected the power, and was on her way back to Pete. The dolphin made no attempt to cross the lowered net. He was silent, swimming back and forth before the object in the water.

"He's worried," Melis said. "He senses something . . . not right. He's always been more sensitive than Susie." She stood staring at the object floating just beneath the surface. She didn't want to look at it. Like Pete, she felt a kind of foreboding.

"We don't have to retrieve it now," Kelby said quietly. "I'll come back later and get it."

"No." She edged the boat closer. "As you said, it's not logical that he'd want to blow me up or anything. I'll pull alongside and you can reach over and untie it from the net."

"If that's what you want." He bent over the side and plunged his hands beneath the water. "It's fastened with rope. It will take me a minute. . . ."

She didn't care if it took him a decade. She hoped the damn thing would sink to the bottom of the sea. He'd put the lanterns down in the bottom of the boat, but light speared out over the water and she could see that odd glittering surface. She was starting to shake.

Gold. It looked like gold.

"Got it." He pulled the wooden panel onto the boat and examined it. "But what the hell is it? Pretty carved fretwork. This looks like gilt paint, but there's no message painted on it."

Golden lacy fretwork.

"You're wrong. There's a message," she said numbly.

Golden lacy fretwork.

"I don't see—" He broke off as he lifted his gaze to her face. "You know what it is."

"I know." She swallowed, hard. Don't be sick. "Throw it back into the sea."

"You're sure?"

"Dammit. Get *rid* of it."

"Right." With all his strength he hurled the panel back into the sea.

She turned the boat and headed back to shore.

"Melis, you have to raise the net," Kelby said quietly.

My God, she'd forgotten. She'd never forgotten to safeguard the island in all the time she'd been here. "Thanks." She turned the boat and headed back to the net.

He didn't speak again until they were once more on their way back to the cottage. "Are you going to tell me what message Archer sent you?"

"Archer?"

"Wilson says his name is Hugh Archer. If he's the same man who leased that cruiser in Greece."

"Why didn't you tell me?"

"I didn't have a chance. I just found out tonight and you were in no mood to listen. You were afraid for your dolphins."

She was still afraid. So much ugliness. She couldn't imagine the degree of ugliness in Archer that had led him to send her that panel.

"You didn't answer me. Are you going to tell me what that panel meant to you?"

"No."

"Well, that's succinct. Then will you tell me if it's a onetime contact or the opening play?"

"There'll be more." She cut the engine at the pier. "Soon. He'll want to hurt me again."

"Why?"

"Some men are like that." Was she talking

about the past or present? They were blurring together. "He probably liked hurting Carolyn. Power. They like power. . . ." She started toward the house.

"Melis, I can't help you if you're going to leave me in the dark."

"And I can't talk to you right now. Leave me alone." She went into the house and straight to her room. She turned on all the lights and huddled in the chair, staring at her phone on the bedside table where she'd thrown it. She had to stop shaking. He'd call her soon and she had to be ready.

God, she wished she could stop shaking.

He didn't call back.

She gave up and went to take a shower when the first light of dawn broke over the horizon. The hot water felt good on her chilled body, but it didn't relax her tensed muscles. Nothing would do that until the waiting was over. She should have expected him to draw it out.

Waiting had always been a form of torture for her. He would know that. He would know everything.

Kelby was sitting in a chair and nodded at the carafe on the table when she came out on the lanai. "I made fresh coffee when I heard you stirring." His gaze raked her face. "You look like hell."

"Thank you." She poured the coffee. "You don't look very spry yourself. Have you been out here all night?"

"Yes. What did you expect? When you ran into that room, you looked like a Holocaust survivor who'd been thrown back into Auschwitz."

"And you were curious."

"Yeah, you could say that. If you don't want to give me credit for concern. Are you going to talk to me?"

"Not yet." She set her phone on the table before she sat down on the lounge chair. She stared out over the water. "He . . . has my files. I told Carolyn things I've never told anyone. He knows exactly what will hurt. He's trying to find a way to manipulate me."

"Son of a bitch."

"Isn't that why you followed me from Athens? You needed to find a hook to make me tell you about Marinth. He wants the same thing you do."

"I don't believe I appreciate you comparing the two of us."

"No, there's no one on earth as low as this bastard."

"How comforting."

She should probably apologize. She was so exhausted it was difficult to think. "I didn't mean— It's just that I'm caught and I have to fight my way out. I don't know who or where to— I wouldn't have told you I wanted to come to terms if I'd thought you were like him."

"Then the offer is still open?"

"Yes, did you think I'd let him intimidate me?" Her lips tightened. "I'd never give in to him. I'll never let him get what he wants."

"We don't know what he wants yet."

"Marinth. He told me."

"Archer is a big-time arms dealer. I don't know how he could even have become involved. I can see him skimming some cream off the top of a very rich find, but he's—"

"He's an arms dealer?"

"Yes." His gaze narrowed on her face. "That struck a note. Why?"

"Because I may know how he became involved. Phil needed money for the expedition. I'm sure that's why he wanted to contact you. But Archer might have heard about Phil and got in touch with him."

"Heard what?"

She didn't answer for a moment. It was difficult to trust anyone when she was so used to protecting Phil. But Phil was dead. She didn't need to protect him any longer. "We . . . found tablets. Bronze tablets. Two small metal chests, but they were both filled with tablets."

"In Marinth."

"They weren't with the ruins. We didn't discover the ruins. Phil thought they'd been separated from the city by the force that destroyed it. Or maybe the tablets had been secreted there even before the cataclysm. It didn't matter. Phil was over the moon."

"I can see why."

"They were written in hieroglyphics, but they were a little different from any seen in Egypt. Phil had to be very careful to choose a translator he could trust, and it took over a year for him to get them deciphered."

"Jesus."

"That excites you. It excited him too." She paused. "Me, too, at first. It was like discovering a brand-new world of knowledge and experiences."

His gaze narrowed on her face. "But something turned you off. What?"

"Sometimes new worlds aren't all that they're cracked up to be. But Phil was happy. He'd been studying thermal vents on the ocean floor, and one of the tablets gave him something he thought would change the world. A formula for creating a sonic apparatus that could tap the vents and possibly the magma at the earth's core. It would furnish geothermal power that would be both cheap and clean. He was going to save the world."

"He invented this apparatus?"

"Yes, it took him a long time, but he did it."

"And it worked?"

"It could have worked. If it had been used as he intended. He went to a U.S. senator who was big on environmental issues. They gave him a lab and a team to complete his work on the device." She moistened her lips. "But he didn't like what was happening there. There was too much talk about volcanic effects and not enough about geothermal energy. He thought it was likely they intended to use it as a weapon."

"A sonic gun?" Kelby gave a low whistle. "That could be one hell of a weapon. Earthquakes?"

She nodded. "Absolutely."

"You're very certain."

"There was an . . . incident. A tragedy. It wasn't Phil's fault. He'd already grabbed his notes and the prototypes and gotten out of there. He promised me he'd give up on trying to make the apparatus operable." She grimaced. "But he didn't give up on Marinth. He started searching again."

"And you think that Archer found out about the experiments and decided he wanted a piece of the action?"

She shrugged. "There were some unsavory types being hired for the project. It's not impossible."

"So Archer may not be after Marinth at all. Do you have Lontana's research?"

"No prototypes." She paused. "But I have the tablets, the translations, and the work he did for the government."

"Shit. Where?"

"Not here. Do you think I'd tell you?"

"No, I guess not. But you might be safer

if someone besides you knew where they were."

She didn't answer.

"Okay, don't tell me. I'm not into sonic bombs anyway."

"No? Most men like war toys. The idea of being able to wield enough power to shake up a planet appeals to them."

"You're generalizing again. And I'm getting pretty pissed off about—"

"Someone's coming." She jumped up and headed for the house. "Don't you hear Pete and Susie?"

"No, you must have built-in antennae." He got up and followed her. "And it doesn't have to be visitors, does it?"

"No, but it is." She went through the house and out the front door. Relief surged through her. "It's Cal and Nicholas Lyons. That's right, I forgot they were coming this morning."

"You obviously had a few other things on your mind." He stood beside her on the pier watching Cal lower the net. "And they are a little early. They must have left before dawn."

She stiffened. "Why would they do that?"

"I've no idea." His gaze narrowed on the boat. "But they're no threat to you, Melis. I

don't know about Cal Dugan, but Nicholas
is straight. I've banked my life on that any
number of times."

"I've known Cal for years. I'm not worried that he might— But everything's different now. I don't know what's going to
happen next."

Cal was waving at her as he replaced
the net.

She waved back and began to relax. She
was being overanxious. Cal appeared completely casual and at ease.

"Okay?" Kelby asked. "Pete and Susie are
swimming back. Everything should be all
right with your immediate world. How
about going inside and letting me scramble
some eggs for the four of us?"

"I'll do it. I need to keep busy." She
watched Cal and Nicholas near the pier.
"Hungry?" she called. "You must have left
Tobago too early for breakfast."

"Yeah, I'm starved," Cal growled as he
drew alongside the pier. "I was going to take
Lyons to that little seaside restaurant for break-
fast, but he got a burr in his pants about getting
here right away. I told him it was nothing."

"What was nothing?" Kelby asked.

"This was left outside Cal's door," Lyons

said as he reached down to lift the object at his feet. "It had Melis's name on it."

"It's just an empty birdcage," Cal said. "I could see how you'd worry if there was a dead bird or something. It's kinda pretty. I've never seen one painted gold before."

Kafas.

She could feel the pier shifting beneath her feet. Don't faint. Don't be sick. That would make him happy. Power. Remember they love power.

"Melis?" Kelby said.

"It . . . was Archer. It had to be him."

"What do you want me to do with it?"

"I don't care. I don't want to ever see it again. Do whatever you like with it." She jerkily turned on her heel. "I'm going for a swim. You feed them, Kelby."

"Sure. Don't worry about it."

How could she worry about anything when she couldn't think of anything except that damn golden cage?

Kafas.

Nicholas gave a low whistle as he watched Melis disappear into the house. "Big trouble?"

Kelby nodded. "And the cage is only the tip of a very ugly iceberg." He turned to Cal. "Take the damn thing and tear it to pieces. Make sure she never sees it again."

Cal frowned, troubled. "I didn't mean— I didn't think it was anything to worry her." He took the cage and headed up the pier. "It was . . . pretty."

"I tried to tell him," Nicholas said. "Pretty doesn't always cut it. What's the problem?"

"An arms dealer named Hugh Archer who probably killed Lontana and Carolyn Mulan and her secretary. He was here last night outside the net doing a little harassing."

Nicholas's gaze shifted to the net. "Then he probably has a watch on the island. Want me to take a boat and scout around and see what I can see?"

"That's exactly what I want you to do."

"I thought you would. May I have break-fast first?"

"I suppose. Melis gave me orders to feed you."

"Orders? Really?" Nicholas grinned. "I think I may like this island."

Chapter Seven

Archer's call came at nine that night.

"I'm sorry to have kept you waiting, Melis. It must have been very distressing for you. But I did want to make sure that you had the full impact. Did you like the birdcage? It took me quite a long time to spray-paint it. I'm such a perfectionist."

"It was sadistic and stupid. And I wasn't at all distressed by your cat-and-mouse game."

"You're lying. You hate waiting. It brings back too many memories. You said that yourself. I believe it was on tape three."

"I got over it. I got over a lot of the traumas you're salivating over."

"Actually, you're right. I did find the tapes titillating. I adore little girls. But I believe I'd find you equally exciting now. I'm going to be very disappointed if you give me those research papers too soon."

"I'm not giving you anything."

"That's what your friend Carolyn said. Do you want to end up like her?"

"You son of a bitch."

"No, it wouldn't be like her. I have to fit the punishment to the person. As I said, I'm a perfectionist. I believe you're missing Istanbul. I think I should endeavor to find a place for you. I've never been to the one in Istanbul, but there are other *Kafas* in the world. Albania, Kuwait, Buenos Aires. I've been a patron of them all."

"I bet you have." She had to steady her voice. "It's what I'd expect of you."

"And I believe I enjoy your particular niche best of all."

The cage. The golden fretwork. The pounding of the drums.

"You can't speak right now? I can tell this is very difficult for you. Did you know that Dr. Mulan was very concerned about your prognosis? You're too controlled. She was afraid that something would trigger you and you'd become unbalanced. You have such a pleasant life. I'd really hate to see that happen. An insane asylum is a cage too."

"Are you threatening to send me over the edge?"

"Why, yes. In those sessions you were walking a fine line, you were in the depths of hell. I believe dredging up old memories might send you back there. Periodic calls that bring everything in the past to the present. You don't need that kind of torture." He chuckled. "Of course, I much prefer to inflict the real thing, but this will be very enjoyable."

"Listen to me. I'm not going to let you send me around the bend. I'm not going to let you kill me." She paused. "And *Kafas* is my past, not my future. Carolyn taught me the difference."

"We'll see," Archer said. "I don't think you're as strong as you think you are. There were times when you were too frightened to sleep because you were afraid you'd dream. Did you sleep last night, Melis?"

"Like a rock."

"That's not the truth. And it's going to get worse. Because I'll be here to remind you of every detail. I'd say a week or so and you'll be ready to crumble. You'll beg me to take those tablets and research and leave you alone. And then I'll sail to your side and relieve you of them. I do hope it won't be too late for you."

"Screw you."

"By the way, does Kelby know about *Kafas*?"

"What do you know about Kelby?"

"That you're holding Marinth out as a carrot and you shared adjoining rooms in Nassau. I imagine you're giving him a very good time. I think I'd enjoy discussing *Kafas* with him."

"Why?"

"From his rather flamboyant reputation I'd judge he's a man of varied experience. I imagine he'd appreciate the same type of play I do. What do you think?"

"I think you're a sick son of a bitch." She hung up.

So much evil. She felt as if she'd touched something slimy. She felt dirty . . . and scared. Jesus, she was scared. The muscles of her stomach were tied in knots, and her chest was so tight she could scarcely breathe.

There are other Kafas *in the world.*

Not for her. Never for her.

Forget what he'd said. He meant to frighten her. Terror gave him the power.

Christ, she couldn't forget it. He wasn't going to let her forget one minute of the memories she'd confided to Carolyn.

Deal with it. That's what Carolyn would have said.

Her phone rang again. She wouldn't answer it. Not now. Not until she was stronger.

The phone was still ringing when she half ran out of the bedroom and onto the lanai.

She stood by the French doors and breathed in the moist warm air. Ignore the phone. He couldn't touch her as long as she was here on the island. She was safe.

She was lying to herself. She'd never be safe. Not as long as there were men like Archer in the world. There would always be risk and moments of terror like this. She would have to accept and deal with it as Carolyn had taught her. She would have to find strength within herself. It was the only—

"Are you going to go for another swim with your dolphins?"

She stiffened and turned to see Kelby walking toward her across the lanai.

"No."

"What a surprise. It seems to be the number-one escape route." His gaze went beyond her to the bedroom. "Your phone is ringing. Are you going to answer it?"

"No. It's Archer. I've already talked to him."

"Would you like me to answer it?" His lips tightened. "I assure you, I'd be delighted."

"There's no point." She closed the French doors to muffle the ringing. "I'm the one he wants to hurt."

"Well, he's certainly accomplishing that. He's putting you through the wringer."

"I'll get over it." She crossed her arms tightly over her chest. She wished the ringing would stop. She should go in and turn down the volume. No, then she wouldn't know when he'd given up. She'd imagine the phone ringing and ringing. . . .

"What does he think he's going to get out of harassing you?"

"He wants to drive me crazy. He thinks I'll give him the tablets if he can make me stressed enough," she said jerkily. "He wants to keep gnawing at me until I bleed to death. Like Carolyn. She bled to death. But I'm not going to let him do it to me. I won't be helpless again. That's what he wants. That's what they all want. I won't go crazy and I won't—"

"For God's sake, shut up." His arms closed around her. "And don't stiffen up on me. I'm not going to hurt you. I just can't stand to see you like this. It's like watching someone being crucified."

"I'm okay. He didn't hurt me. I wouldn't let him hurt me."

"The hell he didn't." His hand reached up to cup the back of her head, and he rocked her back and forth. "Shh, it will be fine. You're safe. I won't let anything happen to you."

"Not your responsibility. I have to deal with it. Carolyn said I had to deal with it."

"Deal with what?"

"*Kafas.*"

"What's *Kafas*?"

"The cage. The golden cage. He knows about it. That's why he sent me that birdcage. He knows everything about me. I feel as if his dirty fingers are on my soul. Though he'd rather have them on my body. He's one of them. I can tell. I can always tell when they—"

"Melis, you're not yourself. You'll regret—"

"No! I'm not out of control. I'm fine."

"Jesus, I didn't mean you were going off your rocker." He pushed her back and looked down at her. "You have a right to be upset. I only meant I wasn't going to listen to anything you'd regret telling me later. I don't want you feeling about me the way you do about that bastard Archer."

"You're not like him. I'd be able to tell. I couldn't stand you touching me if you were like him. And why should I tell you anything? It's none of your business." She took a step back. "I'm sorry. You meant well. I was— I have to come to terms with it. It just came as a shock and sent me spiraling."

"You're still not in good shape." He looked away from her. "Archer thinks he knows something about your past that could hurt you. Is it possible he could blackmail you?"

There was a note in his voice that surprised her. "What would you do if I said yes?"

"I might cancel the bargain and just go after Archer for free." His smile was cold. "I don't like blackmailers."

She stared at him in surprise. "He can't

blackmail me. I got over worrying what the world thought of me a long time ago."

"Too bad. I really wanted to break someone." He met her gaze. "And don't go telling me that's the typical male reaction. I'm not in the mood."

"I wasn't going to say that. I'm all for you breaking Archer. If I don't get him first." She moistened her lips. "He knows about you. He believes we're lovers. He may try to go through you to get to me. He seems to think that knowing about *Kafas* will bother you."

"Since we're not lovers, he's out of luck, isn't he?"

"Yes, and I don't care what he thinks, what you think. I don't care."

"Then I wish to hell you'd stop shaking."

"I will." She started to turn away. "I'm sorry I upset you. I won't bother—"

"For God's sake, that's not what I meant."

"It's my problem. I have to deal with it." She drew a deep breath. "But there may be some good in that filth he's throwing at me. If I can convince him he's breaking me, we may be able to turn the tables on him."

"And you want me to help you spring the trap?"

"Yes, it might be easier now. He's going to want to talk to me." She smiled without mirth. "He wants to be my new best friend. He's licking his lips with anticipation."

"For God's sake, you're not going to listen to that filth and let him hurt you again?"

"Oh, yes, as long as he thinks he has a chance of sending me over the edge, I'm the one who has the upper hand. But I can't cave in too quickly or he'll be suspicious. I have to wait until he thinks he's won."

"If you can stand it." His gaze went to the French doors leading to her bedroom. "You don't seem to be doing too well at the moment."

"I have to get used to it. It's . . . difficult."

"Really? What a surprise." His voice was rough. "It must be a little like being drawn and quartered. But I'm sure you'll become perfectly accustomed to it. You'll deal with it."

"Yes, I will." Her lips tightened. "But it doesn't help to have you so angry and sarcastic."

"It's my only weapon at the moment," he said harshly. "What the hell do you expect? I feel helpless as hell, and when I feel helpless I get mad." He started to walk away and then glanced over his shoulder. "But do me a favor, dammit. Don't take his call again tonight. That would be a little too much for me."

She was silent a moment. "Okay, I won't answer it. Who knows? It might make him all the more eager to talk to me tomorrow."

He muttered a curse before disappearing into the house.

He was gone, but she still felt an explosive lingering tension that was like the acrid smell of lightning after it had struck. His response had been almost as draining for her as Archer's call.

Was the phone still ringing?

She drew a deep breath and opened the French doors. The phone was silent, but it would start again. Archer still thought of her as a victim. He wanted to bring her down, use her, destroy everything she'd built from the ruins of her life. He'd use every weapon those records and tapes had given him.

She wouldn't let him. She was strong enough to fight him and win. She would listen to his filth and let him think he was breaking her.

Then, when the time was right, she'd break him.

Lyons gave a low whistle as Kelby came into the living room. "You look like you're a tad annoyed. Anything to do with Melis and the birdcage?"

"Everything to do with them." He'd really handled the situation with kid gloves, Kelby thought in disgust. Just yell at the woman, vent all your frustration, and then walk away. "And that son of a bitch Archer. He's trying to drive her to a breakdown. Sweet. Really sweet."

"Can he do it?"

"No, she's tough. But he can make her life hell, and she's going to let him do it. She thinks she can lure him into a trap."

"Not a bad idea."

"It stinks. The whole thing stinks."

"So what are you going to do?"

"I'm going to find Marinth. Make myself a legend. And sail away into the sunset." He pulled out his phone. "But first I have to have a ship. I'm calling the *Trina* and having the crew sail it to Las Palmas."

"Is that where Marinth is?"

"How the hell do I know? She says it's in that area. Of course, she could be lying. She doesn't trust me worth a damn. Who could blame her? I have a hunch she's not been able to trust many men."

"Are you still going to need me?"

"You're damn right. First, I'm going to call the *Trina,* then I'm going to call Wilson and find out what we know about Archer." He dialed the *Trina.* "I'm going to clear the decks before I make my exit. And Archer is going to be the first one overboard."

The sun was bright, the water was silky smooth against her body as she moved through the waves. Pete and Susie were ahead of her as usual, but they came back every little bit to make sure she was all right. She'd always wondered if they thought she was slightly handicapped. It must seem odd to them that she was so slow when their sleek bodies were so wonderfully equipped to tear through the water.

Time to go back. She could see Kelby standing on the edge of the lanai, watching them. He was wearing khakis, deck shoes, and a white pullover shirt, and he looked lean and powerful and vitally alert. It was the first time she'd seen him since last night, and she experienced a ripple of uneasiness. She hadn't expected to feel this . . . connection with him. It was as if that moment of intimacy last night had woven a bond between them.

Crazy. That feeling was probably only on her side. Kelby appeared cool and even a little distant.

"You're wearing a swimsuit." He leaned over to take her hand and pull her onto the lanai. "What a disappointment. Cal said you frequently swim in the buff."

"Not with guests around." She took the towel he handed her and started to dry off. "And I seem to have more than my share these days."

"I believe I had an invitation. Though you did have an ulterior motive." He sat down in the lounge chair. "Have you talked to Archer?"

"No, I promised you I wouldn't. I turned off the phone. I'll turn it on again when I go in to dress."

"I talked to Wilson last night and got a profile on Archer. Do you want to know what kind of monster you're dealing with?"

"Monsters are monsters. But I suppose I should find out everything I can about him."

"No, Archer's in a class by himself. He grew up in the slums of Albuquerque, New Mexico. He was running drugs by the time he was nine and was picked up for suspected murder of a fellow student at his high school when he was thirteen. It was a particularly gory murder. He took a long, long time torturing the kid before he killed him.

"The state couldn't make a case and he walked. Archer disappeared the next day and presumably went to Mexico. His rap sheet reads like an encyclopedia after that. He went from drugs to arms, and that became his specialty. At twenty-two he formed his own group and went international. He's done very well in the past twenty years or so. He has investments in Switzerland and owns a ship, *Jolie Fille,* that he uses for business. It's usually docked in Marseilles, but he uses it to transport weapons cargoes to the Middle East. The bastard loves money, power, and has never lost that streak of sadism. Some of the stories regarding what he did to rival gang leaders and victims are damn chilling. In that way I guess it served him well. Nobody wanted to be on his shit list."

"None of this surprises me," Melis said. "I

knew what he was. I saw what he did to Carolyn. Are we going to get a photo of Archer?"

"As soon as Wilson can get his hands on one." He paused. "This isn't necessary, you know. Don't take the phone calls. You don't have to stand that kind of punishment. Archer will follow us when we leave for Las Palmas."

She stiffened. "Are we leaving for Las Palmas?"

"As soon as I hear the *Trina* is in port and outfitted."

"You're definitely going to help me? What about proof and bond?"

"Everyone's entitled to roll the dice once." He grimaced. "But I'm cutting down the odds. We go after Marinth first. Then Archer. But there's a chance we may be able to take down two birds with one stone if he follows us to Las Palmas."

"It's still a stalemate. I have to trust you."

He nodded. "But you know I'm aching to get my hands on the son of a bitch. It's not much of a gamble for you." He paused. "One more thing. The tablets and translations are mine."

"No, I may need them to bait Archer."

"You can have them on loan, but from this moment they belong to me."

She was silent a moment. "You drive a hard bargain."

"I've been coached by experts. It's going to be a very expensive gamble if you don't come through for me."

"I'll keep my promise. I'll give you what you want."

"Now I need to know one thing right away. What kind of equipment am I going to need? What's the probable depth?"

"The ocean floor was only sixty meters where we were exploring. Unless there's a drop in the area, scuba should be fine for initial exploration."

"No submersible. That'll cut the expense way down."

"Take it where you can." She paused. "Because getting there may be even more expensive than you think. You're going to have to find a plane you can outfit with tanks to transport Pete and Susie. Then you're going to need a bigger tank when they arrive in Las Palmas."

"What? No way. I know you're fond of

Pete and Susie, but I'm not footing the bill to take your aquatic friends with you. Do you know how much money that would—"

"They have to go."

"I'll leave enough men on this island to protect them from any threat. They'll be okay."

"We can't find Marinth without them. They're the only ones who know the way."

"I beg your pardon?"

"You heard me. We found Pete and Susie in waters off Cadora, one of the Canary Islands, when Phil was looking for Marinth. They kept getting in our way, riding the wake of the boat and swimming with us when we were underwater searching. They were young, not more than two years old. It's unusual for young dolphins to leave their mother or their chosen subgroup, but Pete and Susie were different from the beginning. They seemed to crave human contact. I gave it to them. They'd show up at the *Last Home* in the morning and then leave at sunset. I never saw them after dark. Maybe that's when they went home to their mothers or their group. I didn't care. The daylight hours were enough for me. I didn't really want to search for lost cities, and this was my chance to study wild dolphins at close range. I spent more time with them underwater than I did searching for Phil's city."

"Which probably didn't please him."

"No, but he was over the moon when I followed the dolphins to an underwater cave and found the tablets."

"They intentionally led you to them?"

"I don't know. I think they did. Though I can't prove it. They may have just wanted to play in an area familiar to them."

"And Lontana reaped the benefit."

Her lips tightened. "He went crazy with excitement. He thought the dolphins could lead him to the actual city. He and the other men he'd hired at Las Palmas dove every day for weeks with the dolphins. Trying to herd them, even scare them, into going away from the boat so they could follow them. I wanted to strangle him. I told him to stop, but he wouldn't listen to me. All he could think about was Marinth."

"Did he get what he wanted?"

"No, Pete and Susie didn't show up one day. Three days later we heard that two young dolphins had been caught in fishermen's nets off Lanzarote. It was Pete and Susie, and they were sick and badly dehy-

drated. I was furious with Phil. I told him if
we didn't take the dolphins back to the island
and get them well, I'd broadcast the news of
the tablets we'd found to the four corners of
the earth."

"I'd say that would do the trick."

"He didn't like it. He didn't have much
money, and transporting dolphins isn't
cheap. But we flew Pete and Susie home and
here they've stayed."

"But I'd wager Lontana didn't want them
to stay here. Did he go back to the Canaries
and try to find Marinth without them?"

"Yes, but the underwater terrain there is a
maze of reefs, caves, and ledges. Unless you
accidentally stumbled on Marinth, you
could search for a hundred years without
finding it."

"And he didn't put pressure on you to let
him use the dolphins again?"

"Of course he did. Particularly after he
had the tablets translated. It seemed the
Marinthians used dolphins constantly in
daily life."

"How?"

"They were a fishing community, and the
dolphins helped herd the fish into the nets.
They warned them of sharks in the area.

They even helped the children learn to swim. For centuries the dolphins were an integral part of their life."

"So? What has that got to do with finding Marinth?"

"Dolphins are still a mysterious species to us. There's a possibility there may be a genetic memory passed on to the generations of dolphins that came after Marinth's destruction. Or they might just cling to a habitat that's proved beneficial to them. Either way, Phil was sure that we should give Pete and Susie another crack at finding Marinth."

"And you refused to consider it?"

"You're damn right. Transporting dolphins is highly stressful to them. It was his fault they almost died in those nets. Phil could just find Marinth on his own. They'd already given him the tablets."

"But you think Pete and Susie could find it?"

"If their mother or any dolphin they know is still near the ruins. Each dolphin has its own signature whistle, and they'd be able to follow it with no problem."

"But Lontana wasn't able to get them to go to her."

"He was harassing them and they didn't

know Phil well enough to trust him. Yes, I think there's a good possibility that they can lead us to Marinth. They found the tablets. And the Marinthians who wrote the tablets spoke of the dolphins as their little brothers. Well, their little brothers were probably the only species to survive, and their descendants are still out there." She added fiercely, "Do you think I want to take Pete and Susie? They're happy and safe here. If I could see any way to get out of it, I would. So bite the bullet. They're going to travel first-class, Kelby."

"Okay. Okay." He gazed at Pete and Susie playing in the water. "But they'd damn well better have a great sense of direction."

Chapter Eight

There were seven messages on her cell phone when she went to her room that evening.

She cleared them without listening and then turned the phone back on. All right, Archer, go for it. I'm ready for you.

She was lying to herself. She could feel her muscles tense at the thought of answering another call from that bastard. Get over it. She'd made a decision and she had to live with it.

The phone rang again at exactly midnight.

"I wasn't pleased at being ignored," Archer said. "I thought you cared about those dolphins."

She stiffened. "What the hell are you talking about?"

"I take it you didn't listen to my messages."

"Why should I listen to that filth?"

"Because I want you to do it. And because if you don't, your dolphins will have an accident. I don't have to invade your little paradise. Maybe poison injected in a fish? I'll find a way."

"They're only study subjects. No great loss."

"That's not what Lontana told me."

She paused. "And what did he tell you?"

"About Marinth, about the dolphins. When I came to him to make him an offer for the sonic-gun plans, he tried to divert me. He told me all about you and Marinth and the tablets. I tried to tell him I wasn't interested in Marinth, but he didn't seem to want to discuss the sonic gun."

"He'd been stung before by crooks like you."

"I know. But if he didn't want to play

with the big boys, he should have stayed home on that island. The potential is too great to ignore. I have three buyers right now clamoring for the right to give a first bid. And there are signs that there may be other sharks buzzing around. I want Lontana's research papers."

"I don't have them."

"Not on the island. Lontana told me that you didn't have them there. I think he was trying to protect you. But he did let it slip that you knew where they are. So tell me."

"You're lying. He wouldn't have made me a target."

"He still thought I was going to invest in his lost city at the time. He was rather naive, wasn't he? And very, very stubborn. Like Carolyn Mulan. Like you."

"You're damn right I'm stubborn. Do you think I'd give you anything I could keep away from you?"

"But you can't keep it away from me. You may be able to resist for a while, but I've listened to your tapes. I know how delicately balanced you are."

"You're mistaken."

"I don't think so. It's worth a shot. So

here's how it's going to be. I'm going to call you twice a day and you're going to answer and listen. We'll talk about *Kafas* and the harem and all the lovely events of your childhood. If you don't answer, I'll kill the dolphins."

"I can pen them close to the house."

"Dolphins don't take well to pens for any extended period. They often become ill and die."

"How do you know?"

"I've been researching. A good business-man always does his research."

"Businessman? Murderer."

"Only when frustrated. I usually get what I want and I've grown spoiled over the years." He added softly, "I do hope you give in before I totally break you. I feel as if I know you very well. At night I lie in the dark and pretend I'm with you. Only you're much, much younger. Do you know what we're doing?"

She closed her eyes. Smother the anger. Ignore the panic. Breathe slowly. Breathe deep.

"You're not answering."

"You said I had to listen, not talk."

"I did, didn't I? And you're being very

obedient. That deserves a reward. Good night, Melis." He hung up.

It was over.

But it would start again tomorrow. Only it would be worse, uglier, more obscene. He would blend the present with the past into a nightmare whole.

She got up and headed for the bathroom. She would take a shower and try to feel clean again. She could take this punishment. Only twice a day. Just block his words from her mind. Think about what he'd done to Phil and Maria and Carolyn.

And think about what she was going to do to him.

TOBAGO

"The *Trina* has left Athens," Pennig said as he came out on the terrace. "Jenkins said it left port last night."

"Destination?" Archer said.

"He's not sure. He's asking questions."

"He'd better do more than that. It probably means that we can expect them to leave the island soon. Make sure that we know what they're doing every minute."

Pennig hesitated. "Maybe we should get out of here. We're too close to that island. I told you that Cobb said Lyons has left the island several times. This evening he saw him gunning it in the direction of Tobago."

"I'll think about it, but he can't know where we are." Archer gazed thoughtfully out at the beach. "It seems Kelby is moving and shaking. I didn't think he'd wait long before he started putting out feelers. Our sweet Melis is evidently giving him what he wants."

"Why? She wouldn't help Lontana."

"But I wasn't on the scene then. She's feeling threatened." And would feel more threatened, Archer thought with a surge of anticipation. Melis Nemid was proving to be very exciting. When he'd first listened to those tapes and read the records, he'd only been interested in finding a weapon. Yet now he could visualize every scene, imagine every emotion she had felt all those years ago. It was incredibly arousing. "She'll pay Kelby anything he wants to save herself."

"The tablets and research?"

"Maybe. I'd guess he's more interested in Marinth, but from what I've heard, he likes

control and he goes after the whole tamale."
He smiled. "But he can't have it. I'm the one
who's going to get those research papers."

And Kelby couldn't have Melis Nemid either. The more Archer came in contact with
the woman, the more he realized that his relationship with her must continue to give
him this exquisite pleasure. There were so
many ways to twist and hurt her.

He had to explore every single one before
he brought her to the end.

It was the middle of the night when Kelby's
cell phone rang.

"I've found the stakeout," Nicholas said
when Kelby answered. "Black-and-white
motorboat. He's in a cove on an island two
miles from here. Close enough to keep an
eye on Melis, but not too close to be noticed. My boat's about half a mile away,
masked by some overhanging trees."

"You're sure he's the one?"

"I'll ignore that insult. I'm breathing
down his neck. He'll see you as you leave
the island. You'll have to head toward
Tobago and then double back. Are you
coming?"

Kelby swung his feet to the floor. "I'm coming. Give me directions."

The man in the black-and-white motorboat was tall, gray-blond, and was using a pair of high-powered binoculars to observe Lontana's Island.

Kelby lowered his own infrared binoculars and turned to Nicholas. "Can we expect someone to relieve him?"

"Probably. I've been here since midnight and I didn't see anyone but him. But sitting out on a boat in the middle of beyond isn't too comfortable."

"Maybe he's on the night shift." Kelby glanced at his watch. "It's still a few hours until dawn. You go back to the island and I'll take over here."

"You're going to follow him when he's relieved?"

"You know it. If Archer was here the other night, then he may still be in the area. He evidently has a hands-on mentality."

"And so do you," Nicholas said. "Why don't you delegate this one to me?"

He shook his head. "I really want this bastard. Go back to the island and keep an eye on Melis. But I don't want her to know about this in case it doesn't pan out."

Nicholas shrugged. "Whatever you say." He started the engine of his boat. "Keep in touch."

Kelby settled back in his own boat and picked up the binoculars again.

Dawn had barely broken when Dave Cobb tied his boat at the pier at Tobago and strode to his hotel on the dock.

The shabby lobby of the Oceanic Hotel smelled of some kind of cleaning solution and the tropical flowers in the vase in the center of the reception area. The odor was as distasteful to him as everything else connected with this town, Cobb thought as he took the elevator up to his room on the third floor. He'd wanted Pennig to set him up downtown, but the bastard had wanted him available at the dock.

He called Pennig as soon as he got in his room. "Nothing much important to report," Cobb said when Pennig answered the phone. "Like I told you, Lyons left yesterday evening and took off in the direction of Tobago. Kelby left the island about three this morning."

"Same direction?"

"Yes, Tobago."

"That's not unimportant, Cobb. I told you yesterday that Lyons's movements were very important."

"But you won't let me leave to go after him. Dansk is going to let you know when they come back to the island. I'm getting in a hot shower and going to bed. How much longer are we supposed to sit out there staring at that damn island?"

"Until Archer says you can stop. You're getting paid."

"Not enough," Cobb said sourly. "Twelve hours in that damp, moldy boat is too long. I'm a city boy."

"Would you like to tell that to Archer?"

"I'm telling you." Shit, maybe he'd better backtrack. Archer was a sadistic son of a bitch, and Pennig wasn't much better. He'd heard too many stories for some of them not to be true. "I'm doing my job. Just get me out of that boat as soon as you can."

"When the job's done." Pennig hung up.

Screw him. Cobb crashed down the receiver and headed for the shower. He wouldn't have taken this job if he'd been in the money. He'd been a little flattered that a big player like Archer had picked him, but he liked action, not sitting around on his ass.

He turned on the shower and let the hot water stream over him. That was better. It had gotten chilly toward dawn, and he'd been tempted not to wait for Dansk and to just come back to Tobago and tell Pennig to stuff it. One more night and he might still do it. The money wasn't that good and he— What the hell!

The shower door had opened.

"Did anyone ever tell you how vulnerable a man is in the shower?" Kelby asked softly. "You can slip on a bar of soap or get scalded or—"

Cobb grunted and lunged toward him.

Kelby stepped aside and gave him a karate chop to the carotid artery. "Or someone like me may do serious damage to your nervous and skeletal systems. Let's talk about it, shall we?"

Melis was sitting at the kitchen table having coffee the next morning when Nicholas

Lyons came into the room. "Ah, that's what I need. May I?"

"Help yourself."

"I will." He poured himself a cup and sat down across from her. "Kelby's gone to Tobago to try to track down two tanks for your Flipper friends. He asked me to tell you."

"He moves fast."

"Always. Your hair's wet. Have you been swimming with Pete and Susie?"

She nodded. "Every morning. They're good company."

"Some people wouldn't understand that concept. But since I'm a shaman, I've no problem with animal-spiritual interaction. Maybe you were a dolphin in another life."

She smiled. "I doubt it. I get too impatient when they don't understand what I need from them."

"But they give you what you need, don't they?" He lifted his cup to his lips. "They interest you, they amuse you, and they prevent you from being lonely. That's important when you're a loner like you."

She leaned back in her chair. "You think I'm a loner?"

"Oh, yes. There's a wall around you a

mile thick. No one comes in. Except maybe your friend Carolyn."

"You make me sound very cold."

He shook his head. "You're kind to your dolphins; you're nice to Cal. From what he told me, Lontana wasn't the easiest man to live with and you were very patient with him. You were practically ripped apart when Carolyn Mulan died. You're not cold, just wary."

"I can't tell you how happy I am you've come to that conclusion. I had no idea you had me under your microscope since you've been here."

"I'm a student of humanity, and you're very interesting."

Her gaze narrowed on his face. She was again aware of the complex shadings of his character. What was behind that seemingly frank open smile? "So are you. Why are you coming with us? Marinth?"

He shook his head. "I like money and I like Kelby. And there are enough fireworks going on that I thought it might be like the old days. Like you, I'm a loner, and I don't let many people in."

"Fireworks? You were in the SEALs with Kelby, weren't you?"

He nodded. "And we bummed around the world together afterward for a few years. Then we parted company and went our own ways."

"Considering his background, it's difficult imagining Kelby in the SEALs." She looked down into the coffee in her cup. "Everything I've read about him paints a rather undisciplined picture. Was he competent?"

He was silent a moment. "That's a loaded question."

"Is it?"

"Let's see, let me use my shaman powers to see what's behind it. Archer's a very dangerous man. You want to know if Kelby can give you Archer's head in a basket?"

She nodded. "That about covers it."

"I do like a woman who doesn't pussyfoot around." He studied her. "What do you think about Kelby?"

"He's tough. Tough enough?"

"How hard do you think just SEAL basic training was for Kelby? It's supposed to be a level playing field, but he was a rich boy with media swarming all over him. There are a hell of a lot of ways for other recruits to make life miserable, and they used all of them on Kelby."

"You too?"

"Sure. I can be as sadistic as anyone else. Maybe more. I've always believed in tests. Testing yourself, testing others. It's the only way to get ahead of the game. You set the bar and then you go for it. If you fail, you get out of the way and let someone else have his turn and you don't bitch if you get bruised. Survival of the fittest."

"That's a pretty harsh philosophy."

"Maybe it's my Native American heritage. Or it could be slum-kid mentality. Either way it works for me."

"You're proud of your Indian heritage, aren't you?"

"If you're not proud of who you are, then you're in trouble." He smiled. "I joke about it, but I can see myself back in frontier days stalking, tracking. The hunt always excites me. It could be that was why I became a SEAL." He shrugged. "Anyway, Kelby took the punishment during those days of basic training and didn't back down. He was stubborn as hell." He grinned. "And later he got back at every one of us."

"It sounds like he has a good deal of endurance."

"Endurance?" His smile faded. "You

could say that. You want to hear endurance? We were on a mission inside Iraq during the Gulf War, and aerial reconnaissance had located a small underground biological-warfare facility in the north. They sent our team on a hush-hush mission to destroy it. They didn't want to arouse public disapproval of the war by exposing the fact that the troops could be subjected to germ warfare. Everything went wrong from the get-go. We blew the facility, but we had two dead and Kelby and I were captured by local tribesmen before we could reach the helicopter site.

"They were still lying about biological facilities, so they stuffed us in this tiny jail in the desert and sent word to Saddam that they'd captured two American SEALs. Saddam sent word back that he wanted confessions and repudiation of the American war effort. I'm not sure why they chose to work on Kelby first instead of me. Maybe they found out his background and wanted to show the weakness of capitalist moguls."

"They tortured him?"

"Big time. Three days. They didn't allow him food or water and kept him in a hot box for most of the time. He had two broken ribs and was a mass of bruises when they tossed him back in the cell. But he didn't break. Like I said, too stubborn. I didn't think he could survive an escape, but he did and took two guards down. We hid out, trekking through the hills and over the border. We weren't able to radio for a helicopter until five days after we escaped." He smiled crookedly. "Yes, I'd say he has a certain amount of endurance. And I don't envy Archer having him on his trail. Is that what you wanted to know?"

It was more than she wanted to learn. She didn't like the idea of Kelby as a victim—even one who'd overcome all odds. The mental vision of Kelby in that cell, bruised and in pain, was too disturbing. "Yes, that's what I had to know." She poured another cup of coffee. "Thank you."

"No problem." He pushed his chair back. "Now, what are we going to do this morning?"

"We?"

"Kelby says I don't let you out of my sight until he gets back."

"I don't need you. I'm safe here on the island."

"I'll just make double sure. Are we going to go play in the water with the dolphins?"

"Play?" She tilted her head, considering. "That wasn't my intention, but why not? Go put on your swim trunks. Pete and Susie would positively love playing with you." She smiled slyly. "Ask Cal."

"Archer was in Tobago," Kelby said curtly when Nicholas answered the phone four hours later. "At the Bramley Towers. He's not now."

"He flew the coop?"

"Hell, yes. Cobb was the guy on the stakeout, and he said Pennig was nervous about you leaving the island and heading for Tobago. Evidently Archer got a little uneasy and took off."

"Do we know where?"

"Cobb was hired in Miami. I called Detective Halley in Nassau to see if he could put a trace on Archer in Miami. And I told him to come and pick up Cobb and his buddy Dansk."

"Didn't Cobb know where Archer could be located?"

"Believe me, if Cobb had known, he would have told me."

"I don't doubt it," Nicholas said. "I'm just

surprised you decided to turn Cobb over to Halley."

"He's small potatoes. I got what I wanted from him. You go pick up Dansk and deliver him to Halley at the airport."

"Delegating at last? I suppose I don't get to have fun like you did?"

"Dansk doesn't know anything either. It wouldn't be worth your time. Just give him to Halley. You can leave right away. I'm on my way back to the island."

"That's good to hear. Your Melis has a malicious sense of humor. She let me in for a watery interlude with the dolphins that outraged my dignity."

"She's not my Melis, and anyone, human or mammal, who takes you down a peg gets my vote. Call me if you have any problem with Dansk."

Chapter Nine

"Did everything go well today?" Melis asked Kelby. "You look tense."

"I'm not tense."

"Did you arrange for the tanks?"

"Tanks? Oh, yes, I took care of it." He turned to look at her. "Do you want coffee?"

"Not right now. It's almost sunset. The guys should be coming to say good night."

"I think I'll make a pot for myself."

She watched him as he strode into the house. If Kelby wasn't tense, he was definitely edgy. He'd been charged with energy since he'd come back this afternoon. But she didn't know him well. Maybe that was natural for him when he was in high gear.

But it didn't make her uneasy, she realized. She was becoming used to him and there was even a tentative trust emerging.

Her phone lying on the table rang.

She tensed and then slowly answered it.

"Why didn't you call and tell me Lontana had been killed?"

"Kemal?" Relief surged through her. "It's so good to hear your voice."

"All you have to do is pick up the phone. You're the one who distanced herself. I'm always here for you."

"I know." She closed her eyes and could almost see his dark mischievous eyes and that smile that had warmed her heart when she'd thought it would always be cold and barren. "How is Marisa?"

"Wonderful." He hesitated. "She wants a child."

"You'd make a wonderful father."

"True. But it would only make things more difficult for her. I won't have that. We will wait. But that's not why I called you. I only heard today about Lontana. How are you? Do you need me to come?"

"No."

"I knew that would be your answer. Melis, let me help you."

"I don't need help. How did you find out about Phil?"

"Did you think I wouldn't keep an eye on both of you? That's not my nature."

No, his nature was to protect and surround those he cared about with warmth and love. Thank heaven he hadn't found out about Carolyn. "It was difficult at first, but I've adjusted. It would be foolish of you to come to my rescue when I don't need it. But thank you for calling."

"No thanks are necessary between us. We're two of a kind." He paused. "Come to San Francisco."

"I'm fine here."

"Do you need money?"

"No."

Kemal sighed. "Don't close me out, Melis. It hurts me."

And she would never hurt him. "I truly don't need anything, Kemal. Take care of your Marisa. I'm used to being alone. It doesn't bother me."

"It bothers you. Don't lie to me. We go back too far. You've never learned to open up and let people near you."

"Except you."

"I don't count. But your friend Carolyn does. How is she?"

"I haven't seen her for a while," she said carefully.

"Well, at least try to keep in touch with her." His tone lightened. "Or come here and let me get to work on you. You've always been one of my unfinished masterpieces."

"That only makes me more unique. Don't worry about me."

"Impossible."

"I'll come to you if I need you. Good-bye, Kemal. Say hello to Marisa for me."

He was silent a moment. "I always think of you with love. Remember that, Melis."

"I love you, too, Kemal," she whispered. She hung up.

Her eyes were stinging as she gazed down at the phone. His voice had brought back so many bitter memories, but she would not have missed that call.

"Melis."

She looked up to see Kelby standing in the doorway with a coffee carafe and two cups on a tray. She swallowed to ease the tightness of her throat. "You were quick. I think I could use that coffee now."

"I wasn't quick. I've been standing here for the last five minutes." He came toward her and set the tray down on the table with a resounding thump. "Archer?"

She shook her head.

"Don't lie to me," he said roughly. "He tore you up."

"I'm not lying." She paused. "It was Kemal, an old friend."

"Is that why you look like you're going to— Who the hell is he?"

"I told you, he's my friend. No, he's more than that. He's my savior. He took me from *Kafas*. Do you know what that meant to me?"

"No, and I'm not sure I want to know."

"Why not?" She smiled crookedly. "Aren't you curious?"

"Of course I am." He was silent a moment. "I've thought about it. But I don't want to know bad enough to be accused of putting smudges on a soul. That's pretty serious stuff."

"Christ, did I say that? How melodramatic." She drew a deep breath. "This is different. You're not stealing anything from me. I don't care if you know about *Kafas*. Carolyn once told me that only the guilty should feel shame. I refuse to feel ashamed. At some point Archer will probably call you and drop some poison in your ear anyway."

"It's not good enough for you not to care. Do you want to tell me?"

She did want to tell someone, she realized. That conversation with Kemal had brought too many memories to the forefront. She was choking on them, and there was no Carolyn to free her. "Yes, I . . . think I do."

He looked away from her. "All right, then tell me about *Kafas*."

"It means *golden cage*. It was sort of a special club in Istanbul." She stood up and walked over to the edge of the lanai. "And adjoining it was an even more special place: the harem. Velvet couches. Golden fretwork panels. It was very luxurious because its patrons were either important or wealthy. It was a brothel that catered to every sexual taste. I was an inmate there for sixteen months."

"What?"

"It seemed like sixteen years. Children live so much in the present they can't imagine life changing. So if they live in hell, they think it's going to go on forever."

"Children?" he repeated slowly.

"I was ten years old when I was sold into the harem. I was eleven when I left."

"Christ. Sold? How?"

"The usual trade in white slavery. My parents were killed in an auto accident when I was a toddler. I had no relatives, so I was placed in an orphanage in London. It was a nice enough place, but unfortunately the administrator needed money to pay his gambling debts. So, periodically he'd claim one of the children was a runaway. They ended up in Istanbul." Don't think. Just say the words. Get it over with. "Of course, they had to be very special types for him to get the money he needed. They thought I was perfect. Blond, skin with the fresh bloom of childhood, and I had a quality they treasured. I looked . . . breakable. That was important. Pedophiles love to prey on fragile children. It makes them feel more powerful. The owner of the brothel thought I'd even be suitable for regular customers when I was a little older. So I was a true prize."

"What was the owner's name?"

"It doesn't matter."

"It matters. I'm going to rid the world of the son of a bitch. What's his name?"

"Irmak. But he's already dead. He was murdered before Kemal took me and the other children away from the harem."

"Good. This is the Kemal who called you?"

"Kemal Nemid." The words came easier now. Kemal was part of the good times as well as the nightmare. "He's the man who brought me from Turkey to Chile. He was closer to me than a brother. I lived with him for almost five years."

"I thought you lived with Luis Delgado."

"How did you know I—" Her lips twisted. "Of course, you'd try to find out anything that might give you an edge. Am I telling you anything you don't know?"

"Wilson didn't find out about this *Kafas*," he said grimly. "Only about your life in Chile and Luis Delgado."

"Delgado was Kemal. His background was a little shady and he thought it best to buy us new ones. He called me Melisande—"

"And then he dumped you and you had to go live with Lontana? Great guy."

She whirled on him. "He *is* a great guy," she said fiercely. "You don't know anything. He would never have deserted me. I'm the one who ran away from him. He was going

to the United States and wanted me to go
too. He was going to start a new life."

"Then why cut and run?"

"I would have been in the way. He'd been
tied to me for five years. He'd done everything for me. I was on the verge of a breakdown after I left *Kafas*. He got me a doctor,
he sent me to school, and he was there for
me whenever I needed him. It was time I let
him go."

"For Christ's sake, you were sixteen. I
wouldn't have let you go off with Lontana."

"You don't understand. My age didn't
matter. I hadn't been a child for a long, long
time. I was like that little girl in *Interview
with the Vampire,* a grown-up frozen in a
child's body. Kemal always understood that
about me." She shrugged. "Phil was done
with his research on the oceanic vents off the
coast of Chile and was going off on an ex-
ploratory trip to the Azores. I went to the
Last Home and asked him to take me with
him. I'd known him for years. He and Kemal
got along fine after Phil started to hire out
the *Last Home* to the Save the Dolphin foundation's observation trips. Phil and I meshed
well, and he needed someone to keep his

books, deal with his creditors, and keep his feet on the ground."

"And Kemal didn't come after you?"

"I called and talked to him. He made me promise to call him if I was ever in trouble."

"Which you probably didn't do."

"What's the good of letting someone go if you jerk them back? He also persuaded me to accept his paying for my education and the fee for going to an analyst. I didn't really want to keep on with the sessions. I didn't think they were helping much. I was still having the nightmares."

"But then you found Carolyn Mulan."

"Then I found Carolyn. No mumbo jumbo. No pity. She let me talk. Then she'd say yes, it was ugly. Yes, I can see how you'd wake up screaming. But it's over and you're still standing. You can't let it beat you. You have to deal with it. That was her favorite phrase. Just deal with it."

"You were lucky to have her in your corner."

"Yes, but she wasn't lucky. If she hadn't known me, she'd still be alive." She shook her head. "She'd hate me blaming myself. That was one of my problems. It's easy to teach children blame. If I wasn't bad, why was I being punished? Somewhere inside I thought it was my fault I ended up at *Kafas*."

"Then you really were crazy. That's like saying someone tied to the railroad tracks is to blame if the train runs over them."

"Carolyn agreed with you. It took us a long time to get me over that hurdle. She said blame wasn't healthy and I should deal with it. So I'll deal with it." She stared him in the eye. "But I'll also deal with Archer. He doesn't deserve to live. He's worse than those men who came to screw a little girl in a white organdy dress. He reminds me of Irmak. He deals in death as well as sex."

"And you're ready to take him on all by yourself. You're going to let that pervert murmur in your ear and you'll just take it. Isn't that sweet?"

He had been so outwardly calm that she hadn't realized the fury that was seething beneath. She noticed it now. It was tensing every muscle of his body. "I won't have to do it by myself. You're going to help."

"How kind of you to let me have a small part." He took a step closer to her. "Do you have any idea what I'm feeling right now? You tell me a story that makes me want to run out and carve up everyone who screwed that little girl in the harem. Then you tell me I have to stand by and watch Archer hurt you again."

He *was* angry. She could feel the rage vibrating through him. "I hate being helpless too. But that little girl doesn't exist any longer."

"I think she does. And what do you mean by offering to go to bed with me? How the hell do you think I'd feel when I found out that I'd screwed a victim from that damn place?"

"I'm not a victim. I've even had sex since that time. Twice. Carolyn thought it would be good for me."

"And was it good for you?"

"It wasn't unpleasant." She looked away from him. "Why are we talking about this? You turned me down anyway."

"Because there's not a doubt in my mind it would have happened. I'm like all those other sons of bitches who wanted to screw you. Shit, I still want to do it." He whirled and moved toward the sliding glass door. "Which, considering the story you just told me, makes me feel real good about myself. But don't worry: As your Carolyn would advise, I'll deal with it."

"What are you talking about? You're not like those men at *Kafas.*"

"No? We have at least one thing in common, and it's damn well not our self-restraint."

She watched as the door slid forcefully closed behind him. Once again he'd surprised her. She wasn't sure what she'd expected, but it wasn't Kelby's response. Part sympathy, part anger, part sexual frustration. It had jerked her from the horror of the past to the turbulent present.

But she was also feeling relief, she realized. She had never confided her past to anyone but Carolyn, and it had been strangely cathartic to tell Kelby about *Kafas.* She felt stronger. Perhaps it was the knowledge that Kelby had no medical training and was just an ordinary person. Maybe she hadn't completely lost that trace of blame Carolyn had worked so hard to eradicate. Kelby had not blamed her. He'd blamed the men who'd victimized her. He'd been protective, angry, and . . . lustful. In a way, that lust had been welcome. Her time at *Kafas* hadn't lessened his desire for her. It hadn't twisted it or destroyed it. He'd accepted that period of her life as part of her. Even his anger had been comforting, because it showed that he thought she could handle it. Who would have known that the call from Kemal would bring her this sense of greater peace and strength?

Kemal or Kelby? Kemal had given her gentleness and Kelby anger, and she wasn't sure which had been more valuable.

She only knew when that phone rang and Archer came on the line, she'd be more ready to deal with him.

"Halley picked up Dansk and Cobb a few minutes ago," Nicholas said when Kelby answered the phone. "Do you want me to do anything here in town or come back there?"

"Come back here. I need to get away for a while."

"You sound uptight. Things not going well?"

"Why shouldn't they? It's such a bright, beautiful world filled with kind, caring people. It's enough to make a man weep with joy."

Nicholas gave a low whistle. "I'll be back in an hour. Is that soon enough?"

"It will have to be." Kelby hung up, left

the house, and strode down to the pier. Nicholas couldn't get here soon enough for him. He was filled with pity, anger, and frustration and was ready to explode. He needed to get out on the water, tear through the waves, and have the wind blow some of this damn emotion away.

If he couldn't control it, he had to get away from it.

Swim toward the arches. . . .

No, that wouldn't work. He mustn't identify Melis with Marinth. She was the key, not the objective.

So sit down on the pier and wait for Nicholas.

And try not to think of a little golden-haired girl in an organdy dress.

"I know you don't understand," Melis whispered as she looked down at Pete and Susie in the pens. They were definitely unhappy. The dolphins hated the enclosures that Cal had helped build near the lanai a few days ago. "I wish I could explain it to you."

"Can't you?" Kelby said from behind her.

She looked up to see him coming toward her. He'd been gone all day, but he'd evidently just showered, because his hair was wet. He was barefoot, without a shirt, and he looked slightly rakish. "What do you mean?"

"I was beginning to think you could talk to them. There's definitely a bond."

She shook her head. "Though sometimes I feel as if they can read my mind. Maybe they can. Dolphins are strange creatures. The more I learn about them, the more I find I don't know." She glanced at him. "Did you get the ice-making machine?"

"They're installing it in the jet now." He grimaced. "The pilot was a little confused about the necessity of it. I had to convince him we weren't planning a giant margarita party."

"We have to keep the guys cool in the tank. It's absolutely necessary. Cool and wet and supported."

"Support. That's why you're going to keep the dolphins in those foam-lined slings?"

She nodded. "Dolphins' bodies are built for the buoyancy of water. When you take them out of the water, their own body weight presses down on vital organs and injures them. There's not going to be enough water in those transport tanks to do the job."

"Stop fretting. I've done everything you've told me about making it safe for them. After we board those dolphins on the plane tomorrow, they're going to be more comfortable than we are. They're going to be okay, Melis. I promise you."

"It's just . . . they're helpless. They trust me."

"And they should. You're a woman to trust."

She looked at him in surprise.

"If you're a dolphin," he amended with a faint smile.

"I didn't think you'd commit to a statement like that without qualification."

"Hell, no." He sat down beside her and dangled his feet in the water. "Then you'd think I'd gone soft."

"No way." In these last days she'd found that he was dynamic and forceful but not inflexible if he could be shown he was wrong. "You're too stubborn to change."

"The pot calling the kettle . . ." He took a fish out of the bucket on the lanai and threw it to Susie. "She hasn't lost her appetite." He threw another fish to Pete. The male tossed his tail and ignored it. "We may have problems with him."

"He can't be bribed." Her gaze was on his hands, now lying on his knees. Beautiful, tanned, strong hands with long, capable fingers. She had always been fascinated by hands. Kelby's were exceptional. She could imagine them either at hard labor or playing a piano. He was very tactile. She had noticed the tips of his fingers brushing over the lip of a glass, fingering the rattan on the arm of the lounge chair. He obviously liked to touch, caress, explore. . . .

"Well, is he?"

She jerked her gaze back up to his face. What had he asked? Something about Pete. "He's a male, and they're usually more aggressive. But Pete has always been gentler than the norm. It's probably because he hasn't had the opportunity to travel with a male group as most dolphins do."

"They don't stay with the band?"

"No, the females generally stay with a female pod and the males go off and join a male pod. Males usually bond with another male as a buddy, and the relationship sometimes lasts for life. That's why the relationship between Pete and Susie is so unique. As I said, Pete's unusual."

"And you've made a pet of him."

"I've *not* made a pet of him. I've made sure they could both survive on their own. But I hope I've made them my friends."

"Shades of Flipper?"

"No, it's a mistake to think of dolphins as being like us. They're not like us. They live in an alien world where we couldn't survive. Their senses are different. Their brain is different. We should accept them as they are."

"But can they be friends with humans?"

"For thousands of years there have been stories of dolphins and humans interacting. Dolphins saving human lives. Dolphins helping fishermen with their catch. Yes, I believe there can be friendship. We just have to accept them the way they are and not try to see them in our image."

"Interesting." Kelby threw Susie another fish. "Are they brother and sister? Or can we expect little dolphins to appear on the horizon?"

"They're not brother and sister. I had DNA taken when I first got them to the island. And they're not sexually mature yet."

"And they're over eight?"

"Dolphins live long lives. Forty, fifty years. They sometimes don't mature sexually until they're twelve or even thirteen, but eight or nine isn't that uncommon. So it shouldn't be long for Pete and Susie."

"How do you feel about that?"

"What do you mean?"

"Now they seem caught in a sort of jubilant childhood. Things will change."

"And you think I'd mind?" Her lips tightened. "I'm not a cripple. I've dealt with dolphins and their sexual urges for years. Dolphins are a very highly sexed species. By the way Pete plays with his toys, I'd judge he's going to be particularly sexual. There's nothing obscene about sex in nature. I'd be glad to see the dolphins' lives sexually fulfilled."

"I don't think of you as crippled," he said quietly. "You're stronger than any woman I know. You survived something that would have broken most people. Hell, you even keep your scars hidden most of the time."

"Because no one wants to think about anything bad happening to children. It makes them uncomfortable." She shifted her gaze to his face. "Didn't it upset you?"

"It didn't make me uncomfortable." He grimaced. "It made me mad. For you and at you. I was all set to have a hell of a good roll in the hay, and you stopped me in my tracks."

She moistened her lips. "I didn't mean to tease you. I was upset and it was pure instinct. A throwback to *Kafas*. I knew it was something a man would value."

"You can say that again. Pete isn't the only one who's highly sexed." He got to his feet. "But I just wanted to tell you that you don't have to worry. I can't promise not to have my moments, but I'm usually in control."

"Are you? And is that what this chat is all about?"

"We're going to be together a lot. I don't want you tense."

"I'm not tense." As he looked at her skeptically, she amended, "I'm not nervous or afraid of you. You just disturb me sometimes."

"Disturb you?" His gaze narrowed on her face. "How?"

"I don't know." It wasn't true. She knew all too well. She was too aware of him. He dominated any room he entered. She jumped to her feet. "I have to go check the thickness of the padding in the slings. I'll see you at dinner."

"Right." He rose to his feet. "It's Nicholas's turn to cook, so don't expect much. He says it's not included in the shaman job description."

"I may be too busy to—" Her phone rang, and she went rigid. Not now. She had too much to do and her nerves were always in shreds after a phone call from Archer.

"Don't answer it, dammit." Kelby's demeanor was as taut as her own. "You told me he'd hurt the dolphins if you didn't talk to him, but they're safe in the pens."

"They won't always be in the pens. Besides, he has to think I'm afraid and weakening." She vaguely heard him mutter an oath as she pushed the button. "You're early, Archer."

"That's because I'm taking a jet in a few hours and I couldn't bear not to talk to you. I so enjoy our conversations."

"Where are you going?"

"Where you're going. Las Palmas. I understand the *Trina* arrived there last night."

"What does that have to do with me?"

"Do you think I haven't been keeping close watch on you? Kelby may have gotten to Cobb and Dansk, but it was easy for me to hire more men. And he really hasn't tried to keep the leasing of that Delta cargo jet a secret. Taking those dolphins must pose all kinds of problems for him. Kelby must be completely besotted with you to put up with it. What did you have to do to persuade him?"

"Nothing."

"Tell me."

"Screw you." She paused. "Cobb and Dansk?"

"Don't tell me you don't know he took out two of my employees who were watching the island? Of course, they were very amateurish or he wouldn't have been able to—"

"He probably didn't consider it important enough to tell me."

"Or maybe he knows how weak you are. Only good for one thing."

"He *doesn't* think of me that way."

"Your voice is shaking. I could tell you were crying last night before I hung up. Why don't you give me the plans and let me go my way?"

She was silent a moment. Let him think she was trying to recover her composure. "I wasn't crying. You were imagining it. I don't cry."

"Close enough. You've been near the breaking point several times in the last few days. It's not going to end, you know. I'll be waiting for you in Las Palmas."

"Good." She didn't try to keep the trembling from her voice. He would think it was caused by fear instead of anger. "I'll tell the police you're on your way. Maybe they'll arrest you and put you away for the rest of your life."

"I have too many contacts to let that happen. You're not talking to an amateur. And there's a very influential leader in the Middle East who can pull strings to get me whatever I need. He loves the idea of a sonic gun."

"He's not going to get it."

"He will. You're coming along quite nicely. Now I'm going to put on tape two and you're going to listen. It may be my favorite of all of them. When it's finished, there's going to be a quiz, so don't try to block it out."

Then she could hear her own voice on the tape.

She could see Kelby's gaze on her face and

feel the fury that electrified every muscle of his body. She turned her back on him and walked to the edge of the lanai.

"Son of a bitch!" She heard the slamming of the glass door behind him as he left the lanai.

She was barely conscious of him leaving. She could see why this tape was Archer's favorite. It was full of pain, torment, and graphic detail, destined to bring back hideous memories.

Hold on. She wasn't that girl any longer. Don't let him win.

Kelby was in the kitchen furiously chopping up carrots on the butcher block when she came in from the lanai. He didn't look up. "Finished?"

"Yes, he knows we're going to Las Palmas. He's been having the *Trina* watched. He's been having you watched too. He knows we're taking the dolphins."

"I never tried to hide it." His butcher knife bit deep into the wood. "I was hoping he'd step up to the plate so I could take him out."

"You're not supposed to use a butcher knife for chopping carrots. You'll cut off a finger."

"No, I won't. Archer isn't the only one who knows how to use a knife."

"I thought Nicholas was supposed to cook tonight."

"He needed help and I need the therapy. I wanted to feel a weapon in my hand." He still wasn't looking at her. "Nice call?"

"Not too bad."

"Don't lie to me. I saw your face."

"Okay, it wasn't my best moment. Why didn't you tell me about Cobb and Dansk?"

"Why worry you? I didn't get Archer."

"Because I don't want to be kept in the dark. Because Archer used it against me."

"Okay, next time I'll tell you when I take out one of those bastards. What else did you talk about?"

"He played one of Carolyn's tapes."

"She should have burned them."

"How could she know?"

"We know now. I'll burn them. And after I catch Archer, maybe I'll burn him too. Over a slow-roasting fire like the pig he is. At the moment I'm thinking a knife is too clean for him."

She tried to smile. "May I stick the apple in his mouth?"

He glanced up, and she took a step back at the ferocity in his expression. "I'm not being funny, Melis. You may be able to put up with Archer's sadistic bullshit, but I can't take much more of this crap. I can't stand seeing *you* take it."

"It's my choice."

"Until I get a line on Archer. Then all bets are off. You wanted help taking him down. You'll get it."

"You listen to me, Kelby. I want help, not protection. You're not closing me out. I'm the one who— Oh, shit." Blood was pouring out of Kelby's thumb. "I told you to get another knife." She ripped off some paper towels, wrapped them around his thumb, applied pressure, and raised his hand over his heart to stop the bleeding. "Oh, sure, you know about knives. I'm surprised you didn't cut it to the bone."

"It wasn't the knife." His tone was surly. "I was distracted."

"And making threats. It serves you right." After the bleeding stopped, she rinsed and dried off his hand, squirted some Neosporin on the cut, and then applied a Band-Aid to his thumb. "Now tell Nicholas to finish making dinner. He's got to do a better job than you."

"Whatever you say."

She glanced up at the curious note in his voice. He was looking down at her and a ripple of shock went through her. She was suddenly aware of their closeness, the heat of his body, the hardness of the hand she still held. She took a step back and released his hand.

"That's right, Melis." He turned back to the cutting board. "It's much better not to touch me."

She stood there uncertainly for a moment and then turned to leave.

"Or maybe I'm wrong." His soft voice followed her. "At least you're not thinking about that damn tape anymore, are you?"

Chapter Ten

"Be careful." Melis watched in agony as the dolphins were lowered in their slings into the tanks on the jet. "For God's sake, don't let them fall."

"It's okay, Melis," Kelby said. "We've got them."

"Then let's get the hell out of here." She wiped the sweat from her forehead. "It's seven hours until we get to Las Palmas and they're stressed already."

"It's not only the dolphins that are stressed," Kelby said. "Tell that pilot to get in the air, Nicholas."

"I'm on my way." Lyons headed for the

cockpit. "It's going to be fine, Melis. We've got it covered."

"It's not fine." Melis climbed the three steps of the ladder to Pete's tank and gently touched his nose. He felt silky smooth beneath her palm. "I'm sorry, boy. I know this isn't fair to you. I'll get it over with as quick as I can."

"Susie seems to be taking it okay," Kelby said as he came back from looking at the female in the second tank. "She's got her eyes open now. She had them closed all the while we were loading her."

"She was scared." She hadn't realized Kelby had noticed. He had been running to and fro, talking to the pilot, and supervising the loading of the dolphins for the past forty-five minutes. "Pete's just mad."

"How can you tell?"

"I know him. They react differently to almost everything."

"Sit down and buckle up. We have to take off."

She climbed down, sat in the seat, and fastened the belt. "How long will it take to get the guys to the tank at the dock in Las Palmas?"

"Twenty minutes tops." He fastened his own belt. "I've arranged for some marine-biology students to help release them into the tank. They're eager as hell to help, and they'll be glad to watch them for you. The tank's seventy feet long and should be okay for the short time they'll be in it before we turn them loose."

"Did you make sure the sides of the tank have bumps and protrusions?"

"As per your instructions. But why?"

"The sound has to be deflected. Their auditory system is so highly developed that it would be very disturbing to have their clicks and whistles bouncing off a smooth surface." The plane was taking off, thank heaven. The ascent was smooth and gradual as she'd instructed, but Melis could still hear Susie's worried clicking. As soon as they leveled off, she was releasing her seat belt.

"I'll check Pete." Kelby was already climbing the ladder. "You see if you can quiet Susie."

"Be careful. He might snap at you."

"Yeah, you told me. He's mad." He looked down at Pete. "He seems fine. What else can we do?"

"Just check them frequently to make sure they're wet and try to keep them calm. Jesus, I hope this is a smooth flight."

"The pilot said that the weather should be quiet. No reason for any turbulence."

"Thank God." She stroked Susie's bottle nose. "Hang in there, baby. It's not going to be so strange. You're going back to the womb."

Susie clicked mournfully.

"I know. You don't believe me. But I promise nothing bad is going to happen to you." She glanced at Kelby. "And I'd better be telling the truth."

"I promised you nothing would happen."

She shook her head wearily. "And I don't have the right to blame you if it does. I'm the one responsible for the dolphins." She gave Susie a final stroke and climbed down from the tank. "And I'm the one who came to you and offered a bargain." She sat down in the seat. Lord, she was tired. She hadn't been able to sleep last night worrying about Pete and Susie. "And you've done a good job with the transport."

"Damn right." He sat down across from her. "But I believe I won't make it a habit. Too traumatic. After I get the dolphins home to your island, that's the end of it." He paused. "If you want them back. You might decide to set them free."

"I don't think so. If it was a pristine world

uncontaminated by man, there's a possibility. But there are too many hazards we've created for them: Pollution. Fishnets that entangle and kill them. Even tourists in their boats getting too close to bands of dolphins."

"I'm guilty there." He smiled. "I remember when I was a boy on my uncle's yacht, I'd beg him to let me go out and touch them whenever we saw a large band."

"Did he let you?"

"Sure, he let me do anything I wanted to do. My trust fund was paying for his yacht. He wanted to keep on my good side."

"Maybe he just wanted to be kind."

"Maybe. But I still got the bills for the yacht after I reached my majority."

"Did you pay them?"

He looked out the window. "Yes, I paid them. Why not?"

"Because you liked him?"

"Because those trips on the yacht were my salvation. And salvation isn't free. Nothing is free."

"I believe you did like him. Is that when you decided you wanted a yacht like his?"

He nodded. "Only bigger and better."

"You certainly got it. Why did you name it the *Trina*?"

"I named it after my mother."

She gazed at him in surprise. "But I thought—"

"That I had no great fondness for my mother? Thanks to the media, I guess everyone in the world knows that we haven't been on speaking terms since I was a kid."

"Then why name your ship after her?"

"My mother was a great manipulator and very ambitious. She married my father because she wanted to be the premier social hostess on two continents. She got pregnant with me because it was the only way she could retain control of my father. He was a little fickle and had already been divorced once."

"How do you know that?"

"I was present during one of the screaming fits she had with my grandmother. Neither of them was overly careful of my tender feelings." He shrugged. "Actually, I was glad I was there in the room. Before that day she had me fooled. After my father was killed in an accident, the custody suits started. He left me everything and she was furious. But whoever controlled me controlled the money, and she was quick to jump into battle. Every kid wants to think well of his mother, and she was very talented at playing the weak, helpless victim. She was a true Southern belle. All tears and accusations against my grandmother. I guess she was practicing for her time on the witness stand and trying to influence me to testify for her."

"What about your grandmother?"

"She cared about my father and she cared about the money. She hated Trina, and I was an impediment and a weapon in Trina's hands."

"Pleasant."

"I survived. It wasn't as if I was in *Kafas*, like you. Most of the time I was in boarding schools or on my uncle Ralph's yacht. The only really nasty episodes were when I was pulled into court or forced to go home and have Trina fawn over me for the press. I kept that at a minimum by being a wild little son of a bitch whenever I was around her."

"But you still named your ship after her."

"A little hidden joke on my sweet mama. It cost a bloody fortune and she's living on a budget these days. A generous budget, but not on the scale she'd like." He smiled. "And I'm in complete control of the *Trina*. I call the shots just as I do with her budget.

There's definitely a malicious satisfaction in that."

"You must hate her."

"I did, for a while. I've mellowed with time. That pretense of weakness and fragility really fooled me. I was an idealistic kid and I wanted to go and tilt at windmills to protect her. Until the day I found out that I had to protect myself from her. It was an enlightening experience." He stood up. "I'm going to go back and get some more ice for the tanks. You said that they had to keep cool, and Pete was moving his tail around quite a bit."

She nodded. "I'll check on Susie." She got to her feet and headed for the tank. A sudden thought occurred to her. "Kelby."

He glanced back over his shoulder.

"I look— Most men think I look . . . breakable. Do I remind you of your mother?"

"At first, the way you look aroused a certain resentment." His lips twitched. "But I guarantee you never reminded me of my mother."

LAS PALMAS

"They're so beautiful." Rosa Valdez gazed down in admiration at Pete and Susie in the seventy-foot tank. "And they're truly a magnificent species, aren't they, Melis?"

"They're fascinating, all right," Melis said absently. Susie had been freed of the sling after being lowered into the tank, but she was just lying on the floor of the enclosure. She'd seemed in good shape when they'd reached the dock. Why wasn't she moving? Pete was wondering too. He was worriedly swimming around her.

"It's a true honor for you to let us help you with them," Rosa said solemnly. "We students help at the aquarium, but this is different. This is the real thing."

"I appreciate the help." If Susie didn't start moving, she'd have to jump in and see what—

Pete was gently nudging Susie.

Susie's tail switched back and forth.

Pete gave her a shove with his nose that was far from gentle.

Susie hit him with her tail and then swam up to the surface and started clicking indignantly at him.

Melis breathed a sigh of relief. No trauma. Susie was just being a drama queen. She turned to Rosa. "Thanks. I couldn't have gotten them settled without you and Manuel."

"It was our privilege," Rosa said. "My professor was very excited that we're going to be permitted to take care of the dolphins until you're ready to release them. We're going to keep journals for extra credit."

She was so serious, Melis thought with amusement. Serious and eager and young. What was it like to feel that young? "You say there are other students coming to help tomorrow?"

"Marco Benetiz and Jennifer Montero. They both wanted to be here tonight, but we didn't want to overwhelm you."

"I believe I would have been able to take it." Melis turned to the ice chest beside the tank. "They have to be fed. I purposely didn't feed them before or during the trip because I didn't want to deal with sickness or fecal material in those close quarters. Would you and Manuel like to do it?"

"Could we?" Rosa was opening the ice chest before Melis could do it. "How much? Do we hand-feed or do we just toss it into the tank?"

"I'll show you." She hesitated. Might as well teach them to protect the dolphins while they were helping out. "But you must make sure that nothing is fed to the dolphins that isn't in the ice chest. Sometimes people like to toss human food to the dolphins, but that mustn't happen. Do you understand?"

Rosa nodded. "Of course."

"And since this is a new environment, Pete and Susie have to be monitored twenty-four hours a day. Someone has to be here watching them every minute."

"We would do that anyway. We've already set up shifts of two so that we can complete our journals."

"Good." She bent over the ice chest. "They like whole fish. I only serve them cuts in emergencies. You can toss it to them. Later I'll show you how to hand-feed. It's quite an experience to feel . . ."

"Satisfied?" Kelby was standing at the end of the pier when she left the tank an hour later. "The kids are eager enough anyway."

"That's an understatement. They'll have their eyes glued on the dolphins every minute of the day."

"And that's a good thing," Kelby said. "You won't have to worry about any interference with them on the job. I've had every student on the roster checked out with the university to make sure they're bona fide, but I'm still having Cal stand sentry duty."

He meant interference from Archer. Who else? He seemed to dominate every thought these days. "Any sign of Archer?"

"No. I'm having Nicholas scout the taverns and hotels around the docks to see if he can come up with any info. But Archer may be using his ship, the *Jolie Fille.*"

"He'll want to know what we're doing here in town. He can't do that sitting out at sea." She stared out at the twilight-cloaked horizon. Was he there, waiting? They had arrived in Las Palmas four hours ago and he still hadn't phoned her. "How long do we have to stay here?"

"Probably another two days. The *Trina* hasn't finished being outfitted yet. Wilson had to arrange the loan of a navy underwater sonic imager, and it's not due to get here until tomorrow."

"Very fancy."

"I have great hopes. The technology didn't work so well when scientists used it to try to find the Greek lost city of Helike, but this imager is worlds ahead of the one they used there."

"Pete and Susie are a better bet."

"Maybe. If their mamas decide to answer their whistles. How are dolphin memories?"

"Excellent."

"That's good. Why did Lontana choose the waters around the Canary Islands to search for Marinth? I'd have thought he'd stay closer to Egypt."

"A hunch. The Marinthians were supposed to be master seamen, so the Canary Islands aren't such a stretch, and the topography of some of the islands lent itself to the legend."

"How?"

"They're volcanic, and that means possible earthquakes, and some scientists think they're ripe for tsunami waves."

"That would go along with the part of the legend that says the sea took Marinth back."

She nodded. "Phil was studying vents in this region when it occurred to him that this area could definitely be the place. Have you checked us into a hotel?"

"Hotels are a risk. We're staying on the *Trina*. It's docked only about ten minutes' walk from here and I can control security while we're on it."

"I don't care where we stay. I just want a bed."

"That's right." His expression was grim. "That bastard hasn't been letting you sleep much."

"I can't sleep long tonight either. Six hours tops and then I have to get back to the dolphins. Will you send a messenger back to tell the kids where I'll be?"

"As soon as we get to the ship." He took her elbow. "Come on. I'll have Billy make us a snack and then you can hit the hay."

Billy? Oh, yes, the cook. That day on the *Trina* seemed a hundred years ago. "Is the entire crew on the ship?"

"No, just Billy. Except for two sentries to guard the tank, I gave the rest shore leave. I don't know how long we're going to have to be gone. Maybe I don't have quite so much faith in Pete and Susie as you do."

"I never said I was sure. I just think the chances are good." She glanced sideways at him. "You've kept your word. You've done everything I've asked. I know how much you want this. I'll try not to disappoint you."

"I won't be disappointed. If we get

Archer, I'll consider it a win. Sometimes I think I want Archer almost as much as I do Marinth."

"*Almost* is the key word." The *Trina* was just ahead and it was as beautiful as she remembered it. "Nothing is as important as Marinth. I understand. It's like a fever."

"There are fevers and then there are fevers." He helped her up the gangplank. "I don't think it's wise to discuss fever at the moment."

"Why not? It was always Phil's dream to—" She forgot what she was saying. *Heat.* She looked away and drew a deep breath. "Okay, we won't talk about fever."

"Coward," he taunted softly. "I thought you'd meet the challenge."

"Then say what you mean." She forced herself to look back at him. "Don't play with words. I'm not good at games."

His smile faded. "Neither am I. You caught me off guard. I didn't expect you to feel it too."

She hadn't expected it either. It had come like a lightning strike—hot, searing, intensely sexual. She was still in shock.

"It's okay," he said quietly. "I'm not going to take advantage of a weak moment." He nodded at the stairs leading to the cabins. "I told Cal to put your suitcase in the first cabin on the right. I think you'll have everything you need."

She didn't want to leave him, she realized in astonishment. "Thank you." She moved slowly toward the stairs. Jesus, what the devil was happening?

She was neither stupid nor innocent. She knew what was happening. It was just that it had never happened to her before.

She looked back over her shoulder as she reached the steps. He was still standing there watching her. Strong, vital, and powerfully, sensually male.

Heat.

She hurried down the steps.

She drew a deep breath and opened the door of Kelby's cabin.

"Look, I'm sorry to intrude, but I—"

He wasn't there. Yet it had to be over two hours since she'd left him on deck.

She walked down the hall and slowly climbed the steps to the upper deck. He was standing at the rail looking out at the sea.

"Kelby."

He turned to look at her. "A problem?"

"Yes." Her voice was shaking. "And I don't know what to do about it. I can't sleep and I feel—" She moved to stand in front of him. "But I don't think it's going to go away, so I have to deal with it." She put her hand on his chest. She felt his heart jump and his muscles stiffen beneath her touch. "Carolyn would say it's a healthy development."

"And you respect her opinion. I don't care why or how, just so it happens." He put his hand on her throat. "You're so damn delicate. I'm not the gentlest man in the world. I'll get caught up and I'll go too fast— I'm afraid I'll hurt you."

"Bullshit. I'm not delicate. I'm strong, and don't you forget it."

He chuckled. "I promise I won't forget." His hand moved down to her breast.

She inhaled sharply.

He glanced up swiftly. "No?"

"I wasn't rejecting you, dammit. We're not going to get anywhere if you keep treating me like a cripple. It just felt . . . exciting. It's all connected, isn't it? You touch me there and I feel it . . . everywhere."

"That's the way it works." His voice was

thick. "And sometimes it works very fast. So I think we'd better get downstairs to my cabin."

He tried to get his breath. "Did I hurt you?"

"I don't remember." Kelby had been passionate in the extreme and there might have been roughness. She had no right to complain. After the first few minutes they had both been almost animalistic. She vaguely remembered her nails digging into his shoulders. "Did I hurt you?"

"No, but you surprised the hell out of me."

"It surprised me too. It wasn't like that with the men Carolyn chose. She did her best, but that was . . . clinical."

"I bet she was disappointed."

"Yes, she said we'd try again later. I shied away from it, but if I'd known it was this good, I might have gone along with her."

"I think you should stay with me. I'm a proven product." He drew her closer. "No bad vibes?"

"A few, at first. But then they went away. I guess it was because we were like a couple of bears trying to get at each other. It seemed very . . . natural. If there was a victim in this bed, it was you, Kelby."

"And I'll gladly sacrifice my body again. I'm happy I could please."

She didn't speak for a moment. "It was interesting."

Kelby chuckled. "Not the most enthusiastic comment on my sexual expertise." He brushed his lips on her temple. "And it was more than interesting to you. You were damn hot."

"And that was interesting too." Melis moved closer to him. "It went on and on. I believe you must be like Pete."

"What?"

"You once said you were highly sexed, like Pete. I think you're right."

"Is that a hint? I'm ready."

Oh, yes, he was ready. And so was she. It was incredible that she could want it again so soon. The years and Carolyn must have brought healing. She would have been so pleased. . . .

Kelby raised himself on one elbow. "Where the devil are you going?"

"To my cabin to shower and dress." She

hesitated. "I want you to know that I realize this didn't mean anything to you. I meant to tell you before, but I got distracted."

"I was a little distracted myself, and it did mean something."

She smiled. "A damn good time. But I know you don't have any reason to trust women, and I never realized until tonight that a man can be vulnerable too. I just wanted to tell you that I'm not going to sue you or cry buckets when you go sailing away. No commitments. That's what's so good about what happened tonight."

"Is it?" He was silent a moment. "Then why don't you come back and we'll indulge in some more uncommitted sex."

She shook her head. "I have to check on Pete and Susie."

He threw the sheet aside. "I'll go with you."

"Why? You must have things to do here." She grimaced. "Like sleep. We didn't get much."

"Nicholas is still in town and I don't want you to go anywhere alone."

Archer. How could she have forgotten him? "He hasn't called me yet."

"Thank God. I don't think I could handle that at the moment."

"You can't have someone trailing behind me all the time." She moistened her lips. "Get me a gun, Kelby."

"Okay, but a gun isn't the solution to every problem. You need a bodyguard, and you'll get it. Either me or someone I trust." He headed for the shower. "Archer would love to get his hands on you, and you're not as protected as you were on the island. I'm not going to have to visit a morgue and identify your body because you're being stubborn." The bathroom door closed behind him.

Carolyn lying dead and savaged on that cold metal table.

She shivered as she opened the door to the hall. That memory was like plunging into the depths of icy water. She would take the bodyguard. These last hours had reinforced again how much she owed Carolyn. She wasn't entirely healed, but she was on the way. Debts had to be paid.

And she had to stay alive to pay them.

Archer didn't call her until she'd been at the tank for over an hour. "It's been too long, Melis. Did you miss me?"

"I hoped someone had stepped on you and killed you like the cockroach you are."

"Did you know that cockroaches are supposed to inherit the earth? How did the dolphins tolerate the trip?"

"They're fine. And very well protected."

"I know. I've had the situation checked out. But that doesn't mean I couldn't get to them if I wanted to do it."

"You're here in Las Palmas?"

"Where you are, I'll be. Don't you realize that by now?" He paused. "Until you give me what I want. It shouldn't be hard for you. You're so experienced in giving men what they want. They say children absorb knowledge more quickly and permanently than grown-ups. Isn't it wonderful that that skill and memory will be with you forever? I envy Kelby. You must be showing him a very good time. But perhaps I won't stop at envy. Maybe I'll decide to taste you myself. I'll put you in a little white dress and—"

"*Shut up.*"

He was silent a moment. "Another break in the armor. It's gradually crumbling, isn't it? Give me Lontana's research, Melis."

"Damn you."

"If you don't, I'll be here for the rest of your life. It's no problem for me. I'm quite enjoying it." His voice softened. "But women don't live long in places like *Kafas,* and if I get impatient, I may have to find a way to send you to one. I think you'd tell me what I want to know fairly quickly if I did."

Don't speak. Don't lash out at him. Make him believe he's terrified you into silence.

"Poor Melis. You're struggling so hard. It's not worth it."

"I can't tell— You killed—"

"What difference does it make? They're dead. They wouldn't want you to suffer like this. Give it to me."

"No."

"But that no is beginning to sound more like yes. I hear a hint of desperation."

"I can't help what you hear." She deliberately made her voice break. "I can't . . . help it. Go away."

"Oh, I will. Because you need to think about what I've said. I'll call you back this evening. I believe we'll go over tape one. That was the first day they put you in the harem. You were very bewildered. You didn't understand what was happening to you. It was all fresh and full of pain. Remember?" He hung up.

She remembered all the pain. But for some reason she was less shaken than she'd been when Archer first started calling her. She had claimed she wasn't that little girl any longer, but perhaps she hadn't really believed it. Maybe by inundating her in that long-ago ugliness, Archer had calloused her to the sharpness of those memories. How disappointed he'd be if that was true.

"They're getting along splendidly." Rosa Valdez had come up beside her. "The female let me pet her this morning."

"She's very approachable." Melis tried to block the thought of Archer as she thrust her phone back in her jacket pocket. She couldn't let that bastard disturb her any more than necessary. She had work to do. "Has anyone come around the tank since we put the dolphins in it?"

"No one but the other students on the team." Rosa frowned. "I told everyone that those were the instructions. Is something wrong?"

"No, I just wondered." She turned and headed for the tank. "Did you give the dolphins their toys?"

"Yes. They seemed to feel better after that. Does Susie always wear that plastic boa around her body? She looks very flirtatious."

"She's very feminine. I saw her do the same thing with a length of kelp and decided she needed something more permanent." But evidently Pete hadn't been playing with his plastic buoy in his customary manner or Rosa would have definitely remarked on it. "I thought the toys would help. They don't have enough roaming territory in the tank to combat boredom. It's a temp—"

"Mother of God." Rosa's eyes widened as she stared at Pete. "What's he doing?"

"Just what you think he's doing. He likes to swim around with the buoy."

"But it's on his penis."

"Yes, he sometimes does it for hours." Melis's lips twitched as she added, "He must think it feels pretty good."

"I imagine he does," Rosa said weakly, her fascinated gaze never leaving Pete. "I can't wait to document this in the journal."

"The ship is fast, has a crew of six and a heavy weapon stock," Pennig said. "So it might be difficult to hijack once they're on the high seas."

"Difficult is not impossible. How close are they to having the *Trina* ready?" Archer asked.

"A day or two. They're waiting for some machine or something."

"A day or two," Archer repeated. It wouldn't give him much time to work on Melis. But it might be enough. The last time he'd talked to her she'd shown signs of crumbling. He didn't like the idea of having to call her after she was at sea with Kelby. She might feel freer, safer, isolated on the ship with him.

Should he put pressure by increasing the number of calls?

Maybe.

But he almost hated to disrupt the tempo. He could imagine her waiting, dreading the moment when the phone rang.

"Al Hakim called you last night, didn't he?" Pennig's voice was tentative. "Is he getting impatient?"

"Do you have the audacity to suggest that I'm not handling this right?"

"No, of course not," Pennig said quickly. "I only wondered."

Al Hakim *was* getting impatient. And the last thing Archer wanted was for him to send some of his terrorist partners to scope out the situation and risk them taking over. "Then wonder silently, Pennig. I know what I'm doing."

Going slowly and patiently with Melis was an exquisite pleasure. But patience might be becoming perilous.

He would have to consider the possibility of raising the stakes.

Chapter Eleven

"How are they doing?" Kelby asked as he strolled down the pier toward her. "Is Pete still mad?"

"Not very." Melis handed the bucket of fish to Manuel and turned back to Kelby. "He's quieted down since we gave him his toys."

"Yeah, I saw him playing with one of those toys when I came by here this morning. Interesting."

"I didn't know you were here."

"You were at the market picking out fish for Pete and Susie."

"And Nicholas was right beside me. He didn't appreciate having to carry pounds of smelly fish back to the tank. He said he didn't mind being a bodyguard, but being a beast of burden for Pete and Susie offended his dignity."

"It's good for him." He handed her the canvas tote bag he was carrying. "One thirty-eight revolver, as requested. Do you know how to use it?"

She nodded. "Kemal showed me. He said knowing how to protect myself was the best therapy he could offer me."

"I'm beginning to think better of your Kemal."

"You should. He's a wonderful man."

"Well, maybe I'm not that fond of him. I'm beginning to feel a faint prickling of jealousy."

She gazed at him in disbelief.

"I know. It's surprising me too." He looked down at Pete in the tank. "I need reassurance. Want to come back to the ship and give it to me?"

Their bodies twined, arching, moving.

She felt a surge of heat move through her at the memory. "You don't need reassurance. The first time I saw you I thought you had more confidence than anyone I'd ever met."

"You're right." He grinned. "Just thought I'd play on your sympathy and try to get you in the sack like the unscrupulous guy I am."

"Then you struck out. I don't feel at all sorry for you, and I need to stay with the dolphins. There are two new students arriving this afternoon and I want to meet them."

"Okay." He smiled slightly. "God forbid I compete with Pete and Susie." He turned and started up the pier. "If you change your mind, I'll be at the *Trina*."

She watched him walk away from her. Lord, he was beautiful. As beautiful as the dolphins. And how he'd hate her telling him that. He was all lean, compact muscularity, as firmly rooted to the earth as the dolphins were to the sea. Faded jeans outlined muscular thighs and calves and buttocks that were rock hard. Another surge of heat went through her, stronger, more intense.

Oh, shit.

Screw staying to meet those kids. She'd come back later. She started up the pier after Kelby.

She'd come back afterward.

———

"Just screw me and then get up and walk out the door." Kelby watched lazily from the bed as she dressed. "I feel so used."

"You were." She smiled. "Several times. You asked for it and you got it."

"And I couldn't be more grateful. Unless you came back to bed and did it again."

She glanced out the window. It wasn't twilight yet, but it was close. "I have to get back to the dolphins. Don't you have something important to do?"

"I just did it." His smile faded. "You do know you're something of a miracle, don't you?"

"Of course. I'm smart and I'm healthy and I know how to speak dolphinese—sometimes."

"And you're more giving than any woman I've ever met, and that's a miracle in itself."

"Because of my background"—she finished buttoning her shirt—"I'm finding it pretty much of a miracle too. I never expected to be this lusty. I never expected any of this."

"Do you suppose it could have anything to do with the fact that I'm the best lover in this hemisphere?"

"No, it definitely doesn't have anything to do with that."

"I'm crushed." He paused. "Then why?"

"I don't know. Maybe it's that everything Carolyn taught me suddenly sank in. Maybe it's that I've become so accustomed to sex in nature that I realize that dirtiness isn't in the act but the intent." She tilted her head to gaze at him appraisingly. "And maybe it's because you're not the *worst* lover in this hemisphere." She opened the door. "I'll see you later, Kelby."

He nodded as he reached for his phone. "I'm calling Gary St. George. He'll meet you at the gangplank. I'd go myself, but I'm expecting delivery of the imager."

"Good. That means I can get the dolphins out of that tank tomorrow."

"Or the next day. I have to make sure the imager is in good working order." He raised a brow. "But you know red tape: The machine may not be delivered for an hour or so. Why don't you come back to bed and keep me from being bored?"

Good God, she was actually tempted.

The dolphins.

She shook her head. "I don't want to

wear you out, Kelby. I may have use for you later."

"You're looking good, Melis," Gary said as she came down the gangplank. "More relaxed."

She felt the warmth flood her face. Were he and the other crew members aware how she had become that relaxed? She had the weird feeling everyone must know, that she still wore the imprint of Kelby's body.

"I was worried about you when I put you on that plane in Athens. I've never seen you that tense."

She was jumping to conclusions. Gary hadn't seen her since that awful day in Athens. Naturally he'd comment. "I'm better. How have you been, Gary?"

"Good." He smiled. "It's a fine crew. Kelby hired Terry, and Charlie Collins, the first mate, is top-notch. Karl Brecht doesn't talk much, but that's not bad. I'd rather have quiet than a chatterbox. And I'm going to like working for Kelby. Everyone says he's a hell-raiser but a straight shooter."

"I'm sure he's both."

"I'm glad you gave in about the search."

He strolled beside her down the dock. "I never did understand why you were so set against it. Phil really wanted to find Marinth."

"I never stood in his way. I just refused to help him."

"It made him hot as a firecracker. Particularly those last months before he died."

"You're not going to make me feel guilty, Gary. I made the right choice for me and the dolphins."

"I didn't mean you were wrong, Melis. You had to do what you had to do. I'm just glad that you're going ahead with it now. It'll mean a fat bonus for the crew if we find it. Kelby's very generous."

"Don't get your hopes up. There are a lot of variables."

"Phil thought you could find it if you tried. He talked about it all the time. Toward the last it was all he could think about."

"I know, Gary." A sudden thought occurred to her. "Phil was trying to get funding for an expedition. Did you meet the man who was negotiating with him?"

He shook his head. "I knew there was someone. He went ashore five or six nights in a row to meet with him. The first few times he came back higher than a kite. But then I could tell it had fizzled out. The last time he came back in a hurry, weighed anchor, and we took off right away."

"And he started getting rid of the crew." That must have been the point when Archer had started in pursuit. When he had failed with Phil, he eliminated the only man who knew about Marinth and that blasted sonic apparatus. Phil's death would have had a double benefit because it would have drawn her to Athens and made her vulnerable. "Why couldn't he have just forgotten about that damn city?"

"He never really hit a big bonanza." His brow furrowed in thought as he gazed at the tank on the pier just ahead. "Just that one galleon. He would have been famous and rich. Maybe it was something no one else had done. No one could take that away from—" He stiffened beside her. "Where's Cal? It was his turn for sentry duty at the tank."

She stopped. "What?"

"He was complaining because he was always having to watch the dolphins. It was his turn to—"

His knees buckled and he was falling to the ground.

"Gary!"

A round hole had appeared in the center of his forehead. Blood . . .

A black sedan was barreling down the dock toward her. The back door swung open as it neared where she stood, frozen.

"No!" She started to run, her hand reaching into the tote. The gun. Get the gun.

The sedan was almost even with her. Someone was leaning out the back door.

Oh, my God. Cox.

Melis lifted the gun. She heard a curse and the back door slammed shut as she got off a shot. It ricocheted off the side of the door.

The driver. She tried to aim, but there was no way while she was running. She shot anyway.

The glass shattered and the car suddenly swerved toward a warehouse on the right. Then it swerved back and was coming directly toward her.

No time to run away. No time to think.

She dived off the dock into the water.

Kelby was angry. Every muscle in his body was breathing fury as he strode into the warehouse toward her. He handed her a canvas bag. "I brought you dry clothes."

"Thank you." She drew the blanket the police lieutenant had given her closer around her. "But I need to shower before I get into clean clothes. I feel like I'm coated in salt. I believe they're almost through with me. Lieutenant Lorenzo said he'd be back in a few minutes."

"Are you okay?" he asked jerkily.

She nodded. "I'm not hurt. They didn't want to hurt me. They just wanted to get their hands on me." She shivered. "They killed Gary."

"I know."

"And one of the students was struck on the head and has a concussion. It's Manuel." She rubbed her forehead. "I think that's what they told me. Poor kid."

"It's Manuel Jurez. He'll be okay."

"Cal was shot too. But he's going to live. Archer and his men must have tried to hedge their bets by making sure I was vulnerable at the tanks if he couldn't get me while I was on my way there." She moistened her lips. "Cal was shot in the shoulder, and Archer had him thrown into the dolphin tank to get rid of the body. He should have drowned, but Pete and Susie wedged him between them and kept him above water."

"Hooray for Pete and Susie."

She met his gaze. "Cal thinks so."

He was silent a moment. "So do I."

"Then why are you being sarcastic?"

"Because I came in this drafty warehouse and saw you sitting there looking like a drowned rat. Because all hell broke loose and I wasn't here to stop it. Because I had to have the police call me and tell me what happened. Why the hell didn't you do it?"

"I was busy, dammit."

"Didn't it occur to you that I might want to help?"

"No." Her voice was uneven. "I wasn't thinking very clearly."

He stared at her for a moment and then muttered an oath. He fell to his knees beside her and took the edge of the blanket and dabbed at her cheek. "Why didn't you dry your hair? Water's running down your face. . . ."

"I have to wash it anyway. I stink from the seawater." She tried to stop trembling. "You were right. The gun didn't do the job, Kelby. I tried to shoot them, but it didn't work out. After I jumped into the water and swam under the pier, they took off. The car was abandoned six blocks from the docks. Lieutenant Lorenzo thinks I wounded the driver. There was blood on the seat."

"Good. I hope it was Archer."

"No, Archer was in the backseat. He was the one who opened the door and was ready to pull me into the car."

"How do you know? We don't have a photo yet."

"Cox."

"What?"

"Carolyn said that name on the phone. I think she was trying to help me identify Archer. She was a big fan of late-night TV and classic sitcoms. She even had tapes of her favorite shows that never went into reruns. We used to stay up until all hours eating popcorn and talking and watching Nick at Nite."

"And?"

"She had a tape of a show called *Mr. Peepers* with Wally Cox. He played the quintessential meek, scrawny, milquetoast character. Archer looks like Wally Cox."

"*Milquetoast* doesn't jibe with Archer's reputation."

"But an appearance of weakness might

have fueled that sadistic streak. When we get the photo, I'll bet it looks like Wally Cox."

"No bet. It makes sense." He got to his feet. "We're not waiting any longer on your lieutenant. You need a hot shower and a change of clothes. He can just come to the *Trina* if he has any more questions."

She nodded. "Right after I go check Pete and Susie. The lieutenant said they were okay, but I need to see for myself."

"I knew you'd be concerned, so I sent Terry and Karl to the tank to stand guard. Nothing is going to—" He stopped. "I'm wasting my breath. Come on. We'll see your lieutenant and then go to the tank."

Susie clicked excitedly the minute she saw Melis. It was as if she was trying to tell her what had happened. Pete was silent, but his tail switched nervously as he swam around the tank.

"See, I told you they were fine," Kelby said. "Maybe a little upset, but what else can you expect?"

"Yes, they're fine," she said softly. "More than fine."

"They really saved Cal's life?"

"No doubt about it. He was unconscious when the medics went into the tank after him. It's not that unusual. There are stories through history about dolphins saving swimmers." She called softly to the dolphins, "You did good, guys. I'm proud of you."

Pete suddenly rose to the surface in a high jump that splashed water out of the tank.

"Is that a reply?" Kelby asked.

"It could be." She nodded. "Yes, I think he's proud of himself too."

"Then can we go back to the *Trina*? You haven't stopped shaking since we left the warehouse."

She didn't want to go. Danger had come too close. She had lost Gary and had come close to losing Cal. She couldn't stand the thought of losing the dolphins.

"Archer's not about to come back tonight," Kelby said. "Besides the guards I put on the dolphins, the entire dock is crawling with police. He'd be nuts to come back."

"He is nuts. You saw what he did to Carolyn." She waved her hand as he opened his mouth. "I know. I know. There's a difference. I don't believe he'd come back tonight either." She turned and started up the pier. "We'll go back to the ship."

Kelby was sitting in a chair in her cabin when she came out of the shower. "Feel better?"

"Warmer. Cleaner. Not better." She sat down on the bed and started towel-drying her hair. "I didn't expect this to happen. I thought I'd fooled him. I thought he'd wait until I gave in and turned the research over to him."

"Maybe he got impatient."

"I made a mistake. I shouldn't have taken for granted that he was predictable. Maybe Gary would be alive if we'd been more careful."

"Your Carolyn would say that you're coming pretty close to blaming yourself. She wouldn't like it."

"No, she wouldn't. She'd hate it." She tried to smile. "You seem to know how Carolyn would react better than I do."

"I'm getting to know you. And she's a big part of you."

"I guess you're right. Okay, no blame."

She tossed the towel aside. "But I'm not staying around here and running any more risks. The dolphins are sitting ducks in that tank. Archer could have killed them after he got rid of Manuel and Cal. I don't care if the ship is fully outfitted or not. I have to go to the police station and give the lieutenant a statement tomorrow morning, but after that we leave Las Palmas. We have to find Marinth fast and then go after Archer. He's getting too close."

He nodded. "I'm not arguing. No one could want to be under way more than I do."

"No, of course not." She smiled with an effort. "Marinth is on the horizon."

"You're damn right. Did you expect me to deny I still want it? But first we'd better address the matter of Lontana's research and the tablets. You said they were here?"

"Not exactly here. They're on a tiny island some distance from Lanzarote."

"What island?"

"Cadora. It's hidden on the slope of an extinct volcano on the north side of the island. Cadora has only a few thousand people living there, and most of them are on the coast. It's a pretty place. Phil and I rented a cottage there for a while." She made a face. "Of course, when we needed supplies we had to go to Lanzarote. Cadora wasn't a shopping mecca."

"Hidden? I'd think Lontana would have had them under lock and key in a bank vault somewhere."

"You didn't know Phil. He didn't trust banks. He put everything in a large chest and buried it. He always told me that pirates buried treasures that weren't found for centuries."

"The world was a bit less crowded then."

"His world wasn't. It was full of dreams." She felt a sudden sadness. "So many dreams."

"Will you trust me to go get the tablets and research and place them somewhere safe?"

"No." She saw him stiffen and quickly said, "It's not a question of trust. I may need them as bait for Archer. They stay where they are. I don't want them buried in a vault where they won't be accessible."

"And you don't trust anyone but yourself."

"I don't think you're interested in his research."

"But the tablets and translation are a draw for me. And you know it."

"Naturally. You can have them—after we get Archer." She turned to the bed. "I need to rest. I have to get up early tomorrow. Good night."

"I'm dismissed?"

"I'm not going to your cabin. I don't feel like sex right now."

"Do tell." He stood up. "No, you're hurting and hollow and feeling a little scared." He took a step closer. "And you're not going to admit any of it." He took her in his arms. "Jesus, you're difficult as hell. Stop stiffening up on me. I'm not trying to jump you. I'm just trying to show you that sex isn't the only thing I value in you." He pushed her down on the bed and drew the sheet over her. "Though I have to admit it's way up there." He lay down beside her and wrapped his arms around her. "Now, relax and go to sleep. You're safe."

Safe. She let her breath out in a shaky sigh as her muscles gradually went limp. She hadn't realized she'd been afraid until this moment. She'd been pushing the fear away since the moment she'd seen Archer in that car. "Gary's dead, Kelby," she whispered. "I was talking to him and the next minute he was dead. I didn't even hear the shot. The lieutenant said the gun must have had a silencer. Gary was saying how excited he was about Marinth and talking about Phil and then he fell and—"

"I know." His fingers were making soothing spirals on her back. "The first time I saw a friend die, when I was in the SEALs, I couldn't believe it happened so fast. It didn't seem right that he didn't have any chance to prepare. Later, I thought maybe it was a mercy. He didn't see it coming and it was over in a heartbeat. Try to think of Gary that way."

"Archer killed him because he was in the way to me. He took all his years and just snuffed them out. Phil, Carolyn, Maria, and now Gary. I can't let him go on."

"We'll get him."

"He doesn't care. . . . He'll do anything. He's like Irmak. He even said he'd like to put me back in *Kafas*. He'd like to watch me being hurt and used and— That scares me. He knows it. He knows about the dreams."

"You dream about *Kafas*?"

"Yes, but in them I'm not a little girl

anymore. I'm back there, but it's happening now."

"It won't happen." His arms tightened around her. "I won't let it happen."

In this moment she could believe he was telling the truth. That there would never be another *Kafas,* that Archer would not be allowed to destroy her. "It's not your responsibility. I have to deal with it. Carolyn would say I had to—"

"Shh. I have the greatest respect for Carolyn, but she was a hard-liner. It's okay to lean a little."

She *was* leaning. She felt enveloped, absorbed in his strength. It probably wasn't good for her. She should push him away.

Not now. She needed to recover a little of her own strength. Tomorrow would be soon enough. "Thank you. You're being very kind. I'm . . . grateful."

"Don't worry. I'll find a way to collect."

"Marinth?"

His lips gently brushed her temple. "No, not Marinth."

"Coffee?"

Melis opened drowsy eyes to see Kelby

standing by the bed with a cup and saucer in his hand. He was fully dressed and looked as if he'd been up for hours. "Thank you." She sat up and reached for the cup. "What time is it?"

"A little after ten." He dropped down into the chair with his own cup of coffee. "You slept like a rock. You must have needed it."

"I guess." She didn't remember anything after the moment she had drifted off. "How long have you been up?"

"A few hours. I had some arrangements to make."

"What kind of arrangements? Departure?"

"There were a few other preparations to take care of." He took a drink of coffee. "I talked to Cal in the hospital and got the name of Gary's next of kin. He has a sister in Key West. I called her and broke the news. She wants his body shipped to her for the funeral. Wilson's on his way here to take care of the details."

"I was going to do that."

"I thought you were. But Wilson excels at details."

"Gary was my friend, Kelby."

"Exactly. So I can't see him wanting to

cause you any more stress. God knows you have enough." He went on, "I called Lieutenant Lorenzo, and he's going to send a police car for you at eleven. He said you should be finished by two and he'll give you a police escort back to the ship." He sipped his coffee. "We should be ready to leave by five. How do we set the dolphins free?"

"You anchor out to sea and I take the tender close to the tank. We open the sea door and let the dolphins out. They'll be confused, but I'll talk to them and hopefully they'll follow the tender back to the ship. Dolphins usually love to jump and swim in a ship's wake."

"Hopefully?"

"They could just take off. I've attached radio tags, so if they do, I'll probably be able to find them again."

"Hopefully. Probably." His gaze fastened on her face. "You're scared you'll lose them."

"You're damn right I'm scared. I'm scared they'll become disoriented and end up in some fisherman's net. I'm scared they'll know they're home and go to wherever their family is. I'm scared Archer is out there somewhere ready to stick a harpoon in them. I need them to keep close to the ship, and I'm not sure I can make them understand."

"But you think you can."

"If I didn't think I could, I wouldn't have brought them. I'm relying more on their instinct than any communication. I told you that sometimes I think they read my mind. I hope this will be one of those times." She set her cup on the nightstand. "I want to go check on the dolphins before I go to the police station." She swung her legs to the floor. "They're going to have another high-stress day, and I have to make sure they're up to it." She headed for the bathroom but hesitated at the door and looked back at him. "Thanks for calling Gary's sister. It would have been very difficult for me."

"It wasn't easy for me either. But it had to be done and I didn't want you doing it." His lips tightened. "I hope that's the last of that kind of duty either one of us will be faced with." He stood up. "I've got a few orders to give the crew and then I'll meet you at the gangplank."

"You're going with me?"

"Everywhere. Every minute. Unless you're with the police, you're not going to be out of my sight. I learned my lesson last night. Never delegate."

"But then it might have been you with the bullet between your eyes." She went rigid as the thought hit home.

"I'm more guerrilla savvy than Gary. I'd have been on the watch. I'll see you on deck."

She still stood there after the door closed behind him. She was suddenly ice cold with panic. She had never imagined that Kelby could be harmed. He was too confident, too tough, too *alive*.

Kelby shot.

Dear God, Kelby dead.

The tank gate was open.

Melis held her breath and waited until Pete and Susie discovered it.

One minute.

Two.

Three.

Susie's snout suddenly emerged through the opening.

"Good girl," Melis called. "Come on, Susie."

Susie erupted in a sonata of clicks as she swam toward the tender.

"Pete."

No Pete.

She lifted her whistle to her lips and blew softly.

No Pete.

She blew louder. "Dammit, Pete, stop being stubborn. Get out here."

His bottlenose snout appeared at the opening, but he didn't come any farther.

Susie clicked nervously.

"She's getting upset," Melis said. "She needs you."

Pete hesitated, but when Susie's clicks increased in volume he swam out of the tank toward the tender.

"Talk about hard to get." Melis turned on the engine. "Come on, let's get to the ship."

Would they follow her or go off on their own? She glanced back twice in the next few minutes. They were following. So far, so good.

No, they'd disappeared!

She breathed a sigh of relief as she saw two silver bodies arch out of the water in a high jump. The dolphins had only dived deep before the jump. They were flexing their muscles and skills after the long incarceration in the tank.

The *Trina* was just ahead, and she could see Kelby and Nicholas Lyons standing on deck.

"It's working?" Kelby called.

She nodded. "They're following. It took a little doing getting them out of the tank. Pete isn't in a trusting mood right now. He's been through too much."

"Can't blame him," Nicholas said. "What can we do?"

"Nothing. I'm coming on board and I'll feed them. Then I'll go swimming with them and sit on deck and talk. We're not going anywhere until they get accustomed to the idea that I'm on the ship and that's where they'll find me." She glanced over her shoulder. The dolphins were still jumping and playing behind her. She guided the tender close to the stern of the *Trina*. "Throw down the ladder and I'll hurry on board while they're distracted. I don't want them getting anxious."

Chapter Twelve

"I brought you a sandwich." Kelby sat down beside her, on the deck. "Billy was getting upset that you refused his dinner."

"Thanks." She bit into the ham sandwich, her gaze still on Pete and Susie. "I don't want to leave them. This period is critical. They've got to become used to the idea of me on the ship."

"And are they?"

"I think so. They're staying close and playing around the *Trina* like they did the *Last Home* all those years ago." She paused. "But at sunset they'd leave me and go wherever home was to them. It's almost midnight and they haven't left me yet."

"Is that good?"

"I don't know. They may sense they're not in their home waters yet. I almost hope they don't go. I have no idea what would happen if they tried to search for their family group and didn't find them."

"If they stay here tonight, can we start the engines at dawn?"

"Yes, but we have to travel very slowly. I want to talk to them. They need to hear my voice." She finished the sandwich. "They already seem oriented to the open sea again, but they've got to connect it with me. I have to be part of the big picture."

"They don't appear to have lost their affection for you." He paused. "Archer hasn't phoned you?"

"No, maybe he's lying low after all the police furor over Gary's murder."

"I wouldn't count on that lasting too long."

"I'm not counting on anything. I'm just grateful for whatever respite I get from him. I need to concentrate on Pete and Susie."

"You're certainly doing that." He took off his windbreaker and formed a pillow with it.

"If you're going to be here all night, you might as well be comfortable." He set it on the deck and stood up. "I'll keep running coffee and sandwiches."

"You don't need to do that."

"Yes, I do." He leaned on the rail and gazed out at the dolphins. "Jesus, I see their eyes glowing in the dark. I never noticed that before. They look like cats' eyes."

"They're brighter than cats'. They have to function in the depths and withstand light levels below the surface that might hurt a human."

"You said the concept of Flipper was way off base, that they were alien. Yet I look at them and all I see is a couple of cute, funny mammals. How are they alien?"

"You name it. Their auditory potential is staggering. Their frequency range is ten times greater than yours. They can actually form pictures in three dimensions with their echolocation and process them faster than any computer."

"Now, that's pretty alien."

"They have no sense of smell. They swallow everything whole, so taste isn't important."

"Touch?"

"Touch is very important to them. They spend maybe thirty percent of their time in physical contact with other dolphins. They don't have hands, so they use every part of their body to caress, to investigate, to carry things around." She smiled. "You've already seen them play."

"I've noticed they rub and stroke each other. But that makes them seem more human than alien."

She nodded. "But there's one other difference. We don't think they sleep. If they do, it's with half their brain. And a Russian scientist measured their REM and they don't dream." She gazed out at Pete and Susie. "That seems the strangest thing to me. They don't dream." She shrugged. "Of course, that could be a blessing."

"Or it could be the reason they haven't come back onshore where they started and taken over. You can't accomplish much without a dream."

"Maybe they have another way to dream. The way their minds work is a mystery to us." She paused. "But it's a wonderful mystery. Do you know there's a place on the Black Sea where children with mental traumas and disorders are encouraged to play in the sea with the dolphins? Some positive medical progress has been reported and, at the least, the children are soothed and happy when they leave. But the most interesting thing is that at the end of the day, the dolphins are grumpy and disoriented. It's as if they take away the children's disturbance and give them their own serenity."

"That idea is pretty far-fetched."

She nodded. "There's a lot of skepticism about the program."

"But you believe it?"

"I know what they did for me. No one was more disturbed than I was when I arrived in Chile and first saw the dolphins."

"And they brought you peace."

She smiled. "You remember I told you that?"

"I remember everything you've ever said to me." He started down the deck. "I'll see you in an hour with fresh coffee."

She watched him walk away before she lay down on the deck and propped her head on his jacket. It smelled of lime, salt air, and musk and was still warm from his body. The scents were vaguely comforting as her gaze returned to the dolphins.

"I'm here, guys," she called. "No one is

going to hurt you. I know it's a little weird, but we just have to get through this."

Keep talking. Let them hear you and identify you. Keep talking.

They started the engines at six-thirty the next morning. They allowed an hour for the dolphins to become accustomed to the sound and vibration, and then the *Trina* slowly began heading east.

Melis's hands clenched on the rail. Pete and Susie hadn't moved from the area where they'd been swimming. "Come on, we're leaving."

They ignored her.

She blew her whistle.

Pete hesitated and then swam in the opposite direction. Susie immediately followed him.

"Pete, you come back here!"

He disappeared beneath the water.

"Shall I stop?" Kelby asked.

"Not yet."

Susie was gone, too, following Pete into the depths.

Lord, what if they'd left her? What if they'd decided to—

Pete's head suddenly broke the water three feet from where she stood on deck. He chortled gleefully as he rose and paddled backward upright in the water.

She went limp with relief. "Okay, very funny. Where's Susie?"

Susie's bottle nose appeared next to Pete and clicked shrilly as she tried to imitate him.

"Yes, you're both wonderful. Showtime's over," Melis said. "We're leaving."

And they were following. Cutting through the water after the *Trina*. Playing and riding the wake.

"It's a go?" Kelby asked.

"It's a go," Melis murmured. "Give them another hour and then you can up the speed."

"Good. Otherwise it would take us a week to get to Cadora." He gazed at the dolphins jumping in the wake. "God, they're beautiful. Makes me feel like a kid again."

She was feeling the same euphoria. Only her joy was mixed liberally with relief. "They're feeling like kids too. That was definitely a practical joke Pete pulled on me."

"Do you still have to talk to them?"

"For safety's sake. But if they keep jumping, they won't pay any attention to me. How long until we get to Cadora?"

"Depends on the dolphins." He turned and headed for the bridge. "At least before sunset."

Her relief was abruptly gone.

The sun setting in Pete and Susie's home waters. Instinct and genetic memory would go into play.

Would they leave her?

Cadora loomed dark and mountainous against the pink-lavender sky. The sun was setting in a blaze of fiery glory.

And Pete and Susie were still hovering nearby, even though Kelby had cut the engines.

"Now what?" Kelby asked.

"Now we wait." She leaned on the rail, her gaze on the dolphins. "It's up to you, guys. I've brought you home. Your choice."

"It's been a long time. Maybe they don't realize it's home."

"I think they do. Ever since we got within sight of the island, they've stopped playing and become subdued."

"Afraid?"

"Uneasy. They're not sure what to do."
She didn't know what to do either. She had
never felt more helpless since that moment
years ago when she'd seen the dolphins
caught in the nets off Lanzarote. "It's okay,"
she called. "Do what you need to do. It's
okay with me."

"They don't understand, do they?"

"How do I know? Scientists argue about
it all the time. Sometimes I think they do.
Maybe they don't process information like
we do, but they might be sensitive to tone. I
told you that their hearing is terribly keen."

"I've noticed."

Pete and Susie were swimming slowly
around the ship.

"What are they doing?"

"Thinking."

"They're not doing that clicking thing.
Are they communicating with each other?"

"They do communicate without sound.
No one's sure how. I'm leaning toward the
theory that says mental telepathy is the
only explanation." Her hands tightened
with white-knuckled force on the rail.
"We'll see."

Five minutes passed and the dolphins continued to circle.

"Maybe they'd settle if you fed them," Kelby suggested.

She shook her head. "I don't want them to settle. I can't force them or persuade them now that we're here. What has to be, has to be. I took them away six years ago and now I've brought them back. They have to be the ones to decide what— They're going!"

Both the dolphins had dived deep beneath the water.

She watched. They didn't surface.

Minutes passed and there was no sign of Pete and Susie.

"Well, it seems they made their decision." Kelby turned to look at her. "Are you okay?"

"No." She said unevenly, "I'm scared they won't come back."

"You have the radio tag."

"But that's different. It wouldn't be voluntary. I'd be interfering in their world." She sat down in a deck chair, her gaze on the horizon now darkening to twilight. "So I wait until dawn and see if they come back."

"You said they did before."

"But that was before Phil harassed them and drove them straight into those damn nets. They might remember that and decide to stay away."

"And they might remember six years of kindness and friendship with you. I'd say the odds are in your favor." He sat down beside her. "We'll think good thoughts."

"You don't have to stay here with me."

"You're not going to bed, are you?"

"No, they might come back tonight."

"Then I'll stay. You wouldn't have let the dolphins go if it hadn't been for me. I feel a certain responsibility."

"I'm the one who's responsible. I knew what I was doing. I needed you and I knew there was a price to pay. Phil told me you had the same passion he did and there wasn't any doubt we'd end up back here." The moon was up and she could see the silver reflection on the dark water. But there was no sign of a dorsal fin anywhere within view. "He was right. Why? Why do you have to find it? It's a dead city. Leave it buried."

"I can't. There's too much to discover. All that beauty. All that knowledge. Who knows what else we can find? My God, even that sonic apparatus would be a blessing if it was used in the right way. Are we supposed to ignore thousands of years of learning and technology?"

His expression was lit with excitement. She wearily shook her head. "You sound like Phil."

"I'm not going to apologize for wanting to bring Marinth to life. I've wanted my shot at finding it since I was a kid."

"That long?"

He nodded. "My uncle brought me all kinds of seafaring and treasure books to read on board. A couple of them mentioned Marinth, and he dug up an old *National Geographic* for me describing Hepsut's tomb. I was hooked. I used to lie in bed and imagine swimming through the city, and everywhere I looked there was adventure and wonder."

"A child's fantasy."

"Maybe. But it worked for me. There were times when I needed to get away from all the bullshit happening around me and I'd focus on Marinth. It was a great escape hatch."

She shook her head. "Not for Phil. It was El Dorado."

"Perhaps that's the most alluring thing about it. It fulfills all needs. It means different things to different people." He paused. "But you said you were excited about Marinth at first too."

"The search turned Phil into a fanatic where Marinth was concerned. He almost killed Pete and Susie."

"That's not all, is it?"

She was silent a moment. "No. The tablets . . ."

"What?"

"The Marinth described in the tablets was everything a man would want it to be. A democracy like the Greeks'. Freedom to work and worship as they pleased. Which was unusual considering they listed an entire hierarchy of gods and goddesses. They encouraged art in all forms and deplored warfare. They were kind to their little brothers, the dolphins."

"So what's not to like?"

"It was everything a man would want it to be," she repeated. "Including a society that used women as breeding animals and toys. No marriage. No equality. No freedom for women. They were slaves or whores depending on their desirability and strength. There were houses throughout Marinth where women were kept for entertainment.

Beautiful houses to please male citizens, who were encouraged to appreciate the finest art forms. Silk cushions and fine tables with bejeweled ornaments." She looked at Kelby. "And what do you bet they had panels of golden fretwork?"

"You identified it with *Kafas*."

She nodded. "After I read the translations I had nightmares about it. I kept getting the two confused in my head."

"And that was one of the reasons you wouldn't help Lontana. I can see how you'd feel like that, but you wouldn't forbid studying the Renaissance because politically it was rife with corruption."

"Maybe it wasn't reasonable. Maybe you and Phil are right about the good outweighing the bad. But I didn't want to have anything to do with it."

His lips tightened. "Until I forced it on you."

"Until Archer forced it on me. Carolyn would say you should watch that tendency to blame yourself. It's not healthy."

He smiled. "Okay, I'll watch it." His gaze shifted to the sea again. "And I'll watch out for your dolphins. Dawn?"

"I hope."

His smile faded. "Me too."

The dolphins didn't come back at dawn. Two hours later there was still no sign of them.

"You don't know how far they had to swim to meet with their groups," Kelby said. "Maybe the dolphins moved their territory in the last six years."

"Or maybe they were thrown a hell of a welcome-home party," Nicholas said. "I'm never up early on the morning after."

They were doing their best to make her feel better, Melis knew. It wasn't working, but she forced a smile anyway. "Stop trying so hard. I'm okay with this. We'll just have to be patient."

"You're not okay with it. You're holding on by your teeth," Kelby said. "We'll give them another eight hours and then start to track them."

"Tomorrow."

He shook his head. "I'm not watching you sit vigil through another night like last night. I know you want them to come back on their own, but they'd better get a move on it." He turned on his heel and headed for the bridge. "Four o'clock we start after them."

"He means it, Melis," Nicholas said. "If that whistle you wear will do any good, you'd better start using it."

She shook her head in despair. "Nothing will do any good if they don't want to come."

"You want me to do a little shaman magic?"

"No, but a prayer might help."

"No problem. Christian, Hindu, or Buddhist? I don't have any influence in any of the other religions." His hand touched her shoulder in comfort. "You should remember that old saying about as the tree is bent, so it will grow. The dolphins have affection for you. They won't forget."

"They're not here." She shook her head. "But they will be. I just have to be patient."

At noon the dolphins had still not come.

Nor had they shown by two-thirty.

At three-fifteen a huge explosion of water broke five feet from where Melis stood at the rail.

Pete!

He clicked loudly and rapidly as he back-pedaled and then dove into the sea.

"Where's Susie?" Kelby had run to stand beside Melis. "I don't see her."

Neither did Melis. But Pete wouldn't have left Susie.

"Over here." Nicholas was on the opposite side of the ship. "Is that a dolphin or a shark out there?"

Melis ran to the rail. A dorsal fin was homing toward them, a dorsal with a *V* in the center. "Susie."

Her head jutted out of the water and she clicked furiously at Melis as if trying to tell what had happened to her.

Then Pete was beside her, urging Susie closer to the ship.

"It's about time you got here. I've been waiting for—" Melis broke off. "She's hurt. Look at her dorsal." She dove off the ship into the water. As soon as Melis's head broke the surface she was calling to the dolphin. "Closer, Susie."

"What the hell are you doing?" Kelby asked. "Get back on board and suit up."

"I want to take a look at it first and see if we need to get her out of the water. If it's bleeding, it'll attract sharks."

"And you'll be dinner."

"Hush, I'm busy." She examined the dorsal. "If it was bleeding, it's stopped now. I think she's okay." She swam around Susie, checking her out. "No other wounds." She patted Susie on the nose. "See what happens when you go honky-tonking out on the town?"

Kelby threw her a line. "Get out of the water."

She caressed Pete's nose, then grabbed the line and headed for the ladder. "Nicholas, get them some fish, will you?"

"Right away."

He was tossing herring into the water by the time she reached the deck. She took the towel Kelby handed her and stood drying off while she watched Pete and Susie devour the fish. She couldn't stop smiling.

"It's good to have them back," Kelby said. "I never imagined I could become so attached to a couple of dolphins. I was beginning to feel like the father of a delinquent teenager."

"What a concept." Melis went back to the rail and stood looking down at Pete and Susie. "Maybe they had reason to be delinquent. I think that was an abrasion, not a bite, on Susie's dorsal."

"And that means?"

"Other dolphins often express their displeasure by rubbing against invaders. They're not gentle. There's a possibility Pete and Susie weren't welcomed enthusiastically. It could be that they had some interaction problems to work out before they felt comfortable about leaving the band."

"They're here now." His gaze lifted to the sky. "But they only have four or five hours until sunset. Will they leave again?"

"I think so. Unless they had a really rough time and are scared. But they don't look scared. They're blessedly normal. And if they came back once, they'll do it again."

"How do you know?"

"They remember the pattern we formed six years ago."

"And they like you," Nicholas said over his shoulder.

She grinned. "Hell, yes, they like me."

"So what do we do next?" Kelby asked.

"As soon as Nicholas finishes feeding them, I suit up and let them get used to swimming with me in these waters."

"I said *we*. They're going to have to get used to me in the water too." He raised his hand when she started to protest. "I'm not going to be like Lontana and harass them. You call the shots. But you know damn well it's dangerous to swim without a buddy."

"I have two buddies."

"Well, now you have three. And I'm the one with the shark gun." He turned and headed for the cabins. "I'll go suit up while you have a discussion with Pete and Susie and tell them to be nice to me."

It was just before sunset when Kelby reached down a hand to help Melis back on the *Trina*. "They didn't range very far from the ship." He took off his goggles. "Maybe they are afraid."

"We'll know soon." She took off her compressed-air tank and moved over to the rail. Pete and Susie were still playing in the sea. "I couldn't have asked for a better partner down there. You're very good in the water, Kelby."

"What did you expect? This is what I do for a living."

She smiled. "Besides clip coupons?"

"Wilson does that for me." His gaze went to the dolphins. "It was weird being down there with them. It's their world. It makes you feel kind of inadequate."

"How do you think they feel when they're beached?" She shook her head. "Only with them it's life or death."

"It could be life or death for us in their domain too. But we have all the apparatus to keep us alive."

"Unless it goes wrong. Then we could freeze to death in minutes. Their bodies just make the adjustment to furnish them with more heat. They're incredibly well suited for the sea. It's almost unbelievable that they originated on land. Almost every part of their body is— There they go."

The dolphins had gone underwater, and only a dull gleam of silver showed beneath the surface as they swam away.

No use lingering here, staring after them. "That's it." She turned and headed for the cabin. "I've got to strip down and get in a shower."

"Would you like to see the sonar imager first?"

She stopped. "What?"

Kelby gestured to a cumbersome tarp-wrapped bundle in the middle of the deck. "I had Nicholas get the crew to bring it up from the hold. I wasn't sure we were going to get cooperation from Pete and Susie. It's pretty cool."

He reminded her of an eager little boy. "By all means, show me."

He swept the tarp off the long yellow metal machine. "It's the latest technology. See, it's attached to the back of the ship and we pull it behind us. The sound waves bounce off the bottom of the ocean floor, and they're measured and transferred to the graphs on the machine. It can even tell us what's several feet under the bottom down there. It's much more sophisticated than the one they used at Helike. That one they called the fish, but this one they nicknamed—"

"Dodo bird?"

He frowned. "Dynojet. And why the hell are you laughing?"

"Because it's funny. Those extensions on each side look like little wings." She went around to the head of the imager and started to laugh again. "Oh, my God."

"What's wrong?" He followed her to look at the head. He muttered a curse. "I'm going to kill Nicholas."

Two eyes had been drawn on either side of the head, complete with sweeping long lashes.

"Are you sure it was Nicholas?"

"Who else would defile a fine machine like this?"

"You have a point. It looks like a pelican or some weird cartoon bird."

He scowled. "Maybe it does. But dodos are extinct, and this is the latest technology."

"I think you said that," she said solemnly. "Sorry. I called it the way I saw it." He appeared so disappointed that she added, "But your dodo is a nice, cheerful color."

"Thanks for those patronizing words. At least I won't have to coax the imager into helping us, like you do Pete and Susie."

"I'm afraid I'd rather rely on the dolphins." She turned away. "I'll see you at dinner."

"Billy will be pleased," Kelby said. "He was developing a complex about you avoiding his meals."

"We wouldn't want that." She smiled at him over her shoulder. "There's little enough that's normal around here."

"I like this norm," he said. "Even though you laughed at my imager. I've not seen you smile this much since I met you."

"I'm happy," she said simply. "Things have been bad lately, but these last hours were good. And I refuse to feel guilty for letting myself enjoy them."

"By all means." A smile softened his face. "Enjoy."

Archer phoned an hour later, as she was going out the door of her cabin.

She stopped and looked at her phone on the nightstand. Jesus, she wanted to ignore it.

It rang again.

Bite the bullet. She turned and went back to the phone and answered it.

"You were very naughty," Archer said. "And you know how naughty little girls are punished."

Her hand tightened on the phone. The ugliness washing over her was almost overpowering. She'd hoped that the period of freedom from Archer's venom would permit her to regroup, but it hit her with the same force. "Did you expect me to just let you pull me into that car?"

"I admit I expected you to freeze like a

rabbit. I certainly had no idea you'd shoot poor Pennig."

"I hope I killed him."

"You didn't. You grazed his neck, and he bled quite a bit. He was very angry with you. He begged me to let him have the privilege of chastising you, but I told him that I couldn't bear to relinquish you. I have far too many plans."

"You weren't too eager to execute them after you failed at Las Palmas."

"It was discreet to stay out of sight for a while. However, don't think I didn't have someone keep an eye on you. At the moment you're near the lovely island of Cadora." He paused. "And you've freed the dolphins. Don't you think that's risky?"

"Are you going to go after them with a harpoon? I'd like to see Mr. Peepers in a wet suit."

There was a silence. "That's not the first time I've been compared to that weakling. I don't believe any comparison makes me angrier. Yes, I'll kill the dolphins. I was planning on waiting until you've been in a house like *Kafas* for long enough so that you won't care what I do. But I've changed my mind.

You need to be punished now. I can't think of anything that would hurt you more than killing your fishy friends."

Fear knifed through her. There was a note in his voice that was dead serious. She'd been too defiant. It was so hard to remember when she was so filled with anger. It was time to backpedal. "The dolphins?" She didn't have to fake a tremor in her voice. "I didn't think you meant it. You'll hurt Pete and Susie?"

"You're frightened? I warned you. You should be more obedient. If you're very good and give me the research right away, I might reconsider."

"I . . . don't believe you."

"I'm being pressured to turn that sonic weapon over to my friend in the Middle East. That's why I pushed a little hard myself in Las Palmas."

"Pushed," she repeated. "A good man died there."

"And you got scared and took your dolphins and ran away."

"Yes, I was afraid. Why shouldn't I be? You keep at me. I can't sleep. I can't eat." Her voice was uneven. "And now you tell me you're going to kill Pete and Susie."

"Poor child."

"I'm hanging up."

"No, haven't you learned I'm in control? We're going to talk a little longer about *Kafas* and what I'm going to do to the dolphins. Then I decide when we hang up. Are you listening?"

She waited a moment and then whispered, "Yes."

"That's a good little girl. Now we're going to pretend we're back at *Kafas* and I'm just coming into your room in the harem. . . ."

Chapter Thirteen

"You took long enough," Kelby said with a smile when she walked into the main cabin. "I've had to pacify Billy for the last ten— Jesus." His expression turned grim. "Archer?"

"He was in very good form." Her lips tightened. "But so was I. I convinced him I was on the edge of breaking. I was really pitiful. A few more times and he'll think he has me."

"It was the usual bullshit?"

"As ugly as usual, but he's added something new to the mix. I think he's decided to change his focus. And there's something you should know. He told me that he has someone keeping an eye on us. He knew we'd freed the dolphins." She paused. "And he said he's going to kill them. It's my punishment for what happened in Las Palmas."

"He's threatened to hurt them before."

"I don't think it was a threat this time. I think he meant it."

"We won't let it happen." He met her gaze. "But if you want to take Pete and Susie out of the area and pen them, I won't object."

"They wouldn't be any safer. He'll go after them wherever they are. They're probably at less risk with the whole ocean to hide in. With all those hundreds of dolphins swimming around, how is he going to zero in on Pete and Susie? If we can keep him away from the ship and watch Pete and Susie like a hawk when they're with us, it may be enough." She shook her head. "God, I hope so."

He nodded. "And I'll have the crew keep watch on the water whenever they're near."

"I was just going to ask you to do that." She looked at the beautifully appointed table. "I don't believe I'll have dinner. I'm not in the mood. Explain to Billy, will you?"

"Explain that son of a bitch is making you

bleed inside? That's hard to believe and harder to understand." He rose to his feet. "Come on. Let's get some air. Unless you'd rather go lick your wounds."

She shook her head. "I'm not bleeding. I won't give him that satisfaction. At first, listening to him was terrible. Now it's still bad, but I've learned how to handle it."

On deck now, she moved out to the rail and drew a deep breath. "It's good out here—fresh, clean. Lord, it's so blessedly clean."

He didn't speak for a moment. "Let's scrap Marinth for the time being. I think we should go after Archer."

She looked at him in surprise. "That's not what you said on the island. I didn't have collateral, so it was Marinth first. Then Archer."

"I've changed my mind. I'm entitled."

She shook her head. "I promised you Marinth. I'll keep my promise."

"Screw your promise. I'll trust you, dammit."

She thought about it and then shook her head. "If you'd made the offer before I talked to Archer tonight, I would have taken it in a heartbeat. After what happened in Las

Palmas it seemed crazy not to go after him first."

"But not now?"

"The sooner we find Marinth, the sooner I can concentrate on finding a foolproof way to keep Pete and Susie safe. That's my primary concern. Besides, he may be coming to us if he's after the dolphins."

"That's true. But what if there isn't a Marinth? What if those tablets are all that's left of the city?"

"Marinth first." She turned to face him. "Now, shut up about it, Kelby. There's something important I want to ask you."

"I can hardly wait."

"Don't be sarcastic." She moistened her lips. "Will you let me go to bed with you?"

He went still. "Now?"

She nodded jerkily. "If you don't mind."

"Hell, no, I don't mind. You know better than that by now. I'm just curious. After that call from Archer I wouldn't think it would be high on your agenda."

"You don't understand. He's so filthy, he makes me feel filthy too. I choke on it." She tried to smile. "But it's all lies. I'm not filthy. I don't feel dirty with you. You're *clean,*

Kelby. Everything's natural and right. I feel like I do when I'm swimming with the dolphins. I need to feel that right now."

He stared at her for a moment and then reached out and gently touched her cheek. "Nothing a man likes more than to be compared to a cold dip in the ocean with a couple of aquatic mammals."

"They're very special mammals," she said unevenly. "And it won't be cold. *I* won't be cold." She took a step closer and laid her head on his chest. "I promise."

"She's getting close, Pennig." Archer smiled as he gazed out at the horizon. "I think I may have her soon."

"Good," Pennig said sourly. "I want to see her hurting."

"You will. As a reward for that wound, I may let you visit her in the bordello I sell her to. There's nothing like sexual domination to sweeten the punishment."

"I don't want to screw her, I want her dead."

"You have no imagination. Death isn't first, it's last." He tilted his head, considering.

"But she may be feeling a little too safe. I shook her when I threatened the dolphins, but we have to keep the pressure high. She was actually quite insulting. It made me very angry. I think we may have to show her she can't do that."

"How?"

He picked up his phone. "By making sure she knows that there's no place on earth or sea that she's safe from me. . . ."

Melis was still sleeping.

Kelby very carefully and quietly got out of bed and quickly dressed.

He paused at the door. She hadn't stirred. It was unusual for her to sleep this soundly. She was ordinarily up at dawn and moving around with restless vitality. Now she looked like a weary little girl, all tousled and warm, and so goddamn beautiful it made his throat tighten to look at her.

So don't look at her. There were things to do.

He turned and left the cabin.

He found Nicholas on deck. He didn't waste words. "Archer has a man close enough to know we've freed the dolphins. He's threatened to kill them," Kelby told Nicholas. "We need to know where he is and make sure he doesn't get any closer."

"It's a big ocean." Nicholas grinned. "But I'm a big man. You're smart to pick someone so exceptional for the job." His smile faded. "He called Melis?"

"Last night."

"Bastard. We've got to do something about that son of a bitch—soon."

Kelby nodded. "My thought exactly. We not only have to find the sentry, we have to find the mother ship. And as discreetly as possible. I don't want Archer to know we're zeroing in on him."

"You think he's on the *Jolie Fille*?"

"It makes sense if he's staking out Melis. Wilson said his ship left Marseilles before we departed from Lontana's Island."

"And we're going to take out the *Jolie Fille*?"

"Probably."

Nicholas smiled. "Thank God for small favors. Now, this is a man's game. I was getting tired of baby-sitting dolphins."

"We're all baby-sitting the dolphins." He

looked out at Pete, who had just surfaced. "Let's hope they return the favor when Melis and I are forty meters underwater."

The dolphins were probably only toying with her, Melis thought. At first, they had seemed to have a purpose, but for the past hour they'd been swimming through caves and around rocks and coral reefs. She could swear they were playing hide-and-seek.

Kelby swam up to her and signaled they should surface.

She shook her head and swam after Pete. One more try. The dolphins had led them farther from the ship than ever before in the last three days. The water was murkier here than it had been a short distance away. It was difficult to see Susie, who was swimming ahead of Pete. They disappeared behind a huge rock.

Melis swam around the boulder.

No Pete. No Susie.

Kelby swam in front of her and jerked his thumb upward. He was clearly exasperated.

Well, so was she, but she wasn't giving up until she tried one more time to locate the dolphins. Kelby could just be patient until she had her chance.

She made the universal sign of derision with one finger and swam around him.

Five minutes later she still hadn't caught sight of Pete and Susie.

That was it.

She signaled Kelby she was going up and slowly started the journey toward the surface.

She tensed as something brushed against her leg. She looked down to see a dorsal streaking away from her. Susie?

Kelby was behind her with the shark gun in his hand. He shook his head as if reading her mind. Not a shark. He made a swimming motion with one hand.

A dolphin. But it hadn't been Susie or Pete. Through the cloudy water she could see that this mammal was bigger than either of them, and he was swimming with purpose toward—

My God.

Dolphins, hundreds of them. She had never seen a group this big.

Kelby was signaling her, asking her if she wanted to stay and investigate.

She hesitated and then shook her head.

She kept going up. She broke the surface a few minutes later and waved at Nicholas in the tender some distance away. He waved and then sped toward them.

"Where's Kelby?" Nicholas asked as he stopped beside her.

It was what she had been wondering. "I don't know. He was right behind me."

Kelby didn't come to the surface for another two minutes.

She drew a sigh of relief. "So much for the buddy system," she said as Nicholas pulled her into the boat.

"I wanted to see them at closer range," Kelby said as he climbed onto the tender. "They're all big, really big. Aren't males bigger than females? Could they all be males?"

"Not with a group that large. Males do travel in their own subgroups once they leave their mothers, but we're talking about a group of over a hundred males."

He shrugged. "Maybe I was wrong. I didn't want to stay away from you long."

"Or maybe you were right." She could feel excitement stirring as she thought about it. "If the subadult groups are that large, can you imagine how many dolphins are down there?"

"Why didn't you want to stay down and check them out?"

"Males can be aggressive. They might have taken alarm and ganged up on us and attacked."

"Why haven't they surfaced?"

"I don't know. They might have their own fixed behavior patterns. Maybe they'll surface miles from here."

"Are Pete and Susie safe down there with them?" Nicholas asked.

"I hope. They must feel safe with them." She shrugged. "I thought Pete and Susie were just playing, but maybe they wanted to introduce us."

"It would take a while to do the introductions to that many dolphins," Kelby said dryly. "I might pass on it."

She shook her head, excitement growing. "I don't think you would. Dolphins were the little brothers of Marinth. They were protected by the Marinthians, so naturally they would increase in population. These kinds of numbers are unusual. We're looking for the unusual."

"But they haven't been protected for a couple thousand years." He added thoughtfully, "Once established, though, the basic numbers might stay close to the same."

She nodded eagerly. "And there's a large amount of silt down there."

"What's that supposed to mean?" Nicholas asked.

"If an entire island was washed away, wouldn't there be a bigger silt factor?"

"Works for me." Kelby frowned. "Let's go back down."

She shook her head. "Tomorrow. With Pete and Susie. I want to give them a chance to act as buffers for us. Don't make the mistake of thinking all dolphins are like Pete and Susie. They've always been unusual. Dolphins can be as deadly as sharks in some situations. For all we know, those dolphins might have some ingrained genetic instinct to protect Marinth."

"Weird," Nicholas said.

Kelby's brows lifted. "You claim you're a shaman and it's the dolphins that are weird?"

"It's not a claim. And I reserve the right to be weird." He turned the tender. "And I also reserve the right to stay above-water while you're playing with the dolphins. Thanks to Melis, I've already had an experience with Pete and Susie that's unforgettable.

I don't need to be assaulted by a hundred or so."

They'd been back on board the *Trina* for two hours when Pete and Susie finally surfaced next to the ship.

"They seem okay." Melis's gaze raked the two dolphins as they came up to the rail and clicked at her. "No wounds. No trauma. They seem perfectly normal."

"That's good." Kelby's tone was abstracted. "I've been thinking. Maybe we won't go down with the dolphins tomorrow."

"What?" She turned to look at him. "Why not? You were all set to go back today."

"And you said that the dolphins could be aggressive. Let's make a try at letting technology determine if it's worth our while."

She sighed. "The dodo bird."

"I paid a hell of a lot of money for that dodo bird. One day. It can't hurt. It might give us an idea if there's anything unusual on the ocean floor."

"And it might not." Trust a man to be besotted by gadgets. She shrugged. "I guess one day can't matter after thousands of years.

Okay, we'll try the dodo." She saw Nicholas jump into the tender. "Where's he going?"

"Just a little reconnaissance. We don't want to give Archer the advantage of surprise."

She had been so absorbed with the dolphins she'd forgotten about Archer. She wished with all her heart she could afford to do that permanently. "No, we don't want to give Archer anything."

Golden fretwork.
Drums.
Kafas.

She sat straight up in bed, her heart pounding wildly.

"Okay?" Kelby was wide-awake. "Bad dream?"

She nodded jerkily and swung her feet to the floor. "I'm going on deck." She grabbed her robe. "I need air."

He got out of bed. "I'll go with you."

"You don't have to."

"Yes, I do." He slipped his robe on. "Come on. We'll do some deep-breathing exercises and then go down to the galley and get some coffee."

"I'm fine. There's no need—" He wasn't listening. She turned and left the cabin. The night was cool and there was a slight breeze lifting her hair as she went to lean on the rail.

"Nice out here." He didn't speak for a few minutes, then, "Same dream?"

She nodded. "*Kafas*. I half expected it. We're getting close to Marinth. I can't stop thinking about it."

"I could try going after it alone. Pete and Susie know me now."

"No."

"Why not?"

She wearily shook her head. "I don't know." She thought about it. "Yes, I do. It's one of the things I've been hiding from all these years. I was as excited as Phil when I first thought we'd found Marinth. Then I let *Kafas* poison it for me. I shouldn't have let that happen. Hell, men have been sons of bitches to women all through history. Back in the Middle Ages, a council of noblemen even met to decide whether women were beasts or human. The only reason they decided we were human was that they didn't want to be charged with bestiality. But we still managed to survive and gain our independence."

He smiled. "Because you learned to deal with it."

"In spades." She turned to look at him. "So I'll give you your Marinth, and you'd damn well better find something wonderful there. Wonderful enough to make up for those women who didn't get their chance to overthrow those blasted male chauvinists."

"I'll do my best." His hand, warm and comforting, covered hers on the rail. "Are you ready to go get some coffee?"

"Not yet. I need a little time." But the terror was fading, she realized with surprise. It usually took much longer for her to come to terms with it. She gazed out at the water. "Archer didn't call again tonight. It worries me."

"That's probably what he wants to do. He seems to have mental torture down to a science."

She nodded. "He's a terrible man and he must hate women." She grimaced. "I bet he'd be lobbying at the council for the beast theory."

He chuckled. "No bet."

They were laughing at Archer. The knowledge stunned her. Yet letting in the possibility of humor made Archer seem smaller, less intimidating.

"He's just a vicious little man, Melis." Kelby was studying her expression. "We can take him down."

She nodded and smiled with an effort. "Sure we can. I'm ready for that coffee now." She turned and headed for the galley. "I'll make it. You've been very self-sacrificing, listening to my lecture on women's lib."

"Hey, you're preaching to the converted. I've never run across any weakness in my experience with women. I've just tried to survive them."

His mother and grandmother. She had a sudden surge of anger as she thought of that child ripped between the two of them. "There's independence and then there's sheer bitchery." She frowned. "And I don't think I like the idea of you calling your ship the *Trina*. I know it's kind of a twisted joke, but she shouldn't even have that much place in your life."

"You're angry."

"Yes, I am." Angry and protective and scared that she was feeling this way. She drew a deep breath. "Why not? You were nice to me. Usually, I have to rely on the dolphins to keep me company when I have a nightmare."

"Here we go again. Just a substitute for Pete and Susie." He opened the door of the galley. "The story of my life."

She stopped. "You weren't a substitute for— I didn't need Pete and Susie. Even when I was with them after a nightmare, I felt . . . sort of hollow. But I didn't feel alone tonight." She was stumbling and she was probably saying things he didn't want to hear. She hurried past him toward the cof-feemaker on the counter. "That's all. I just wanted to tell you I don't think you'd have given the beast vote at that council. And for the right reason, not the wrong."

"I'm grateful," he said quietly.

"You should be." She turned to face him. "Where's the coffee canister in this stainless-steel jungle? I expect it to—" She inhaled sharply. "Why are you looking at me like that?"

"What?" He glanced away from her. "Oh. Lust. Sheer unadulterated lust." He sat down at the table. "But I'll try to restrain myself while you make the coffee. It's on the top shelf to your left."

"We're within a mile of where we saw the dolphin band." Kelby left the bridge and came down to where the screen was set up on the main deck. "Now we'll see about dodo birds."

The yellow sonic imager was being dragged behind the ship, its huge extensions looking like a pelican's wings.

"Yes, we will." Melis was beginning to be a little excited in spite of her doubts. She glanced at the graph. "It seems to be working okay. Maybe technology *will* triumph."

"It had better. The navy charged me a fortune for this dodo." He shook his head. "Dammit, now you've got me saying it."

"Perhaps you're not as machine-oriented as you'd like to believe." Nicholas leaned on the rail, his gaze on the imager. "It's really pretty stupid-looking. Would you like me to do a little magic to give it soul?"

"No, I would not," Kelby said. "All we need is one of your incantations to make this attempt a disaster."

"Incantation? I was thinking more on the lines of clipping a Stevie Wonder CD to the dodo's neck."

Melis smothered a smile. "Good idea. But I prefer Aretha Franklin."

"Very funny," Kelby said sourly. "We're over the site. We'll see who has the last— Shit!"

Melis's gaze flew to the dodo. "Oh, dear."

Nicholas started to laugh.

Pete had erupted out of nowhere and rammed the imager with full force. The dodo swayed drunkenly before righting itself.

Kelby was cursing. "Call him off. He's trying to sink it."

Melis was afraid he was right. Pete was swimming away to where Susie was waiting, but it was only a matter of time until he'd turn and ram it again.

"No, Pete." She blew her whistle.

The dolphin ignored her. He swam in circles, gaining momentum.

She blew the whistle again.

Nicholas was laughing so hard he had to hold on to the rail. "He looks like a bull pawing the ground before going after the matador."

"I'm going to murder you, Nicholas," Kelby said between his teeth. "Why the hell is he doing it?"

"I don't know. It looks like a bird. But

perhaps he's confused. It could be he thinks it's some weird kind of dolphin or shark. Maybe it's territorial." Melis could no longer hold back the laughter. "I'm sorry, Kelby. I know it's a valuable piece of—"

"Stop laughing."

Melis was trying desperately to do that.

Pete rammed the dodo again, sending it spinning drunkenly in a dizzy circle.

"Jesus." Then Kelby started to laugh. "Oh, what the hell. Sink it, you neurotic mammal."

"No." Melis wiped the tears from her cheeks. "We've got to save that poor, silly dodo." She kicked off her deck shoes. "Faster than a speeding bullet . . ." She dove into the sea and struck out for the dodo. "Hold on. Fear not. I'll rescue you."

"You won't rescue anyone or anything if you don't stop laughing." Kelby was in the water beside her. "I'm going to remember this."

"Is that a threat? I didn't know Pete was going to get pissed."

"No, it's a statement. It's the first time I've seen you really laugh. I like it." He struck out ahead of her. "Now, how do we get Pete to stop ramming the dodo?"

"I've no idea. Swim along with it to show him it's a friend?" The idea was so ridiculous she started to laugh again. "Get in his path and try to deter him?" That wasn't so funny. "Maybe we can use Susie to disarm him. We'll think of something."

"I hope so." Kelby gave a lethal glance back at the *Trina*. "Because Nicholas is getting far too much entertainment out of this."

Chapter Fourteen

It took them over an hour to persuade Pete to leave the imager alone. Melis tried everything from hanging on to the dodo herself to getting Susie to swim beside it. Pete was his usual stubborn self and refused to give up. Finally, Nicholas drove the tender out to the dodo and tossed Pete and Susie fish until the male began to associate the imager with something pleasant.

"Just a fishmonger again," Nicholas said as he helped Melis into the tender. "I was going to bring out the Stevie Wonder CD. You know that quote: *Music hath charm to soothe the savage beast.*"

"It's *breast,* not *beast,*" Kelby said. "And I think Melis would object to you calling Pete savage. He's just misunderstood."

"Well, I guess the fish worked better anyway," Nicholas said. He glanced at Pete and Susie playing in the water. "He seems to have forgotten the deadly dodo. Do you think it survived Pete's attack?"

"It's supposed to be very sturdy," Kelby said. "We'll see when we get back on board and check out the instruments."

The green light was still lit on the control board when they reached the *Trina* ten minutes later.

"By George, it's alive," Nicholas murmured. "This dodo is definitely not extinct. You saved it, Melis."

"Why don't you go tell Billy to fix lunch?" Kelby's gaze was on the panel. "And then bring us a couple towels."

"Are you trying to get rid of me? First a fishmonger and then a cabin boy." Nicholas strolled down the deck. "You've got to promise you won't do anything that might amuse me while I'm gone."

"I'm surprised it's still working." Melis took a step closer to the panel. "If it's as sensitive as you say."

"The imager is sensitive, but the casing is built like a tank and should withstand most things." Kelby bent down and adjusted a knob. "Evidently, including a dolphin trying to sink it."

"Are you saying I didn't save the dodo?"

"Heaven forbid. I wouldn't presume. You're faster than a speeding bullet. . . ." He'd moved around to the graph. "It's just that you had a little help from the lab that— I'll be damned."

"What is it?" She went to stand beside him and looked down at the graph. "Something?"

"We were over the site area all during the time we were trying to finesse Pete into leaving the dodo alone." He pointed to a jagged line on the graph paper. "Something's down there." He pulled up more paper to examine. "Except for a couple of minutes when the dodo was spinning like a top, the imager indicates the same irregularities. Higher and more extreme to the west."

"You're getting excited. It could be another—"

"And it could be the jackpot." Kelby's gaze never left the graph. "Go down and change, Melis. We're going to take the dodo for a little ride to the west and see what we come up with."

Two miles west, the jagged variations on the graph sharpened and horizontal lines appeared.

Another half mile and they saw the dolphins.

Hundreds and hundreds of them, sleek bodies shimmering in the afternoon sun as they swam and jumped and played. Joy. Grace. Freedom.

"My God," Melis whispered. "It makes me think of the beginning of creation."

"Last Home?" Kelby asked.

"It could be," Melis said. The sight of the dolphins was awe-inspiring. She couldn't take her eyes off them. Rays of sunlight were filtering through gray-blue clouds and touching the sea with radiance. The dolphins had been impressive deep below the water, but this display was truly remarkable. It made her throat tighten with emotion. "I guess we'll see tomorrow when we go down with Pete and Susie."

"If those other dolphins let us near it."

"We don't have to use Pete and Susie."

She didn't look at him. "You could get a diving bell or one of your other fancy submersibles to explore it."

"No, I can't. It wouldn't be the same. I don't want to be surrounded by a steel cage when I see Marinth for the first time."

She smiled. "The dream?"

"What else?" His voice was suddenly vibrating with intensity. "My God, it's *here*, Melis."

"I hope so." Lord, he was happy. His expression was glowing, and warmth flowed through her as she looked at him. She couldn't share the dream, but she could share his joy. It reached out and embraced her, enfolded her. She moved a step closer and took his hand.

He looked down at her inquiringly.

"No big thing." She smiled. "I just wanted to touch you."

"That's a very big thing."

"Not right now." She looked back out at the sea and the dolphins joined together in an eternal circle of life and renewal. "Not here. But it's very good."

"Our watcher is using a Ballistic 7.6-meter monohull tender," Nicholas told Kelby when he came back to the ship that night. "Actually, there may be two sentries."

"Two?"

"I saw another motorboat some meters distant, but he was gone before I could get close. It makes sense that there would be two if they needed to keep a twenty-four-hour watch."

"Did they see you?"

"I don't know. But it's no big deal if they did. It would be natural for us to mount our own watch." He made a face. "I don't think I scared anybody away. That tender has as much power and range as yours, Jed. Give him a head start and he's out of sight."

"Can you follow one of them back to the *Jolie Fille?*"

"Maybe. But I'll start my own search anyway. As soon as you come up from the dives at the end of the day, I'll be out of here."

Melis could barely see Pete and Susie swimming ahead of her through the silt-clouded water.

So much for using them as buffers, she thought ruefully. Ever since she and Kelby submerged this morning, the dolphins had practically ignored them.

No, that wasn't true. Because they were moving with purpose. They were intent on something, some destination. They had the same attitude they'd had the other day when Melis thought they were leading her somewhere. When she first noticed that intensity today, it filled her with hope.

Kelby, who had gone ahead, swam back to her and shook his head.

What was wrong?

He made a swimming motion with his hand.

Shark?

Then she saw them herself. The dolphins. A band as numerous as they'd seen yesterday afternoon, here in the depths.

And only yards ahead of them. The sheer mass was intimidating.

And so was the unfriendly interest of one of the males who was swimming toward them.

Jesus.

The male bumped hard against Kelby and then swam toward her.

Kelby unholstered his shark gun.

She emphatically shook her head. The
next minute the male hit her rib cage.

Pain.

Then the dolphin was gone.

But he might be back again, maybe with
reinforcements.

Kelby was signaling for them to go up.

It might be the smart thing to do. They
could come back tomorrow after they figured a way to—

Pete and Susie were back.

Pete was swimming around them in a
protective circle while Susie came and swam
beside Melis.

Melis reached out and patted her nose. *It's
about time you got here, young lady.*

As if in answer, Susie came closer and
rubbed against her.

Melis hesitated and then made a motion
for Kelby to go on.

He started to shake his head and then
shrugged and started forward.

Would Pete and Susie stay with them?

And would it make any difference to the
other dolphins if they did?

She swam slowly toward the band of
dolphins.

Pete continued his protective circling, and Susie stayed on Melis's left side.

Then they were in the center of the mass of dolphins. It was incredible.

And absolutely terrifying.

Please don't leave us, guys, she prayed.

Pete and Susie were still with them.

A female detached herself from the outer perimeter of the band and swam toward them.

Pete instantly swam toward her and made her swerve away from Kelby and Melis. Then he continued his circling around them.

Ten minutes later the dolphin band began to lose interest in them.

Five minutes after that, Pete began to widen his circle as if he sensed they were safe.

But he and Susie still remained with them as they made their way slowly through the band of dolphins.

Then they were on the other side and following Pete and Susie through a grotto and back into the open sea.

But they saw nothing.

The water was murky but clear enough to see the bottom. But the bottom was silt. No columns. No ancient city. No ruins. Silt.

Jesus, Kelby was going to be disappointed, Melis thought.

He didn't show any signs of it. He was swimming faster, stronger, going deeper, closer to the bottom. He was skimming, looking, and then he turned and swam back to her and jerked his thumb upward to indicate they should surface.

Kelby didn't speak until they were back on board the *Trina,* but she could sense an undercurrent of excitement.

"I think it's there," Kelby said as Nicholas helped them strip off their tanks. "Marinth. I'm almost sure it's there."

Melis shook her head. "All I saw was silt."

"Me, too, until I got closer. I saw glimpses of metal fragments jutting up through the silt. You said the tablets were bronze. They could have used metal for other things."

Nicholas nodded. "Microwaves and washing machines."

Kelby ignored his levity. "Maybe. We won't know until we dig Marinth out of that silt."

"Providing it's Marinth and not the remains of a World War Two sub," Nicholas said. "You're not sure."

"I'll have a good idea after I go down again and retrieve some of that metal. I want you to go down with me as soon as I restock the air."

"I thought you'd never ask," Nicholas said.

"No," Melis said. "I go back with you."

Kelby shook his head. "We don't know that the dolphin band will be as tolerant as they were after Pete and Susie appeared."

"And we may need Pete and Susie again. They don't know Nicholas well enough."

"Well, they know me better than I'm comfortable with," Nicholas said.

"I go," Melis repeated. "Someone has to stay on board in case we run into equipment trouble. After we're sure this is the location and that the dolphins are tolerating us, Nicholas can take his turn."

Kelby hesitated. "How are your ribs?"

"Sore. But I'm going."

Kelby looked at Nicholas and shrugged. "She's going."

They brought nothing up but shards of bronze and some other unidentifiable metal on the next two dives.

On the third dive Kelby brought up a long slender cylinder made of the same metal.

Nicholas and the entire crew were waiting as they boarded the *Trina*.

"Something interesting?" Nicholas edged closer to the object in the net. "It doesn't look too corroded. Bronze?"

"It's some kind of metal alloy." Kelby knelt beside the cylinder. "And it doesn't look like a World War Two submarine part to me. Come here, Melis."

She was already beside him. "What?"

"Take a look at the script along the rim of the cylinder."

She inhaled sharply. She hadn't noticed the tiny marks.

"Hieroglyphics?" Kelby asked. "The same as on the tablets?"

She nodded. "They look the same."

"Hot damn." Kelby's smile was exuberant. "I knew it. We've *found* it."

A cheer went up from the crew.

"Go break out the champagne, Billy." Kelby was still examining the cylinder. "I wonder what this is. . . ."

"A spice jar?" Nicholas pointed to one of

the hieroglyphs. "I'd guess this one says chili powder."

Kelby laughed. "Hell, you're probably right. I'm trying to read something profound into it. I guess I'm a little off balance at the moment."

"I think I'll go help Billy choose the champagne. It has to be very special to suit this occasion." Nicholas's expression softened as he said over his shoulder, "I'd say you have a right to go a little dizzy. Congratulations, Jed."

"Thanks." Kelby looked at Melis. "And thank you."

She shook her head. "You don't have to thank me. I made you a promise. You really think this is proof?"

"I think it comes damn close. If we turn up more objects tomorrow, I'd bet we've found it."

"So what's next?"

"I call Wilson right now and send him to Madrid to get me salvage rights and whatever else I need to protect my right to explore it. Otherwise, if there's a leak, the whole area will be teeming with salvage ships trying to strike it rich."

"Will it take long for him to do that?"

"Not if he greases the right palms. Wilson is an expert." His smile faded. "I haven't forgotten Archer. Give me one more day here, Melis. That's all I'll need."

"I wasn't pushing you." She smiled crookedly. "I wish I could forget Archer. I can't do it. He won't let me. *I* won't let me." She paused. "Marinth isn't what you thought it would be, is it? I expected broken columns and ruins. Not just silt."

He shook his head. "When I was a boy, I dreamed of an arched doorway leading to a beautiful city."

"But you don't seem disappointed."

"That was a dream. This is reality, and reality is always more exciting. You can take it in your hands and touch it, mold it." He shrugged. "Maybe I needed the dream then, but I don't now." He grinned. "And who knows what's under that silt? It could be an arched doorway." He took her arm. "Come on, let's get into dry clothes and go drink some champagne."

Kelby wasn't in bed beside her.

Melis glanced at the clock. It was a little

after three in the morning, and Kelby seldom got up before six.

Unless something was wrong.

The dolphins.

She sat up, swung her feet to the floor, and
reached for her robe. A moment later she was
climbing the steps leading to the upper deck.

Kelby was standing at the rail, his head
lifted, his gaze on the night sky.

"Kelby?"

He turned and smiled at her. "Come
here."

There was nothing wrong. He wouldn't
have been able to smile like that if all was not
right with his world. She moved toward
him. "What are you doing out here?"

"I couldn't sleep. I feel like a kid on
Christmas Eve." He slipped his arm around
her. "And in a few hours I get to open my
packages."

His expression had the same luminous excitement that had been there from the moment he'd found the canister. "They may
not be as exciting as the one you unwrapped
today."

"And they may be better." His gaze went
to the sky. "You know, that metal is odd. I've
been wondering—meteorites?"

She laughed. "Or maybe it was brought down by spacemen?"

"Well, anything is possible. Who would have dreamed that a society founded thousands of years ago could be as advanced as they evidently were." His arm tightened around her. "And it's all here for us, Melis. All that wonder . . ."

"Wonder?"

He nodded. "There's so little wonder left in the world. Children are the only ones who have it naturally, and they lose it as they grow older. But once in a while something comes along that reminds us that if we open our eyes and search hard enough we can still find it."

She felt her throat tighten as she looked up at him. Something . . . or someone. "What do you think is still down there?"

"Hepsut wasn't very descriptive. I can't wait to get my hands on those tablets. It may give me an idea where to search, what to expect."

She laughed and shook her head. "You don't want to know what to expect. It would spoil it for you."

He nodded ruefully. "You're right, some of the magic would be gone. And magic's important." He glanced down at her. "It's late. You don't have to stay with me. I'm crazy as a loon tonight."

She wanted to stay. She could tell he wanted to talk, and she wanted to be here for him. And being near Kelby at this moment of triumph had a magic of its own.

Magic and wonder.

"I'm not sleepy. You mentioned arches. If they did exist, what do you suppose they'd be like?"

"You want me to play that game?" He looked back at the sea. "Intricately carved. Maybe inlaid with mother-of-pearl and gold. And when you go through them the streets would be laid out with perfect symmetry. They'd be like the spokes of a wheel that would lead to a great temple in the center of the city. . . ."

"I found the *Jolie Fille* last night," Nicholas said in a low voice to Kelby while he was adjusting his air tank the next morning. "It's anchored about thirty miles south of here."

Kelby's gaze went to his face. "Did you get a good look at it?"

"Big. Sleek. Probably fast. And crawling

with guards. I counted four sentries pacing the decks in the short time I was there. Archer isn't taking any chances on being surprised." He paused. "And I saw a coast guard boat boarding the *Jolie Fille* as I was leaving."

"A search?"

"It looked a lot friendlier."

"A payoff?"

"That would be my bet."

"So outside help is unlikely."

"No loss. Outsiders usually get in the way."

"Good work, Nicholas."

"Only what you'd expect of me. Now we have something to work with. Even if it's not at the top of your list right now." He smiled as he started across the deck to help Melis. "Good luck down there, Jed."

Kelby and Melis brought up four nets' worth of artifacts from the ocean floor the next morning. Some of them were mundane or unrecognizable, but one made Kelby's eyes widen with excitement.

"Melis." He carefully raised the object in his hand. "Look."

She moved nearer. "What is—"

It was a goblet. The gold was dulled and the lapis and rubies were partially obscured by silt, but the craftsmanship was magnificent.

But that wasn't why the sight of it held her spellbound. She reached out a tentative finger and touched the rim. Thousands of years ago some man or woman had drunk from this goblet. Their lips had touched this rim. They had laughed and wept and loved in that ancient city below them. Strange, it had just come from the sea, yet it felt warm. . . .

She looked up and met Kelby's gaze. He smiled and nodded with perfect understanding of what she was feeling.

Wonder.

The afternoon's bounty was not as rich, but there was enough to encourage them to keep them diving.

It was late in the afternoon when Kelby indicated they should go up.

She nodded and pushed upward through the murky water. Lord, she was tired. Her arms felt like lead, and the air tank was a burden she didn't—

Pete swam back and forth in front of her, blocking her way.

Not now, Pete. She definitely didn't want to play. She treaded water, waiting for him to——

Something hard and big brushed by her.

Another dolphin? No, she hadn't seen any sign——

A glimmer of something black and shiny up ahead. Wet suit. Not Kelby. He had a navy blue wet suit, and Kelby was behind her.

Spear gun!

Pete was clicking wildly as he tried to get between her and the man in the black wet suit.

Blood in the water.

Oh, God, he'd shot Pete. She could see the spear sticking out of his side. She swam toward him.

And Kelby was swimming toward the man with the spear gun. She caught a gleam of steel in Kelby's hand as he closed on him. His knife.

They were struggling, turning over in the water.

It was over in an instant.

More blood in the water.

Kelby pushed the man away from him.

No, it wasn't a man any longer; it was a body that drifted toward the bottom.

Kelby was swimming back to her. He motioned for her to go up, but she shook her head. Pete was moving, but sluggishly. She was afraid to take the harpoon out of his side, but she wasn't going to leave him. She tried to nudge him upward. He didn't move.

Then Susie was beside him, nudging, swimming around him, clicking worriedly.

A moment later Pete slowly moved upward toward the surface.

My God, the blood . . .

Chapter Fifteen

Archer didn't call until after midnight.

"What have you done with poor Angelo, Melis?"

"You bastard." Her voice was quivering. "You killed Pete. He wasn't doing you any harm. Why did you have to kill him?"

"I warned you that I'd do it if you didn't cooperate. Did Angelo kill the female too?"

"No."

"Then she'll be next, won't she?"

"No!" Her voice rose. "Kelby killed this Angelo. He'll kill anyone else who tries to hurt Susie. You can't get near her."

"I have other employees, and it's a big ocean. I'll get her. Tell me, did your dolphin suffer?"

"Yes," she whispered.

"I thought he would. I told Angelo to make sure of it. The female will suffer more."

"Dear God," she whimpered, "please don't kill Susie."

"But I have to do it. You won't give me the papers. It's really you who are killing her, Melis. Remember that when you see her die. Good night."

"No, don't hang up." Her voice was panicky. "I'll give you the damn papers. I'll give you anything you want. Just don't kill Susie."

"Ah, at last." He was silent a moment. "And all it took was a dead dolphin. I should have moved before this."

"Don't kill her. Tell me what to do. You said you'd go away if I gave you the papers."

"Stop sobbing. I can't understand you."

She drew a deep breath. "I'm sorry. Just don't hang up. Tell me what you want."

"Is that what you told the men who came to you at *Kafas*?"

"No."

"That's not the right answer. Tell me what I want to hear."

"Yes, I begged them. I said . . . anything . . . anything you want, I'll do."

"That's a good girl." Archer's voice was silky with satisfaction. "You may be able to save your dolphin after all."

"Don't put me through this. Just let me give you the damn papers."

"I'll let you. But you'll do it my way, my rules."

"If I give them to you, you'll leave me and Susie alone, won't you?"

"Of course." He paused. "But you know, I'm going to miss this."

"Where can I bring them to you?"

"Where are they?"

"On the slope of the extinct volcano on Cadora."

"Then we'll go get them together. I can hardly wait. I'll meet you on the dock at Cadora at ten tomorrow night. You won't see me until I want you to. If there's anyone with you, I'll disappear and give the order to kill the dolphin."

"There won't be anyone with me."

"No, I think you're chastened enough for

me to believe that. Good night, Melis. Dream of me."

She probably would dream of him and death and the ugliness of Pete's bleeding. . . .

"Well?"

She turned to Kelby, who was sitting across the cabin. "Tomorrow night at ten. He's meeting me on the dock. If anyone else is with me, he'll no-show and kill Susie."

"I guess he believed you were on the ropes." His lips tightened. "I almost did. The son of a bitch was turning you inside out. It wasn't easy for me to sit through it."

"Do you think it was easy for me?" She was still shivering with revulsion, and she crossed her arms across her chest to try to stop. "It had to be done. This is the moment. I won't have what happened to Pete mean nothing. We have to use it."

"Well, you did." He leaned back in the chair. "And if you think I'm going to let you go alone to Cadora, you're crazy. We made a deal that I'd take out Archer if you gave me Marinth. You sit here and let me do my job."

She shook her head. "I'm the bait. I'm the person who can lead him to the tablets."

"Even if he does believe he's harassed you into going off the deep end, he's going to hedge his bet," Kelby said. "He's going to make sure you're helpless. Just the way he wants you."

Kafas. He wanted to put her in a place like *Kafas.* Don't think about it. It won't happen.

"Then we'll have to make sure I'm not, won't we?" She crossed the cabin to look out the window. "I'm not closing you out of this. That would be stupid. That's why I brought you into it. But I have to be the one to spring the trap."

Kelby muttered a curse. "You don't have to be the one. We don't have to use those damn research papers to get him. I told you that Nicholas found out the location of his ship."

"It's not certain enough. He got away from you in Tobago. He could up-anchor and be gone tomorrow." She could sense his anger and frustration and she spoke quickly, not looking at him. "The chest is in a glade on the west slope of the mountain. It's beneath the only lava boulder in the clearing. It's just a three-foot dig in rocks and sand, so Archer should be able to get to the chest in a few minutes after they move the rock. I think you and Nicholas should wait there in the woods until they finish digging. You're right, Archer will take out insurance. He'll search me for weapons and bring help along in case I'm not the cowed simpleton he thinks. Can you stay out of sight if they search the woods?"

"Hell, yes. What do you think we were trained for? But I don't want to go hide in the woods. I want to go after Archer's ship."

She ignored his last two sentences. "After they find the chest and start going through the papers, they'll forget everything but that. That's the time to go after Archer."

"While you're standing there on top of him? The first thing he'd do is shoot you. You'd be helpless."

"I won't be helpless. Because you're going to hide my gun only a few yards from the cache. There are two pine trees to the north of the glade. Cover the gun with leaves and brush at the base of the one on the left. I'll be ready when you make your move and run toward the trees."

"Let's get this straight. You're *not* faster than a speeding bullet. That was a joke. There's a good chance that he'll shoot you before you reach those trees."

She shook her head. "It's only a few yards.

If you provide interference, I should be okay."

"*Should?* I don't like that word."

"I *will* be okay. Is that better?"

"No." He stood up. "It sucks. You've got it all worked out. You've been planning this for a long time, haven't you?"

"Since the night they found Carolyn's body." She turned to look at him. "He has to die, Kelby. He's an abomination on the face of the earth."

"And you want to do it yourself."

"He's a murderer." She paused. "And he's more than that. He's Irmak and all the dirty, twisted men who came to *Kafas* and raped and hurt me. I never got a chance to punish any of them, but I can punish Archer. I *need* to punish him, Kelby."

He didn't speak for a moment, but the silence vibrated with emotion. "I can see that." He turned away. "And God help me, I'm going to let you do it."

Nicholas was lounging on the bed when Kelby came into his cabin. "He called?"

Kelby nodded.

"Archer's ship?"

"No, Cadora," he said curtly. "I couldn't talk her out of it. Ten tomorrow night. She's the bait. We're the trap. If she lets us spring it."

"You're mad as hell."

"No, I'm scared as hell."

"We could go after the ship tonight and erase the problem. While you were swimming in Marinth, I took the tender to Lazarote and made a few vital purchases. I can have a couple bombs made up in no time."

"No, she needs to be part of it. I'm not going to cheat her."

"So why are you here talking to me? I doubt if it's to vent."

"To get your ass off that bed. We're going to Cadora tonight."

Melis watched the tender roar away to the north and then turn east.

Kelby was going to Cadora.

The chest.

It was her first thought. She had given him both the directions and location. There was nothing to prevent him from taking the chest. Not even conscience. She had told him she'd give it to him after Archer was disposed of.

But they weren't rid of Archer. And if Archer found that the chest was missing, he wouldn't be distracted, he'd be furious and strike like the cobra he was.

And God help me, I'm going to let you do it. Kelby's words had been too passionate and intense to have masked cool calculation.

He wouldn't take the chest. He was probably going to reconnoiter and hide the gun. But no matter why he was going to Cadora, it wasn't to steal the tablets. She had come too close to him not to know when he was speaking the truth.

She went rigid. Jesus, she had come close. Friend, companion, workmate, lover. In the past weeks he had become all of those things to her. She felt a rush of panic. How had it happened? And how would she survive after she left him?

Emptiness. Loneliness.

She knew how to handle both of them. She'd be fine. She'd been a loner all her life.

But she didn't want to be a loner now. She'd found something different, better.

So what should she do? Cling like one of

the women Kelby had grown to hate? She'd promised him she'd never be like them.

And she wouldn't. She'd go when she had to go. She wouldn't be pitiful or helpless. She wanted him, but she didn't need him. She had a life to lead and it would be a good life.

But, dear God, she wished she hadn't been stupid enough to open her mind and body and learn what she would miss.

Wishes didn't do anyone any good. Try to forget.

Remember Archer. Remember tomorrow.

There was no one on the dock.

Melis hadn't really expected him to be there.

But he was there in the darkness, watching her. Even if he hadn't told her, she would have known it.

She jumped out of the tender and tied it before moving up the pier toward the dock. The dock was lined with warehouses and there were only two streetlights on the two-block stretch, but there was a full moon, thank heaven. She could hear sounds of traffic, but it was far away.

Come on, Archer. Here I am. Poor piti-ful me. Come and scoop me up.

She stopped at the end of the pier. Look crushed. Look beaten. Look nervous.

She shifted from side to side. Her gaze darted frantically down the street and then to the warehouses.

"Hello, Melis. How wonderful to see you again."

Her gaze flew to the door of the second warehouse on her right.

Archer.

He smiled gently as he came toward her. Cox. Small. Thinning hair combed back from his high forehead. She had only caught a glimpse in the car in Las Palmas, but there was no mistaking him. She moistened her lips. "I'm here."

"And so frightened. You mustn't be frightened of me. We've grown so close. Like slave and master. Isn't that right?"

"Whatever you say. Just let me give you the papers."

"You know about the slave-and-master game? It's one of my favorites with the little girls at my favorite house in Buenos Aires."

"Please. Let's go."

"She's so eager." He said over his shoulder, "Pennig, I believe we're going to have to let her give me the papers."

"It's about time." Pennig came out of the shadows. It was the same man she'd seen in Athens. But he was wearing a bandage on his throat, and his expression was much uglier. "Stubborn bitch."

"Now, you mustn't be angry with her. Little girls get upset when you're angry."

"She shot me, dammit."

"But she's willing to make amends, and we must be generous. Search her."

Pennig's hands were rough, hurting, as they moved over her body from shoulders to feet. "She's clean."

"I didn't think she could hide much in those khakis and shirt." Archer's gaze went to the deserted pier. "Was it difficult to make Kelby let you come alone?"

"He's got what he wants. Marinth. I'm just an encumbrance now."

"But such an enticing one. I envy him. I'm sure you made the search very enjoyable." He smiled. "But you're getting more upset by the minute, aren't you? I'll be kind and put you out of your misery." He spoke into his phone. "It's okay. Bring the car around, Giles." He hung up. "How far can we go by car?"

"Just past the foothills. The cache is a mile past that point."

A black Mercedes roared around the corner two blocks away and barreled toward them.

"The chest is buried beneath a lava rock in a glade on the side of the mountain." Melis's gaze was on the Mercedes. Christ, it looked like there were three in the car, and with Archer and Pennig it would be five.

"Oh, I almost forgot." Archer turned to Pennig. "Take the box and put it in her tender."

Box?

Pennig was taking a large gift-wrapped box from the shadows and running down the pier with it.

"What is it?"

"Just a little good-bye present. It's a surprise."

The Mercedes pulled up and Archer opened the back door for her. "Then we'd better get going, hadn't we?"

Look frightened at the sight of the men in the car. It wasn't hard to do. She *was* frightened. A protest would be reasonable now. "I can tell you where it is. I don't have to show you. You said you'd let me go."

"After I have the papers," Archer said. "Get in the car, Melis."

She hesitated and then got into the Mercedes.

"How long?" Archer asked as he got in the passenger seat. Pennig rushed up to the car and got in beside him.

"Maybe fifteen minutes," she whispered as the driver started the car. The two men she was sitting with were silent, but their presence was close, smothering.

It was going to be a long, long fifteen minutes.

"A Mercedes stopped at the end of the road," Nicholas said as he ran back into the trees. "Five men and Melis. Archer and Melis are waiting by the car. The other four are on their way up."

It was what Kelby had expected. There was no way Archer would endanger his hide until he was sure the area was secure. He started to climb the tree he'd staked out. "We let them go past on the first go-around.

They'll probably station one man to over-
look the road and one or two here in the
woods. We don't take them out until Melis
and Archer are here."

"It's a terrible temptation," Nicolas murmured as he shinned up the tree several yards
from where Kelby was located. "But I'll try
to restrain myself. I'm closer to the road. I'll
take him out."

"I'll play it by ear. But I want as few
guards functioning as possible when they
unearth that chest."

"The birdcall?"

"Right. Owl. I saw one in the trees."
Kelby drew the camouflage brush around
him as he settled on the second branch.
From this viewpoint he could see both the
road and the rock in the middle of the glade.
Melis was standing by the front bumper of
the Mercedes, and she looked small and in-
finitely fragile from this distance.

Don't think about her.

Think about the business at hand. The
four men Archer had sent up the trail were
close. In a moment they'd be here in the
trees.

Silence. Breathe shallow. Don't move a
muscle.

The man who had driven the Mercedes was standing at the top of the trail and waving a flashlight at them.

Archer muttered a curse.

Melis stared at him in surprise. "What's wrong?"

"Nothing. Giles is giving us the all-clear," Archer said. "Let's go, Melis."

Melis tried not to show her relief. She had been tense from the moment Archer had dispatched his men to search the area. She shouldn't have worried. Kelby had said he and Nicholas would have no problem. But it didn't matter what she should or should not have felt. The fear was there, and she couldn't reason it away. "Let me go back to town. You can see I didn't set a trap for you."

"Stop whining." He took her elbow and nudged her up the trail. "It's very distasteful. You've been very good. I don't want to have to punish you."

She drew a deep, shaky breath. "You won't hurt Susie? I've done everything you said."

"You've made a good start." Archer's eager gaze was on the trees, and his tone was absent. "Don't talk to me. You're not important right now. I'll deal with you later."

They had rolled the rock away and Pennig was digging. Melis and Archer stood together a couple of yards away.

There wasn't much time now, Kelby knew.

One man at the road.

One man seven yards from the tree where Kelby was sitting.

One man about twenty yards on the other side of the glade. He was the difficult target. They'd have to take out the men on this side and then make their way to the other side. The cover was sparse and the man had an Uzi. Archer's men on this side of the glade were armed only with handguns.

Kelby drew a deep breath, cupped his hands over his mouth, and made the sound of an owl.

A beam from the flashlight of the man closest to him immediately circled the trees. It focused on the yellow eyes of the owl in the branches of the tree next to Kelby. At the sudden glare of light, the owl gave a cry of his own and flew from the branch.

The flashlight went out.

Kelby waited.

One minute.

Two minutes.

The soft hoot of the owl. Another hoot.

Nicholas had gotten the man at the road.

His turn.

He threw the rock in his hand at the shrubbery several yards left of where the man below him was standing.

The man whirled and moved toward the shrubbery.

Fast.

Silent.

Kelby was down the tree and a yard behind the guard before he knew he was there. The man started to turn and opened his lips to call out.

Too late. The garrote twisted about his neck, cutting through flesh so that only a gasp came from his lips. He was dead in seconds.

Kelby let the body fall and gave three soft hoots to signal Nicholas. He gave a glance at Melis and Archer. Pennig had already dug at least two feet into the ground.

Shit.

One more guard to take out across the

glade before it was safe to go after Pennig and Archer.

He started moving, low, fast, around the glade toward the man with the Uzi.

"I thought you said it was only a couple of feet down," Archer said. "We should be striking pay dirt."

"Anytime." Melis moistened her lips. There had been nothing but silence from the trees where Archer had stationed his men. It could mean nothing. Or it could mean failure. "I'm only telling you what Phil told me. Phil hated physical labor. He told me that it was stupid to dig deep when we had a rock to roll over it."

"I don't love it myself," Pennig said between his teeth as his shovel bit deep. "If I wanted to be a ditchdigger, I wouldn't have—" He stopped. "I think I've hit something."

Archer moved closer. "Dig, dammit."

"I'm doing it. I'm doing it." He was shoveling faster.

And they were ignoring her.

Melis took a tiny step backward toward the two pines. Then another step.

They were pulling out the chest, breaking the lock.

She took two more steps back.

As soon as they opened the chest and started going through it, she'd bolt and run.

Silence from the trees around her.

Only Pennig's and Archer's hard breathing as they lifted the lid.

"What the hell?"

Empty. Even from here she could see the chest was empty.

Archer was cursing and turning toward her.

She ran, zigzagging toward the pines.

A bullet seared by her ear.

Another yard. She seemed to be moving in slow motion.

A tearing pain in her left side. The force of the bullet sent her staggering the last few steps to the pine trees.

Gun. She had to get the gun. She searched wildly in the brush beneath the tree.

Archer was spewing venom, shouting for his men.

A shadowy figure a few yards from her. Another guard?

Where was the gun? It was so dark here in the shadows she couldn't see anything.

Then she found it.

But the guard was down and Kelby was on top of him. Twisting his neck.

Archer. She had to get Archer.

She couldn't see him. But Pennig was there, coming toward her. His face contorted with rage.

She lifted the gun and pulled the trigger.

He staggered.

She shot him again.

He fell to the ground.

Kelby was kneeling beside her, taking the gun.

She shook her head. "Archer. We have to get Archer."

"No, we have to stop this bleeding." His hand was unfastening her shirt. "Dammit, I told you it was too risky."

"Archer . . ."

"He bolted when none of his men came when he called. Nicholas may be able to catch him, but he had a head start. Nicholas was on this side of the glade with me." His voice was hoarse as he formed a compress and pressed it above the wound. "We have to get you to a doctor. I told you that—"

"Stop . . ." Lord, she was dizzy. "Stop saying I told you so. It would have worked if

the chest hadn't been . . . empty. It shouldn't
have been empty."

"This damn blood . . ." He was cursing
beneath his breath. "Where the hell is
Nicholas? I need him to hold this compress
while I get you back to the car. Screw
Archer. We can deal with . . ."

She heard nothing else.

Red plaid drapes.

It was the first thing she noticed when she
opened her eyes. Red plaid drapes and a
cozy leather armchair in the corner of the
room.

"You're back with us?" A dark, fiftyish
man in a cable-knit sweater smiled at her as
he lifted her wrist and took her pulse. "I'm
Dr. Gonzales. How do you feel?"

"A little woozy."

"You received a wound through your left
side. The bullet hit nothing vital, but you
lost some blood." He grimaced. "Not as
much as your friend Mr. Kelby was afraid
you'd lost. He was rudely intimidating. He
came to my home shouting and threatening.
I almost threw him out. We're not used to

that on Cadora. This is a very peaceful island. That's why I settled here."

"Where is he?"

"Outside. I told him that he could stay
out in his car until you woke. He's a very
disturbing man."

"And this is a peaceful island," she repeated his words. "I need to see him."

"A few minutes won't hurt. I've given
Kelby antibiotics for you, but if you see signs
of infection, get right to a doctor." He
paused. "You know I'll have to report this
bullet wound?"

"I don't care. Do what you have to do.
What time is it?"

"A little after three in the morning."

And she must have been shot sometime
near midnight. "I was unconscious for three
hours?"

"You were coming around, but I gave
you a sedative when I cleaned and sewed up
your side."

Archer.

And three hours was a long time.

"I really need to see Kelby, Doctor."

He shrugged. "If you insist. Though I
really hate to give in to any of his demands.

He should learn patience." He moved toward the door. "Try not to let him upset you."

She was already upset. She had killed a man tonight, she was completely bewildered about that empty chest, and she didn't know what had happened to Archer.

The chest. Try to figure out what had happened to those research papers.

But the question she asked Kelby when he came into the room was, "Archer?"

"I should have known that would be your first thought." He shook his head. "He was already in the car and speeding off when Nicholas reached the road."

"Then it was all for nothing." She closed her eyes as disappointment washed over her. "I risked all of our lives and he's still alive."

"Not for long," Kelby said grimly. "We'll get our chance. He's not going to crawl in a hole. He's going to be mad as hell and want to get back at us." He smiled faintly. "And it wasn't a complete bust. We took out four scumbags who were cluttering the earth."

Her eyes flicked open. "Will there be trouble with the law?"

"I don't think so. The Spanish authorities are very aggressive with arms dealers who supply terrorists, as Archer does. I've called Wilson to come here from Madrid and supply records and mug shots and generally smooth the way. Naturally, he won't tell them we had anything to do with it. But I'd bet when they discover what kind of lowlifes are lying on the side of that mountain, they'll find a way to forget they existed." He smiled crookedly. "Because this is such a 'peaceful' island."

"Dr. Gonzales seems very nice."

"We didn't see eye to eye. But he knows what he's doing. He says we can take you out of here if you promise to rest for the next couple of days. I assume you don't want to hang around here?"

She shook her head. "Will you help me get up?" She looked down at herself. "Where's my shirt?"

"It was too bloody to save." He took off his black shirt. "Wear this." He helped her sit up and carefully put her arms in the shirt. "Okay?"

The room was going around and her side throbbed. "Okay."

"Liar." He picked her up and carried her toward the door. "But you'll be better when I can get you home."

Home? Oh, yes, the *Trina*. That was Kelby's home, and for the past days it had become her home too. Strange . . . "Am I too heavy? I can walk."

"I know you can. But I'm all for efficiency. It's faster this way." He stopped at the door when he saw Dr. Gonzales, and said curtly, "I'm taking her. Thank you for doing your job."

"Thank you for leaving." Gonzales smiled at Melis. "Don't break my stitches, and stay away from violent people like this Kelby person. They're not good for you."

The last sentence was said to Kelby's back as he strode past the doctor toward the car parked in the gravel driveway. Nicholas jumped out and opened the back door. "Why don't you lie down and stretch out? Maybe you can nap."

Melis shook her head as Kelby placed her carefully in the backseat. She didn't want to nap. There was something very wrong and she had to think. "I'm better sitting."

"Debatable," Kelby said as he got in the passenger seat. "But I'm not arguing. I want to get you to the south shore where we left our tender. We'll leave your tender at the dock, and Nicholas can pick it up tomorrow."

As Nicholas started the car, she sat very straight and tried to block out the dull pain in her side. Think. There was a piece missing. And a question she didn't want to ask Kelby.

She had no option. She had to ask him.

"The chest was empty, Kelby."

"I know it, dammit."

She moistened her lips. "Did you do it?"

She saw his shoulders stiffen, and he slowly turned to look at her. "I beg your pardon?"

"You came here to Cadora last night."

He was silent a moment, and when he spoke, each word was precise. "We both knew how crucial it was that Archer be distracted from you. You almost got killed when he wasn't. And you're asking me if I came here and snatched those damn papers?"

Nicholas gave a low whistle. "Oops."

She barely heard him. "I have to ask it. Just tell me yes or no."

"No, goddammit, I did *not* take the papers." He turned around to face the front. "And you'd better shut up until we get to the dock or I just might complete the job Archer screwed up on."

She could feel the rage he was emitting. Rage and hurt. She couldn't blame him. She would have felt the same.

But she couldn't worry about Kelby. She had to think. She was beginning to get a terrible feeling. . . .

Chapter Sixteen

They were a few miles from the dock when she leaned forward and said to Nicholas, "Turn left at the next road."

"What?"

"Just do it."

Kelby gave her a cool glance. "Are you delirious?"

"No. Maybe. I think I know where Phil moved the papers. There's a place on the coast. I have to go there. Please. Don't ask questions."

"You think the papers are there?"

"They might be. I have to go."

Nicholas looked at Kelby.

Kelby shrugged. "Go ahead. Give him directions, Melis."

The cottage was just as she remembered it. White clapboard with blue shutters closed tight. She opened the door and scrambled out of the car before Kelby could help her.

"For God's sake, Melis." Kelby caught up with her as she moved toward the cottage and took her arm. "You're weak as a kitten. You'll be lucky if you don't fall on your face."

She didn't feel weak. The fear-driven adrenaline was surging through her.

"Why do you think they may be hidden here?" Kelby asked.

"We lived in that cottage for a few months while we were searching the area." Her eyes were focused on the front door as she shook Kelby's hand away from her arm. "It's the only explan—"

The front door opened and a figure was silhouetted against the lamplight.

She felt Kelby tense beside her.

He was afraid of that unknown danger. She was afraid, too, but not for the same reason. She took a step forward. "Phil?"

"You shouldn't have come, Melis." He came down the two steps toward her. "I hoped to see you at a happier time."

"Where? At the pearly gates? You're supposed to be dead, Phil."

"As Mark Twain said, the reports of my death are greatly exaggerated."

Kelby took a step forward. "Lontana?"

Phil nodded. "Hello, Kelby. Great job. I knew you could do it. Of course, I could have done it better."

"What?"

"Why, Marinth, of course." He smiled. "I'd like to shake your hand, but that's not in the cards, is it?"

"I don't know yet." He took Melis's arm again. "I do know that I want Melis to sit down. She's been hurt."

"Hurt?" Phil looked at her with concern. "Is it bad?"

"What the hell do you care?" Melis said. "What did you expect to happen, Phil?"

"I care very much," Phil said. "It's not fair of you to doubt I'd worry about you."

"But not enough," Melis said. "You didn't care if you put my head on the block by moving that chest."

"Is that how you were wounded? I hoped

Archer wouldn't try to get those papers from you." He looked pained. "I didn't want to do it. It was necessary. You wouldn't help me, Melis."

"This is beginning to reek," Kelby said. "What the hell did you do, Lontana?"

"He staged his own death," Melis said. "He blew up the *Last Home* himself."

"Do you realize how much that hurt me?" Phil asked.

"How did you get away? Scuba gear and someone in a boat nearby to pick you up?"

Phil nodded. "I was so sad when I saw her blow. I loved that ship."

"But it was worth the sacrifice," Melis said. "It got you what you wanted."

"What?" Kelby asked. "He didn't want to deal with Archer any longer?"

"On the way here I was hoping that was it." She met Phil's eyes. "But I know you, Phil. You'd never have sacrificed the *Last Home* unless it was going to bring you something better. And the only thing you valued more was Marinth. You made a deal with Archer, didn't you?"

"Why would you think—"

"Didn't you?"

He nodded slowly. "I didn't have any

choice. You wouldn't help me. Marinth was lying there, waiting for me, and I couldn't touch it. It was your fault."

"Why, you son of a bitch," Kelby murmured. "So you set Archer on Melis's trail."

"I told you, I didn't want to do it. It's not as if she was the target. We just wanted to make her upset enough so that she'd turn to you to help her. I knew you'd make Marinth a bargaining chip. You know what's important."

"Do I?"

"I tried for six years to get her to use the dolphins. You can understand. I had to have Marinth."

"But you don't have it," Melis said. "Kelby has it."

Lontana glanced away from her. "I may not have the glory, but I'll know that I was the one who made it all possible." He shrugged. "As for any profit, I'm getting older. I don't need much money. All I want is to stay here and watch Marinth come to life."

"And you've been here in this cottage all this time?"

"Except when I was out in the boat keeping an eye on you with my binoculars." He smiled eagerly. "Admit it, Melis. Wasn't it a thrill? I wish I'd been down there with you. When I saw you pull up those nets, I wanted to shout with joy."

"You were in the second boat I saw," Nicholas said.

Phil nodded. "You surprised me that time. And you are . . ."

"Nicholas Lyons."

"Oh, yes, I've heard of you."

"You know a lot about what's been going on, don't you, Phil?" Melis asked slowly. "Do you think I'm idiot enough to believe you'd be content to sit on the sidelines and watch someone else get credit for finding Marinth?"

"Believe what you like."

"I will. But I don't like it." She tried to steady her voice. "Do you know what I believe? I'm beginning to think you're as guilty as Archer. I'm putting together the pieces. What was the deal? Archer was to torment me until I was desperate enough to do what you wanted. What were you going to get in return? And don't tell me it was a chance to stay here and experience Marinth secondhand."

"I never wanted to hurt you, Melis. I

knew Archer couldn't break you. But you had to be urged along."

"Urged?" She had a moment's memory of those nightmare conversations. That hideous moment when she had stared down at Carolyn's body. "Oh, yes, he was very persuasive. But what was your price, Phil?"

He shifted uneasily. "I think you'd better leave now."

"Not yet." Kelby took a step closer. "Let's talk about targets. You said Melis wasn't the target. Who was the target, Lontana?"

Phil started to turn and go back into the cottage.

"It was you, Kelby," Melis said. "From the beginning it was you. All Archer put me through was just to keep us heading toward Marinth. To unsettle me, keep me off balance, make sure I kept on pushing you. He wasn't sure he'd be able to get those research papers from me. Isn't that right, Phil?"

"Nonsense."

"You wanted Marinth. You set Kelby up to find it for you. But what happens after he finds it? I think you told Archer to kill Kelby and destroy the *Trina* so that you could move in on the project. That would be the only payoff that would make sense. Marinth and Kelby's death for your research papers. Why did you move that chest from the mountain?"

He was silent a moment and then he shrugged. "I knew Archer was probably playing a double game. He was aware that you knew where the chest was. If he could get the research from you, he'd do it and leave me out in the cold."

"You mean he wouldn't take me down," Kelby said.

"I'm not admitting anything," Phil said. "Actually, I think I could like you, Kelby. We have a good deal in common."

"Archer *was* playing a double game. He was expecting you to come to the mountain tonight to help me, Kelby," Melis said. "I was surprised he was upset when his men didn't find anyone in the woods. He expected you to be there. Then, if I was lying about the location of the chest, he could still get the research papers from Phil as the price for killing you. Where's the chest, Phil?"

He hesitated. "In the cabinet under the window seat."

"Weren't you afraid Archer would come here and find it?"

"He doesn't know I'm here. I'm not stupid enough to let him get his hands on me. We communicate by phone. He's a barbarian."

"And what are you, Phil?"

"Go get the chest, Nicholas," Kelby said.

Nicholas nodded and started toward the house.

"Those tablets are mine, and so is the research," Phil said quickly. "You can't take them away from me."

"Watch us," Kelby said. "The tablets were found by Melis, and the research came from them. You get nothing, Lontana."

"Stop him, Melis. You know how hard I worked."

"You're incredible," Kelby said. "You actually expect her to help you?"

"I helped her. I gave her a home when she needed it," he said defensively. "If she hadn't been so stubborn, none of this would have been necessary."

"I've got them. Papers and tablets." Nicholas had come out of the cottage carrying a large wooden box. "I'll go put them in the car."

"Don't let him take them away, Melis. I only did what I had to do," Phil said desperately. "I didn't do anything really wrong. There are so many riches down there in Marinth. This sonic device was only the tip of the iceberg. I'm the only one who has the right to explore it. The entire world could benefit from what I find down there."

"Could it?" Melis's voice was uneven. "At the moment I don't really care how the world is going to be a better place because of your lies. I just want to know one thing. When you were trying to persuade Archer to fund Marinth, you evidently told him a good deal about me. You told him about Carolyn and my files?"

He was silent a moment. "I might have mentioned them. He said he needed a hook. We were discussing options."

She felt sick. "Options? My God." Rage seared through her. She took a step closer. "Carolyn died because you told him about her and those files. You son of a bitch. He *butchered* her."

His eyes widened. "She's dead?"

"What did you think would happen when you turned that bastard loose on her? No, you set everything in motion and then just sat here on your island and waited for Marinth to drop into your lap."

"I never intended for her to be hurt."

"Like you never intended for Kelby to be killed?"

He moistened his lips. "I never admitted—"

"You may be a dreamer, but you're not a fool. Somewhere in the back of your mind you must have known what the possibilities were with Carolyn." Her voice was shaking with rage. "You didn't care about Carolyn. You didn't care about Kelby. You didn't care about me. You didn't care about anything but Marinth."

"You're not being fair. I cared about you. I've always been very fond of you, Melis."

"Have you? Is that why you forgot the years we spent together? Is that why you made a deal to kill Kelby? Is that why you let Archer kill my best friend? Is that why you let loose that murderer to tear me apart with his filth?"

"It's not my fault." He tried to smile. "And no one could tear you apart. I know how strong you are. I knew you'd bounce back. You were always a gutsy—"

"It's no use talking to you. You're as much a murderer as Archer, and you don't even realize it. Well, I realize it. Damn you to hell, Phil." She turned and stalked toward the car.

"You never understood about Marinth. I was *right*," he called after her. "It's not my fault every little thing didn't work out. You've got to get them to give back my chest. I need it."

Every little thing? Melis thought in astonishment. Three innocent people had died because of Phil's passion for a dead city. He still didn't realize the enormity of what he'd done. He probably never would.

"I think letting Lontana sit here in his cozy little cottage is a mistake," Kelby murmured as he opened the car's back door for her. "Why don't you and Nicholas wait for me while I go back and make sure Lontana never causes you this kind of grief again?"

She shook her head.

"Why not? He's officially dead anyway."

He meant it. His expression was harder than she'd ever seen it.

She shook her head again.

He shrugged. "Okay. Maybe later. I guess you've gone through enough tonight." He got into the backseat beside her. "Let's go, Nicholas."

"He deserves it, Melis," Nicholas said as he started the car. "You should reconsider."

"I know he deserves it. I . . . just can't handle it right now. He did help me when I needed him. That keeps getting in the way." She wearily rubbed her temple. "And he doesn't even think he's done anything wrong. He has a missing cog in his conscience where Marinth is concerned."

"How did you know it was Lontana?" Kelby asked.

"I didn't know. I guessed. It was all wrong. I was lying in that doctor's cottage and trying to piece it together, but I couldn't. You told me that you didn't do it. And the only other two people who knew where it was buried were Phil and me."

"I could have been lying."

She shook her head. "I knew you weren't. I'm sorry I had to ask you."

"I'm sorry too. I was ready to strangle you."

"I know. But I had to be sure. The other explanation was too wild for me to accept." Her lips twisted. "No, that's not true. It hurt too much to realize Phil could do that to me."

"I think Nicholas should turn the car around."

"No." She leaned her head back on the seat. She was bone-weary and hurting in mind and body. And maybe in her heart. She had mourned Phil in Athens, but the separation she felt now was deeper, sharper, bitter. "If I didn't do it and you didn't do it, then Phil had to have moved the papers. What reason would he have for doing it before his death? The Phil I thought I knew would have told me. Marinth meant everything to him. If he was in danger, he wouldn't chance having all that knowledge lost forever." She paused. "But he didn't tell me. So that led me to start thinking of other possibilities, and I came up with something crazy. Only it wasn't crazy, was it? It was sane and true and so ugly—"

"Hush." Kelby pulled her head down to rest on his shoulder. "It's over, unless you want to change your mind about me going back to see Lontana. I'm at your service."

"That wouldn't change things. I'm always going to remember that he wasn't the friend I thought he was, that he sacrificed me for Marinth. I don't want to remember his death too."

"Have it your way. But it would be a very pleasant memory for me." His hand gently rubbed the back of her neck. "Does your wound hurt?"

"Some." His body felt warm and strong and full of life against her. And, my God, Phil had coldly made a deal to snuff out that life. That was more terrible than all the torture Archer had put her through. He had to be punished. The anger would come, but now she was filled with sadness and loneliness. No, Kelby was gradually shutting out the desolation. How many times had he held her and comforted her like this in the short time they'd been together? She didn't remember and she didn't care. She didn't want to be strong and independent right now. She'd take what she could get.

"But Lontana hurt you more," Kelby said. "And that's not a wound I can heal, dammit."

"I don't want to talk about him anymore." Though she would probably live with that sense of betrayal for the rest of her life. "Are we near the dock?"

"Another five minutes," Nicholas said.

"Good." She wanted to get back to the ship and hide for a little while. There was still Archer to think about, but she couldn't face it right now. She wanted to be away from this island.

Away from Phil in his little cottage overlooking the deep blue sea that held his dream.

It took Lontana three tries to get in touch with Archer. He tried to keep the panic from his voice when he finally reached him. "You promised me that you'd take Kelby out of the picture. You've got to do it now. I've got a ship waiting to take me out and claim salvage rights, but I can't do it with him alive. He and the *Trina* have got to be destroyed right away."

"Where's the research, Lontana?"

"I've got it. Get rid of Kelby."

There was a silence. "Why did you call me tonight?"

"Because you need to—" He drew a deep breath. "You tried to betray me. You tried to get my research from Melis tonight. That's all right, I understand. But now you know that I'm the one who has it and you have to do what you promised."

"How do you know what happened tonight?"

"Call me when you've done what we agreed upon and I'll meet you and give you the research." He hung up.

Archer stared thoughtfully at the phone after he'd hung up from Lontana.

The bastard was scared. And how the hell did he know Archer had tried to double-cross him tonight?

Unless Kelby or Melis had told him.

And how had they been able to tell him? Melis thought Lontana was dead. She certainly would not have his new phone number. Either he would have had to call her—not likely—or she would have had to talk to him in person.

On Cadora.

Yes.

He'd been trying to locate Lontana since they'd struck the deal, and now he had him in his sights. He should have known the elusive bastard would want to be close to Marinth.

Now he could go back to Cadora, scoop

up Lontana and his damn research, and be home free.

Had Archer believed him? Lontana wondered. Jesus, he *had* to believe him. He couldn't let Kelby have Marinth. If Archer got rid of Kelby right away, everything would still be fine. Lontana would find a way of evading Archer's vengeance later. Everything would work out if he just had Marinth.

Marinth.

He left the cottage and walked to the edge of the cliff. He felt his anxiety ebbing away as he stood looking out at the sea. Of course Archer believed him. Marinth had always been his destiny, and fate would not allow him to be cheated. It was waiting for him. He could almost hear it call him.

"Lontana."

He stiffened and looked behind him.

Black hair drawn back in a queue, dark eyes staring at him with implacable ferocity.

His heart leapt with terror.

He turned to run. An arm encircled his neck.

He was dead seconds later.

Kelby met Nicholas at the tender. "Would you like to tell me where you've been?"

"Maybe." He came on board. "How's Melis?"

"Asleep. She was exhausted. She almost fell unconscious when she hit the bed." Kelby glanced toward the east. "Lontana?"

"The poor man fell off the cliff and broke his neck."

"I see. You didn't have to do that. It wasn't your responsibility."

"Melis didn't want you to do it. If she decided later that Lontana should be punished, it would have hurt her to do it herself." He shrugged. "I was the logical choice."

"Why?"

"The crazy son of a bitch was always going to be a threat to you as long as you held on to Marinth."

"But the threat was to me, Nicholas."

"A threat to my friends is a threat to me." He smiled faintly. "It's an old shaman saying." He turned away. "Good night, Jed. Sleep well." He stopped and glanced over his shoulder. "Do we tell Melis about Lontana's unfortunate demise?"

"Not right away. She's had enough to face lately." He hesitated and then said gruffly, "Thanks, Nicholas."

Nicholas nodded and strode down the deck.

Melis slept for a solid eight hours. But when she woke she still felt drugged—and lonely. Kelby had held her until she'd fallen asleep, but he wasn't with her now.

Well, what could she expect? He'd been kind, but he didn't want her leaning on him forever.

And she didn't want to lean. She'd taken a hard blow, but she had to get up and start swinging.

She got out of bed and headed for the shower. Twenty minutes later she was climbing the steps to the deck. Nicholas was throwing fish into the sea and he turned as she came toward him. "Good afternoon. You look a lot better. How do you feel?"

"A little weak and sore. Nothing that food and taking it easy for today won't cure. How's Pete?"

"Hungry." He threw another fish down

to Pete, who was hovering near the side of the ship. "He'll hardly let Susie have any. She doesn't seem to mind though."

"I can see that." Susie was rubbing sympathetically against Pete. "She knows he's hurt."

"Are you sure we shouldn't bring him aboard the ship to take care of him?"

"Not unless we want to kill him. Kelby took out the spear, and I stopped the bleeding and gave him an antibiotic. He'll heal faster in the seawater."

"I thought he was a goner when you brought him back."

So had Melis. That blood had terrified her. It was only later that she'd realized the attack could be used to make Archer believe he'd finally broken her. "We were lucky. Archer's man had to work fast. It was a glancing strike, or it could have done serious damage."

"How soon do you think it will be before he's his old self?"

"Soon. He'll tell us. He knows his body. Nature is a wonderful thing."

"That's good. I like the guy. I like both of them. They kind of get to you." He made a face. "Even though your blasted dolphins have turned me into a nursemaid."

"It's good for you," Kelby said as he came toward them. "You need a little softening."

"The pot calling the kettle," Nicholas said. "One of you will have to do the next feeding. I need to jump in the tender and do a little reconnoitering."

Kelby nodded. "To see if Archer's taken off?"

"It's a possibility."

"He won't go," Melis said. "Even if he didn't still want the papers, he's furious. He'll think we fooled him. We sent him running and he'll want revenge."

"Against you," Kelby said. "This might be a good time for you to stay in your cabin and let us take care of business."

"He'll be just as angry with you. Are we all going to hide under the bed?" She shook her head. "We have to put an end to it." She turned to Nicholas. "I'll take care of Pete and Susie. You spend your time keeping an eye on Archer's ship. We need to know what's happening."

"I agree." Nicholas turned to Kelby. "When I wasn't keeping an eye on the dol-

phins this morning, I did a little firepower
assembly. Just in case." He moved down the
deck. "I'm going to catch a bite to eat before
I take off. It might be a long night."

"Why didn't you wake me up?" Melis
asked Kelby.

"You needed the sleep. Besides that
wound, Lontana gave you a knockout punch.
And there wasn't anything you could do.
From now on it's going to be a waiting game."

She was afraid he was right, and she was
going to hate that waiting. "I hoped it might
end last night."

"It should have. The plan was sound
enough. It just went wrong."

"Thanks to Phil." She gazed in the direction of Cadora. Phil was out there in his cottage, probably still congratulating himself on
his great success. "He was so proud of
himself."

"Stop thinking about him."

"I will. It's still new. I thought he was my
friend."

"It sounded like he still believed it. He's a
little wacko."

"No. It's only that we're all just shadows
to him. Marinth is the reality. I never real-

ized that." She forced herself to look away. "Are you going down today?"

"For one dive. And, no, you're not going with me. I'll take Charlie."

"I wasn't going. I can't risk not getting this wound healed right away."

"The doctor said nothing strenuous for a week."

"I heal fast." She smiled faintly. "I'm like Pete. I'll know when I'm ready."

He paused. "I don't know if you're going to be ready for this. We found a gift-wrapped package in the tender you took to Cadora."

She stiffened. She'd completely forgotten the package Pennig had put in the tender. "Did you open it?"

"No, I wanted to chuck it, but I don't have the right. It's in your cabin." He added roughly, "*You* chuck it. Don't even open it."

She nodded and moved slowly toward her cabin.

What do you have for me now, Archer? What cruel little whimsy?

The box was sitting on her bed. A note was taped to the top. She opened the envelope.

Melis,
I hope I don't have to dispose of you tonight and that we're opening this together. I desperately want to see your face.

She hesitated and then tore off the gold wrappings.

She lifted one corner of the box.

White. Delicate as a moonbeam.

She slammed the lid of the box down.

Damn him. Damn him.

She picked up the box and headed for the door. Destroy it. Throw it overboard.

She stopped and drew a deep breath. She wasn't thinking. Everything had changed. They had no weapons against Archer right now. They might have to turn his weapons against him.

Not this one. Oh, God, not this one.

She forced herself to stride to the closet, tossed the box out of sight, and slammed the door.

She didn't even know if she could live in the same room with it. It would be like knowing a cobra was coiled in that closet.

But she didn't have to live in this room.

She had Kelby, and she'd be safe wherever he was. She was welcome in his cabin, welcome in his bed. It didn't matter that it was only for now. What a good thing to know he was there for her.

Nicholas came back after nine o'clock that night. "It took me an hour or two to locate the ship. Archer up-anchored and sailed ten miles to the east. I was afraid we'd lost him."

"Is he still on board?"

"I didn't find the ship until almost sunset. I didn't stay long and I had to keep far back so that I wouldn't be seen. I don't think he was on deck."

"He's on the ship," Melis said. "He's hovering. Like a bad dream."

"I'd bet he's doing more than forming a black cloud over your head," Kelby said. "He's getting reinforcements. We took out four of his men. It might take a little time to call up more help and weapons."

"Makes sense," Nicholas said. "I'll be able to get a better look at any comings and goings tomorrow. There's a chain of deserted islands about four miles away from where

Archer's anchored. I can set up surveillance from one of them."

"What kind of weapons?" Melis asked.

"He has access to some nasty firepower," Kelby said grimly. "Maybe rocket launchers. No maybe if he decides to come after the *Trina*."

"You think he will?"

"I imagine he's mad enough to do almost anything. There's a possibility."

"Then maybe we shouldn't wait until he gets reinforcements," Nicholas said.

"If he's as angry as I think he is, we might be able to use it," Melis said.

Kelby gave her a wary look. "How?"

"I'm not sure."

"You don't mean use his anger, you mean use you." Kelby added flatly, "No."

"How do you know he hasn't already got those weapons on board his ship? Maybe he's just waiting for more men," Melis said. "Do you want to chance him blowing the *Trina* out of the water?"

"No, and I don't want him to blow you out of the water either."

"We need to know what he's thinking. Let's give him another day."

"And you think we'll know then?"

"Yes. He'll call me. He won't be able to resist. He's only waiting until he thinks he has the upper hand. He's probably seething to do it now, but he can't feel like a failure when he talks to me." She smiled crookedly. "It has to be slave and master."

Kelby gazed at her for a moment. "Okay, one day. That's all." His eyes narrowed on her face. "What are you thinking about? You can't pull the same trick on him again."

"I know. He'll want me now as much as he does the papers. Before I was just a little something extra." She shook her head. "I don't know what I'm thinking. There has to be a way. . . ."

They didn't have to wait a day for Archer to call. Her phone rang two hours later.

"Are you feeling smug?" Archer asked. "Nothing's changed, Melis. I'm alive and you're alive and you still have to give me the papers."

"Some things have changed. Pennig's dead."

"He's replaceable." He paused. "But you're right, there has been one change. I took a little trip to Cadora. You're my only source for those reference papers now. You took them from Lontana, didn't you?"

"What did you expect?"

"You've made it very inconvenient for me. I'm afraid there will be a price to pay. Shall I tell you how?"

"Do you expect me to quiver and weep? That was an act, Archer. I made a fool of you." She paused before adding mockingly, "Mr. Peepers."

"Bitch." He drew a deep breath. "You'll pay for that. I'd almost rather have my hands on you than the papers."

"It won't happen. I'm safe here. Kelby will protect me. He doesn't give a damn about me, but that doesn't matter. I give him what he wants and he keeps all the nasty impotent perverts like you away from me."

She could almost feel the heat of his rage through the phone. "He'll get tired of you."

"I'm too good, and there's only one thing Kelby likes better than sex. He thinks his damn boat was made in heaven. He yells when one of the crew gets a scratch on it. But I manage to quiet him down. I learned a lot at *Kafas*. No, you'll never get another chance at me, Archer." She hung up.

"You gave it to him with both barrels." Kelby raised himself on one elbow on the bed. "He certainly won't think you're a wimp anymore. And a man doesn't like to have his virility questioned."

"I wanted to make him angry." She paused. "So he wouldn't realize I'd deliberately dropped a weapon in his hands."

"What weapon?"

"You."

"Oh, big sex-hungry me, who doesn't give a damn about you? I can't say I liked that description."

"I bet you like it better than impotent pervert."

"That's true."

"I had to switch his focus. He's getting impatient. Somehow he found out that Phil doesn't have the papers. He tried to kill the dolphins and it didn't work. And he's not getting any satisfaction out of talking to me anymore. He senses I'm not a victim any longer. He can't hurt me."

Kelby went still. "He can't?"

She shook her head. "I'm the only one who can hurt me. Maybe I should thank him. He punished me so much that I've developed scar tissue that would withstand almost anything."

He reached out and touched her cheek. "When did you find this out?"

"It's been growing on me." She shook her head impatiently. "We don't have time to talk about me. Archer may be calling back."

"Why?"

"Because when he gets over the first rage at me, he's going to think about what I said."

"And he'll call you back."

"No, he'll call you back and try to make a deal with you. He'll threaten to blow up the *Trina* if you don't hand me over to him."

He nodded slowly. "Because what's a good piece of ass in comparison to a ship like the *Trina*?"

"You have Marinth. You don't need the tablets or the research. You've gotten everything material you wanted from me. All I am is a sex object. Archer understands that concept."

"I don't."

She smiled. "Yeah, but you would have voted the right way at that council of noblemen."

"What's the purpose? Why am I serving you up to him?"

"I need to get on the ship."

"Bullshit."

Her smile faded. "You'll have to be convincing. It's probably best you tell him you have to think it over."

"It's not going to happen," he said flatly. "Not again."

She studied his expression. There was no moving him. "Then buy time. When he calls, pretend you're considering it."

"I'll consider cutting his balls off."

"Kelby. Please. You know we need the time. Stall."

He was silent a moment. "Okay, I'll stall. As long as he keeps his damn mouth shut about you."

It was as much of a concession as she was going to get. She could only hope Archer was brief and to the point.

Chapter Seventeen

Melis's hopes were answered. When Archer called Kelby at eight the next morning, he was on the phone for only a few minutes. Kelby was just as brief, except for one very convincing outburst of obscenities. "You can't get away with that. I'll call in the coast guard." Then he was silent again, listening. Finally, he said, "I'll think about it." And hung up. He stared at her. "You were right. He threatened to blow me out of the water if I didn't turn you and Lontana's research over. When I mentioned the coast guard, he said I could call all I pleased and they wouldn't come. He has them in his pocket."

"Like Nicholas suspected."

He nodded. "And I didn't say any of the things I wanted to say. Satisfied?"

"It was as good as could be expected. Did he give you a time limit?"

"I didn't give him the chance." Kelby got out of bed and started getting dressed. "If I'd talked for another minute with that greasy asshole, it wouldn't have been pretty."

"Where are you going?"

"I can't stay here. I'm about to explode. I'm going on deck to wait for Nicholas to come back from his watch."

She watched the door slam behind him.

He didn't want her with him. He was angry and protective and trying to shut her away from Archer. She'd never seen him more determined. She couldn't allow it. She had to be there when Nicholas got back.

She got out of bed and started getting dressed.

"As far as I can tell, Archer has four men on board," Nicholas said when he came back at noon. "And they're good. They're moving around, watching for boats, watching for swimmers. They have searchlights constantly focused on the water around the ship. Chancy to plant an explosive on the hull. And it will be damn hard to board her without a distraction."

"What kind of distraction?" Melis asked.

He shrugged. "We'll work it out." He looked at Kelby. "I saw Archer. And he received a shipment last night. Four six-by-seven crates."

"No additional manpower? The four men he has would only give him defense."

Nicholas shook his head. "But they could come anytime."

"Then we need to move fast. If we can't plant the explosives on the hull, we probably need a small rocket launcher."

Melis stiffened in shock. "What?"

Kelby ignored her. "How long will it take to get it?"

"Twenty-four hours. Maybe a little longer. My nearest supplier is in Zurich. Do we have that long?"

"Maybe." Kelby glanced at Melis. "We bought some time. He'll probably wait to go after us until he's certain I won't give him what he wants."

"I don't like it," Nicholas said. "We'll tip our hand the minute we use it. They could blow us out of the water if they brought on some of the really big stuff."

"Then we'll have to find a way to not tip our hand. Get it."

He nodded. "I'll get on the phone and start making purchases." Nicholas started up the deck. "But we should keep an eye on the *Jolie Fille* to make sure the status doesn't change."

"I'll take the tender out and stand watch. You get some sleep and relieve me at dawn."

"Right."

Melis waited until Nicholas had gone belowdeck before she turned to Kelby. "Rocket launchers? It sounds like we're going to war."

"Just getting prepared for all eventualities," Kelby said. "I don't want to use that kind of firepower if I don't have to. Very messy."

"And they'll fire back. Nicholas is right, it's more dangerous."

"Maybe I'll decide Nicholas is wrong about attaching the explosives to the hull. We'll see."

"He said you could board it if you had a distraction."

Kelby's lips tightened. "No, Melis, you're out of it."

"The hell I am."

"Listen to me. I understood what you were going through. So I let you talk me into setting Archer up and you nearly got killed. I never want to go through that again." His voice was hard. "You can argue until you're blue in the face. No way."

He turned and strode away from her.

He meant it. There was no doubt about his determination to keep her out of any action against Archer.

And there was no doubt that she couldn't permit him to do it.

Melis watched Kelby's tender disappear beyond the horizon before she went to hunt Nicholas.

He was just hanging up the phone. "Looks like the launcher is a go. But we can't get it before—"

"I need your help," Melis said.

Nicholas gazed at her warily. "I don't think I'm going to like this."

"Neither of you wants to use that

launcher. You and Kelby need a distraction. I can give you one. Only Kelby won't have it."

"Why do you think I will?"

"Because it's logical and there's no time to find another one. I don't want any rockets lobbed onto the *Trina*. Kelby loves this ship."

"I'm not fond of the idea myself." Then he shook his head. "It's too risky. Archer hates your guts."

"He won't hurt me right away."

"You don't know that."

"I know him. I can see into every dirty cranny of his mind. I'm no martyr. I can do this, Nicholas. I just need a little help to divert Archer's attention at the critical moment. What kind of distraction did you have in mind?"

"An explosion to draw the guards away from the rail."

"You can get me a grenade?"

He nodded. "I have something much more sophisticated. Small and easily hidden."

"Then just tell me where and when you want the explosion."

He hesitated. "Kelby will kill me."

"You're going to do it?"

"What would you do if I turned you down?"

"Find another way to do it without you or that explosive."

"I think you would." He was silent a moment more. "Let me think about it." He turned and walked away from her.

"There's not much time," she called after him.

He glanced over his shoulder, and his expression surprised her with its hardness. "Don't push me, Melis. I'm not playing the clown right now. You can't coerce me into doing anything I don't want to do. If I go along with you, it will be because I think it's the smartest thing to do for all of us. It won't be because you're in a fever to get to Archer. I wouldn't do that to Jed. And I damn well wouldn't do it to myself."

She stared after him in surprise and uneasiness as he crossed the deck and gazed out at the sea. She had seen only a few glimpses of this darker, more dangerous Nicholas that he hid so well behind that light facade. She wanted to go after him and try to convince him, but she knew it would be useless. His expression had been remote and totally intimidating. She would have to wait until he came to her.

She sat down in a deck chair, her gaze on Nicholas's ugly/arresting profile. Shaman. The title he used as a joke didn't seem to be so funny right now. He was exuding a quiet force and power that made her wonder if she knew him at all. The man who had painted the eyes on the dodo bird was not this man.

It was over thirty minutes before he left the rail and strode across the deck to her.

"Okay, it's a go," he said curtly. "There's a chance you'll bite it, but you're safer with Kelby and me in the plan. And we need that distraction. I'll take the heat."

Relief surged through her. "Where do you want me to throw the explosive?"

"The engine room or the galley. Either would have enough compressed gas to fuel an explosion."

"And how am I supposed to carry this explosive?"

"The sole of your right deck shoe. There will be a switch to arm and you'll have fif-teen seconds to toss it. So you'd better be damn ready. We've just got to pray he doesn't search you that thoroughly."

"I think I know how to prevent that." She smiled without mirth. "I have a distraction of my own in mind." She kicked off her deck shoes. "Get to work, Nicholas." She turned to leave. "I'm going to go to my cabin and make a few preparations."

"And it might be a good idea to say your prayers. Your chances of getting out of this alive are maybe fifty-fifty."

His voice was cool and without expression, and she glanced back at him. "You're clearly upset about that."

"Oh, I'll be upset if he kills you. So upset I'll have to justify letting you go after him by killing him myself. But since I've made a decision, I won't let emotion interfere. We've just got to get the job done and try to stay alive." He picked up the white deck shoes. "I'll get these ready for you. Nice thick soles. That's a lucky break." He headed toward his cabin. "We'll need all the luck we can get."

She felt sick.

Don't look in the mirror. Don't think about it. Just go up on the deck to Nicholas.

He was standing by the rail next to the tender. "I polished up your deck shoes. No one would ever know— My God." His eyes widened. "What the hell are you dressed up for? Halloween?"

She touched the white organdy empire-waist dress with a shaking hand. "No, but there's an element of horror in it. It's a present from Archer. I described it in one of my tapes, and he had it made up exactly. A child's dress in an adult size. You'll tie my hands and pin that note we wrote to the bodice of this disgusting abomination and send me to Archer with Kelby's compliments." She swallowed. "He knows what putting on this dress would do to me. He won't think I can do it. So he'll deduce that it was Kelby."

"Jesus."

"One, it will add to the veracity of handing me over. Two, seeing me in it will definitely distract Archer. He'll be triumphant. He'll be excited. He likes little girls." She drew a deep breath and slipped on the white deck shoes he'd handed her. "Now, let's get out of here. I want this dress off as quickly as possible."

———

"We can't get any closer without them seeing us," Nicholas said as he cut the motor. He sat and gazed at Archer's ship gleaming in the darkness. "Last chance. Are you sure you want to do this?"

"I'm sure." She held out her wrists. "Tie me. Tight. But make sure I can see my watch."

He took the rope he'd brought and bound her wrists. "This is ugly, Melis."

"He's ugly." Dear God, she was scared as she gazed at the ship. The organdy dress, her bound hands, the feeling of helplessness. She could almost hear the pounding of the drums of *Kafas*. She wanted to scream—or whimper.

But she wasn't helpless. She was doing this of her own free will. So get it started. "One more thing, Nicholas. Knock me out."

"What?"

"Hit me. Make sure I have a bruise, but I'd appreciate it if you wouldn't break my jaw. I want Archer to feel I'm totally helpless when he looks at me through those binoculars."

"I don't like to—"

"I don't care what you like. You know you should do it. Hit me, dammit."

"Then don't look at me."

"Some shaman." She shifted her gaze back to the ship.

"Shamans were magicians, not warriors. Though they did officiate at the burnings at the stake. That's what I feel like I'm doing at—"

Pain exploded in her jaw as he unleashed a right hook.

Nicholas gazed down at Melis crumpled in the seat. She looked like a little girl taking a nap in that dress.

And he felt like a son of a bitch. He was tempted to just turn the boat around and go back to the *Trina*.

He couldn't do it. He was committed, and in these kinds of situations it was often suicide to pay attention to second thoughts. Besides, Melis had gone too far to be cheated. He patted her cheek. "Good luck." He pressed the timer to set the clock on the rescue flare for three minutes, threw his waterproofed bundle into the water, and then followed it. He moved through the water with long, strong strokes. It would take him at least twenty minutes to swim to the island where Kelby was watching the ship. He wouldn't get a warm welcome. By that time Melis should have been brought onto Archer's ship and Kelby would probably know it.

A shrill whistling shrieked behind him.

He looked back over his shoulder to see the rescue flare explode in the dark sky.

"What the hell is it?" Archer ran out onto the deck, his gaze on the rocket. "Destrex, turn on the searchlights." He took the binoculars from the first mate. At first he'd thought they were under attack, but Kelby wouldn't have called attention to himself in this blatant fashion. And the possibility of a true rescue situation was minimal.

His gaze raked the waters in the area of the rocket. Nothing. "Where are those lights, dammit?"

The lights speared out over the water. A motorboat. Engine turned off, rocking on the waves.

"It's too far to blow it out of the water," Destrex said. "Besides, I think it's empty."

Archer focused on the boat.

A glimmer of white . . . He adjusted the focus again.

A little girl with golden hair, her delicate wrists bound with rope.

Melis!

"Yes."

Excitement was tearing through him. Kelby had caved. Nothing could be clearer. He *had* her.

He turned to Destrex. "Go get her. Check the tender to make sure there aren't any booby traps, but bring her to me."

He watched Destrex and the two men lower the boat and glide out over the water. And then focused his binoculars on Melis again. She was obviously unconscious. Had she been drugged? She would have had to be restrained in some way to be forced into that dress. It would have stirred too many nightmare memories of *Kafas*.

But Kelby's forcing her to wear it was the clearest indication that he was giving in on all fronts. He was not only surrendering Melis, he was gift-wrapping her in the packaging Archer had chosen. There was definitely nothing even the slightest bit sentimental about his feelings for her.

Destrex had reached the tender and was checking it out. Then he lifted Melis to one of the men in the boat. They were speeding back.

His heart was beating painfully hard as he watched the boat coming toward him. He wasn't sure if it was hate, lust, or anticipation that was causing the blood to surge wildly through his veins. It didn't matter.

She was coming.

Kelby's grip tightened on the binoculars until the veins stood out on his hands as he saw Melis being lifted onto the ship. She had been limp while in the boat, but now she was stirring.

And by the time she reached the deck she was able to stand.

But only for a moment. Archer's hand lashed out viciously and knocked her to the deck.

"Jed." It was Nicholas behind him.

He didn't lower the binoculars. "Not now, you bastard." One of the men pulled Melis to her feet and was pushing her toward the stairs leading down to the cabins. She disappeared from view.

Kelby whirled on Nicholas. He could

barely speak for the fury that was flaming through him. "You son of a bitch. What the hell are you doing?"

"What Melis wanted. It was her plan from the get-go. You wouldn't let her help, so she went for it."

"With your help, damn you."

"She would have found a way to go alone. You made a mistake, Jed. There's no way of keeping her out of it."

"You didn't give me a chance."

"No, because I'd feel the same way in her shoes. She has to do this. She has a big pay-back coming. She was cheated at Cadora. Besides, we needed that distraction."

The memory of Melis knocked to the deck came back to Kelby. "He's *got* her."

"Then let's go get her before he does her much damage. I brought your wet suit and the equipment," Nicholas said. "Melis is go-ing to set off the explosive at one forty-five. That gives us a little over an hour to swim out there and get in position. When she blows, everyone should rush toward the gal-ley area. That's our opportunity to board. After that, it's up to us. I told Melis to hide after she tosses the explosive and keep hidden."

"If she's still alive."

"She's smart, Jed. She's not going to do anything dumb."

Kelby knew that, but it didn't stop the fear that was eating at him. He had to stop it or he wouldn't be able to function. "Okay, where's the explosive?"

"Her right deck shoe." Nicholas smiled. "I put one of my favorite stilettos and a skeleton key in her left."

"Easy to get at?"

"All she has to do is rip down the back tab and strip off the sole. She can do it with one hand."

"Both hands are tied. Your idea?"

"I told you, it was all Melis. If he doesn't untie her, she can use the stiletto. It will be awkward but doable."

"If she has the chance."

"Yeah. If she has the chance."

"You could have stopped her."

"I chose not to try." He looked him in the eye. "Blame me all you please. It's not going to change a damn thing. It's done."

He was right. It was done. And there was no way Kelby could turn back the clock.

Nicholas's face softened as he saw the despair in Kelby's expression. "I'm sorry it has to be this way. I don't feel good about this either, Jed. I'm worried as hell."

"Worried? You don't have a clue." He turned away. "Let's get going. Where's my wet suit?"

Golden fretwork panels hung on the cabin walls.

Velvet coverlet on the bed.

Melis leaned back against the wall, sick, after the crew member pushed her into Archer's cabin. It was her nightmare come to life. There were even Moroccan lanterns sitting on the floor beside the bed.

Did she hear drums? No, that was her imagination. She closed her eyes to shut out the sight. But it didn't shut out the memories.

Then use all her will and shut them out herself. This response was what Archer wanted from her. Don't let him get anything he wanted.

What time was it? She forced herself to open her eyes and look at the gold-framed clock on the wall. Fifty minutes to go. Fifty minutes to stay in this hellhole of a room. If she stood very still and stared only at the ceiling she could stand it.

The door opened and Archer stood there, smiling at her. "You look like a cringing mouse. Where's your dignity, Melis?"

She straightened with an effort. "You went to a lot of trouble. When did you do all this?"

"As soon as I arrived here from Miami. There was no doubt in my mind that you'd be in this cabin eventually. It was only a question of when. I took a good deal of pleasure out of choosing and matching. I'd listen to the tapes and then send for the merchandise. It kept me from being bored." He shook his head. "I only wish I'd seen your face when you first caught sight of it. I was a little angry or I wouldn't have forgotten I intended to do that." He moved to stand before her and touched the bruise on her chin. "Kelby wasn't as soft about you as you thought, was he?"

"He's a bastard." She stared him in the eye. "Like you."

"Sticks and stones." One finger stroked the pink satin ribbon in her hair. "But you mustn't blame him. You told me yourself that he was nuts about that ship."

"I didn't think he'd sell me down the river for it."

"Haven't you learned that whores are dispensable? There's always another one. But you're rather special. I feel a certain bond with you." He took a step back. "And you look so pretty. Turn around for me."

"Go to hell."

He slapped her. "Don't you remember? Disobedience was always punished." He tilted his head. "But they also used drugs on you, didn't they? I don't want you all bruised to begin with. Maybe I'll go that route."

"No!" She wouldn't be able to function if she was drugged. Forty-five minutes.

She turned around in a circle.

"Again. Slower."

She bit her lower lip and then obeyed.

"Good little girl." He was looking down at her deck shoes. "But where are the shiny patent-leather shoes I sent you?"

She kept her expression from showing the panic she felt. "They had to hold me down to get me in this dress. After I kicked him in the nuts, Kelby decided not to try the shoes."

He chuckled. "He obviously doesn't know how to handle naughty little girls. It takes experience." His smile faded. "But he didn't send the chest with you."

"He doesn't have it. Do you think I'd share that with him? It's *mine*."

He studied her. "No, I can see how you'd need a little insurance. And, after all, he has Marinth."

"And that damn boat."

"Such bitterness. We'll discuss you giving me the chest later. Now, come over to the bed and lie down."

She shook her head.

"Why, you've turned pale. It's such a soft, lovely bed. And do you know what we're going to do in it? We're going to lie together and listen to the tapes. And I'm going to watch your face. I can't tell you how much I missed that when I was phoning you. I wanted to see every expression."

"I . . . can't do it."

"Don't make me use the drugs. It might dull your emotions. Look at the bed."

Red velvet, heaped with cushions.

"Now, go over and sit on it. We'll go slowly. I like slow."

But every moment would be a century. She moved across the room and sat down on the side of the bed.

"You hate the feel of that velvet against you, don't you?"

"Yes." Only two minutes had passed. "I can't *stand* it."

"You'll be surprised what you can stand. We'll explore that after the tapes." He lay down and patted the bed. "Lie down by Daddy, sweetheart. Isn't that what a lot of them said to you?"

She nodded jerkily. "I'll . . . give you the papers if you'll just let me out of here."

"In time. Lie down, Melis."

Two minutes more had passed. "Take the ropes off me."

"But I rather like them. Say please."

"Please."

He took out his pocketknife and cut the ropes. "Lie down or I'll tie you again."

She slowly lay back on the pillows.

Oh, God, it was happening again.

She was going to scream.

No, she could control it. It wouldn't happen. She just had to hold on.

Deal with it.

Was that Carolyn's voice?

"Your expression is priceless," Archer said hoarsely, his gaze fixed hungrily on her face. "I wish I had a camera handy. I'll have to remember the next time." He reached over and turned on the tape recorder on the nightstand. "But I'm too eager right now. I have to watch you. . . ."

Then she heard her own voice on the tape.

Chapter Eighteen

Five minutes to go.

"Two men on the bridge," Nicholas murmured. "One will probably stay at the helm even if the other runs to the explosion. You or me?"

"You do it. I'm heading for the cabins."

"I thought as much."

Kelby's eyes strained as he stared up at the deck. God, he wanted to move now.

Four minutes.

Melis sat bolt upright on the bed and covered her mouth. "Jesus, I'm going to throw up."

"How annoying." Archer sat up in bed. "When we were just getting to the good part."

She bent over the bed, gagging.

"No, you don't. Not on this bed. I have too many plans for it." He jumped up and jerked her out of bed. "The bathroom, bitch." He dragged her over to the adjoining bathroom. "Hurry up. And don't get anything on that dress."

He pushed her into the room and slammed the door.

Alone.

She had been afraid he'd come in with her. But most people didn't like to see others throw up. That didn't mean he wasn't probably right outside the door.

She made gagging sounds as she reached down and stripped the tab on the back of her right shoe. She carefully removed the slender explosive device and set it on the top of the commode. Then she retrieved the stiletto from her left shoe.

"Are you through?" Archer said.

She gagged again. "I guess so."

"Then wash your face and rinse out your mouth like a good girl. You've made me a little angry. I may have to spank you."

She started the water running in the sink. She took a few deep breaths to steady herself. Her hand tightened on the hilt of the stiletto. She had to move. Don't turn off the water. It would give her a few seconds of surprise when she went through the door.

"Melis."

She threw open the door and leapt forward. She had a fleeting impression of the shock on Archer's face as the stiletto entered his upper chest. He started to fall.

Was the wound enough?

No time to check. It was a minute past time. She ran out of the cabin. She'd noticed when they'd brought her down that the galley was right down the hall. She ran toward it.

No one was there.

She armed the explosive.

"What are you doing here?" A man carrying an assault rifle was coming down the stairs behind her.

"I was looking for Archer. He told me to stay in the cabin, but I—"

She hurled the explosive with all her force into the galley, whirled, and hit the floor, covering her head.

The galley exploded with a force that

shook the ship and blew the ceiling. She heard the man on the stairs grunt with pain.

Debris was flying like bullets in all directions. She felt a stinging on her leg but didn't uncover her head to look. Better her leg than her skull. Seconds later she cautiously raised her head. The man on the stairs was lying in a heap on the floor, blood pouring from his forehead.

The shaking had stopped. The other crewmen would be coming to investigate. She had to hide or get out.

Out.

The galley was roaring with flames. She'd be cooked if she stayed down here.

But she could hear the shouts and orders of the men on the deck. She'd walk right into them as she climbed the steps. She was no commando and she wanted to live. Better to hide, as Nicholas had told her.

Okay, wait. She grabbed the assault rifle from the man lying on the floor and ducked behind the steps. Not that she could see what good the weapon would do her. Hell, she didn't even know how to work an assault rifle.

Well, this was obviously the time to figure it out.

Two of Archer's men were running toward the stairs leading to the lower deck.

Kelby aimed and fired. One man down. The other man whirled with a curse, his gun drawn.

Kelby shot him between the eyes.

There was one more crewman. Where the hell was he?

Jesus, black smoke was pouring out of the open door.

He ran toward the stairs.

He couldn't see anything. Smoke stung his eyes. "Melis!"

No answer.

He started down the stairs. "Melis!"

"Don't come down here. I'm coming up."

"Thank God." It wasn't only smoke that was stinging his eyes. "Do you need help? Are you—"

"I need new lungs." Melis was coughing as she came up the stairs. She tried to breathe. "Mine are burning up."

"Archer?"

"Dead."

"Stay here. There's one more crew member to account for."

She shook her head. "Down . . . there."

"Are you sure?"

She nodded at the weapon in her hands. "I took this from him."

"Get your breath. I've got to go see if Nicholas is okay." He took off at a run for the bridge.

Get your breath?

That was easier said than done, Melis thought as she leaned against the rail. She felt as if her lungs were seared. She went to the rail and took several shallow breaths. That was better. Now try a deep breath—

"What a bad little girl."

She whirled to see Archer leaning against the doorjamb. His face was blackened by smoke and he was covered with blood.

But there was a gun in his hand.

She jerked to the side as he pulled the trigger.

The bullet went past her cheek.

She lifted the assault rifle. Aimed quickly but carefully. Fired.

He screamed as the bullets tore into his groin. The gun fell from his hand as he fell.

She kept firing. And firing. And firing.

"I think he's out of commission, Melis," Kelby said gently. He was standing beside her and holding out his hand. "And you're ricocheting a hell of a lot of bullets off everything around him."

She had run out of bullets anyway, but she didn't give up the weapon. "I didn't know how to shoot it. So I just held down the trigger."

"It was effective enough," Nicholas said. "My God, I think you've blown his nuts off."

"It's what I intended. I couldn't think of anything more fitting. Are you sure he's dead?"

Kelby went over and looked down at him. "I'll be damned, he's still alive."

Archer's eyes opened and blazed at Melis. "Bitch. Whore."

Kelby lifted his gun. "But I think it's time he said *sayonara*."

"No," Melis said. "Is he in pain?"

"Big time."

"The wounds are fatal?"

"Yes, some of those bullets tore into his stomach."

"How long will it take him to die?"

"Could be thirty minutes. Could be hours."

Melis slowly walked toward Archer.

"Bitch," he whispered. "Bitch."

"Are you hurting, Archer?" She bent down and whispered, "Do you think it's as bad as the pain Carolyn felt? Do you think it's as horrible as what those little girls felt when you raped them? I hope so."

"Whore. You'll always be a whore." His voice dripped malice. "And I've made you realize it. Everything your Carolyn did for you, I destroyed. I could see it in your face tonight."

"You're wrong. You provided the final cure. If I could go through that nightmare, I'm strong enough for anything."

Doubt flickered over his face. "You're lying."

She shook her head. "Carolyn always said that the way to get rid of a nightmare was to deal with it." She looked down at his bleeding groin. "I dealt with it."

She turned and walked away.

Kelby and Nicholas caught up with her before she was halfway down the deck.

"You're sure you don't want us to put him down?" Nicholas asked. "It would be a pleasure."

"I want him to die slowly. It's not enough, but it will have to do." She looked back at the fire that had broken from belowdeck and was now eating at the timbers of the main deck. "I hope the ship doesn't sink too soon."

"I think we'll get off it just in case." Kelby moved toward the tender. "Let's go."

"One more thing." She stripped off the organdy dress, leaving her in bra and panties. Then she took the pink ribbon from her hair. She tossed both of them on the deck where the fire was creeping toward them. "I'm ready now." She jumped into the tender.

"Jed, drop me off at the island and I'll stick around until the ship sinks," Nicholas said. "We don't want any last-minute slip-ups." He tossed Melis an emergency blanket. "Wrap up. You might get cold."

"I won't get cold." She felt strong, complete, and . . . free.

Archer was screaming in pain.

Kelby started the engine, and the tender moved slowly away from the ship.

Archer was still screaming.

The first tendrils of fire had reached the white organdy dress. The delicate fabric was curling and blackening. Then it was completely aflame.

In a few short minutes the dress and ribbon were gone.

Ashes.

Two hours later, from the deck of the *Trina*, Melis and Kelby saw a flash of light in the east.

"That's it," Kelby said. "The fire reached the arms. It took longer than I thought."

"I wish it had taken even longer."

"Bloodthirsty wench."

"Yes, I am."

"Will you go down and hit the shower now? You've been glued to this rail since we came back."

"Not yet. I'll wait for Nicholas. I have to be sure. You can go."

He shook his head and leaned on the rail, his gaze on the east.

Nicholas arrived thirty minutes later.

"The big boom," he said as he climbed on board. "He was carrying some mega firepower." He turned to Melis. "No last-minute rescues. The bastard's dead, Melis. Blown to hell."

She gazed out to the east.

He's dead, Carolyn. He won't hurt anyone anymore.

"Melis." Kelby's hand was gentle on her arm. "Time to let it go."

She nodded and turned away. It was over. Done.

Time to let it go.

Pete and Susie were gone when she came on deck the next morning.

"Is it okay?" Kelby had come to stand beside her. "You said Pete would know when he was well enough."

"I think it's okay." Melis shrugged. "There's so much about dolphins that is a mystery to me. Sometimes I feel I don't know Pete and Susie at all."

"And other times you know damn well you're learning every day. They'll be back, Melis."

She nodded as she sat down on the deck. "And I'll be here. Are you going to dive today?"

He shook his head. "I'm going to pay a visit to the coast guard. You can't sink a ship without repercussions, even if it's one used for criminal activities. But if they were willing to take a bribe from Archer, then they'll take one from me."

"Money is the answer to everything."

"No, but it's very useful. Call me if there's a problem with Pete."

"I can handle it."

He hesitated as he looked at her. "You're a million miles away today."

"I feel . . . subdued. Maybe a little empty." She smiled faintly. "For weeks I've had only one purpose, and it's not there anymore. I'll be fine once I adjust. When will you be back?"

"It depends on how long and how much money it takes to convince them that Archer's ship accidentally blew up because of the arms he was carrying. The wages of sin." He moved toward the tender. "I'll let you know if I run into any snags."

"You don't have to report in to me." She looked out at the water. "I promised you I wouldn't tie you down."

"It's courtesy, dammit." He frowned. "I *want* to call you."

"Then do it."

"Melis, I can't—" He shook his head. "Screw it. I don't think I could get through to you now." He jumped in the tender. "I'll see you later."

She watched him speed away from the *Trina*. Then her gaze shifted back to the ocean and she waited for Pete and Susie to come back.

They surfaced near the ship two hours later.

Pete looked fine, she thought with relief. Better than fine. He and Susie were cavorting and clicking as usual.

"Hi, guys," she said softly. "You could have waited until I was here before you decided to take a little trip." She stripped off her T-shirt. "I'm coming in. It'll be like old times. I need it to be good today."

She dove into the water. It was cold and clean and familiar. When she surfaced, it was to see Nicholas at the rail. She waved.

"You don't have your air tank," he called. "And you shouldn't be in the water alone."

"I'm not diving. I'm just going for a little swim with the dolphins. It always clears my mind."

"Jed won't like it. He nearly went bananas

when he saw you taken aboard Archer's boat. He's still mad as hell at me."

"I'm sorry, Nicholas." But she struck out in a breaststroke with Pete and Susie on either side of her. That formation lasted for only a moment before they grew impatient and, as usual, swam ahead, coming back to her periodically.

It was different swimming with them today. Since they had arrived here in the Canaries, there had always been a purpose when they were in the water together. Now it was almost like swimming with them at the island.

No, that wasn't true. They had another life now. Before they had been hers. Now they gave her time and affection, but they had joined with their own kind. They had the choice. She shouldn't be sad. It was right and natural.

So was life at this moment. Right and natural and everything coming into focus.

And becoming more crystal clear with every passing minute.

Kelby cut the engine as he neared the *Trina*. The other tender was gone.

Don't panic. Nicholas could have gone to Lanzarote to get supplies or—or what, dammit?

Nicholas hadn't taken the tender. He was walking down the deck toward Kelby.

"Where's the other tender?" Kelby asked as he came on board. "And where's Melis?"

"The tender is sitting at a dock in Lanzarote. And Melis is probably boarding a plane at Las Palmas."

"What?"

"Pete came back. She went for a swim with the dolphins, and when she came back she packed and took off."

"She didn't call me. You didn't call me either."

"She asked me not to."

"What the hell is this? A conspiracy between the two of you?"

"Well, I figured I couldn't be any deeper in your bad books."

"You were wrong."

Nicholas shrugged. "She said she needed to go back to the island. She's been through a hell of a lot. I can see how she'd need some downtime."

"Then why didn't she talk to me about it?"

"You'll have to ask her." He reached in his pocket. "She left you a note."

The note had two lines.

I've gone back to the island. Please take care of Pete and Susie.

Melis

"Son of a bitch!"

LONTANA'S ISLAND

The sunset was beautiful, but she missed having Pete and Susie come to say good night.

And that wasn't all she missed.

Melis squared her shoulders, turned, and left the lanai. She had work to do and there was no use putting it off. She had done what she had to do. What would be, would be.

She went to the bedroom and pulled out her suitcase. There should be some boxes around here. They might smell of—

"What the hell are you doing?"

She went still. She was afraid to turn around. "Kelby?"

"Who else could get past those barriers

you set up around yourself?" he said harshly. "I'm surprised you didn't up the electricity to keep me away."

"I wouldn't do that." Her voice was uneven. "I'd never hurt you."

"You did a pretty good job. Turn around, dammit."

She took a deep breath and turned to face him.

"What kind of note was this?" He threw a balled piece of paper at her feet. "No good-bye. No reason. No *it's been good to know you*. Just *take care of the dolphins*."

"Is that why you came halfway around the world? Because you're angry?"

"It's reason enough." He took four steps and grasped her shoulders. "Why did you leave?"

"I had to come back to the island and pack up. I can't live here anymore."

"And where were you going?"

"I'll find a job someplace. I'm qualified."

"But not back to me."

"It would depend."

"On what?"

"On whether you wanted me enough. On whether you followed me."

"Some kind of a test?" His hands tightened on her shoulders. "Yes, I want you enough. I'd follow you to hell and back. Is that what you want to hear?"

Joy soared through her. "Yes."

"Then why the hell did you take off? I would have told you that when I got back to the ship. All you had to do was talk to me."

"I had to give you the choice. You could have read the note and said, 'To hell with the rude bitch.' I gave you the out."

"Why?"

"I promised you I wouldn't hold you."

"I've been the one who's been holding tight."

"But you had no reason now. You have Marinth. Archer is dead. I had to be the reason. The only reason." She looked him in the eye. "Because I'm worth it, Kelby. I can give you more than Marinth, but you have to give me what I need."

"And that is?"

"I . . . think I love you." She moistened her lips. "No, I do love you. It's just hard for me to say." She took a deep breath. This was even harder for her to say. "And I don't want to be alone anymore."

"Jesus." He drew her close and buried her head in his shoulder. "Melis . . ."

"You don't have to say you love me. I promised I wouldn't—"

"Screw your promise. I never asked for it. I don't want it." He kissed her, hard. "I don't want to be alone either. You had me on the ropes even before we left this place." He cupped her face in his two hands. "Listen to me. I do love you. I would have told you a long time ago if I hadn't been afraid you'd skip out on me. You were so grateful that we were so beautifully noncommittal."

"It was only fair to you."

"I don't want you to be fair. I want you to make love to me and eat with me and sleep with me." He paused. "And when you're absolutely sure I'm the one who you want to spend the next seventy years with, I want a cast-iron commitment. Understand?"

A brilliant smile lit her face. "I don't need to wait to be sure."

"Yes, you do. Because there's no going back with me. You saw how I was about Marinth. Multiply that into infinity and you'll see how hard I'd make it for you to leave me." He brushed a kiss on her forehead. "You'd have to go live with the dolphins."

"I don't have the lungs for it."

"Then you'd better stick with me."

She put her head on his chest. She whispered, "I think you're right."

They left Lontana's Island the next evening.

As the boat picked up speed after stopping at the nets, Melis looked back at the island shimmering in twilight haze.

"It's a beautiful place," Kelby said quietly. "You're going to miss it."

"For a while."

"I'll buy you another island. Bigger, better."

She smiled. "That sounds like you. I don't want an island. Not now. I want to stay on the *Trina* with you." She frowned. "Can't you change that name?"

"Henpecked already. Shall I name it after you?"

"Heavens, no."

"Our first child?"

Her eyes widened. "Maybe," she said cautiously. "You are thinking of commitment."

He grinned. "I didn't say our third or fifth."

"Perhaps *Trina's* a fine name for a while."

"Coward."

"You have Marinth to bring to life. I have to study the dolphins that live there. I have an idea they're going to be different from any I've ever observed. We're going to be busy."

"And you have to take care of Pete and Susie."

She nodded. "Always."

"But you left them in my care."

"If you hadn't come after me, I would have gone back and found a way to watch over them. They're my responsibility."

"You may need an island after all. You told me about all the hazards that threaten wild dolphins. Are you sure you won't want to bring them home to a safe haven?"

"No, I'm not sure. It depends on the conditions. If you have control of the project, you'll have power to protect the dolphins." Her lips tightened. "If not, we may gather all of them up and take them to safety."

He chuckled. "I'm not sure this place would support all those hundreds of dolphins, but we could try."

She shook her head. "I'm going to deed the island to the Save the Dolphin foundation in Carolyn's name. That will be a constant source of irritation to Phil. I'm sure he thought I'd eventually deed it back to him. No ship. No island. He'll have to start over."

"I don't think so."

There was a note in his voice that made her gaze fly to his face. "No?"

He shook his head.

"Dead?" she whispered.

"He had a fall off the cliff."

"You?"

"No. And that's all I'm going to say about it."

Then it must have been Nicholas. She was silent, letting the knowledge sink in. All those years working with and protecting Phil. It seemed strange to realize he was gone. She finally said, "I don't feel anything but relief. I was so afraid. He would have kept on trying to take Marinth away from you, and I couldn't have let that happen. It's everything to you."

He smiled. "Not nearly everything."

"That's good to know." She glanced back again at the island. It looked smaller, lonelier from this distance. So many years, so many memories of Pete and Susie.

Yet there were better years to come,

richer memories to create. So what if she felt just a little sad? Deal with it.

And she knew just how to do it.

She reached out and covered Kelby's hand with her own.

Wonder.